THE PERFECT HUSBAND

IAIN MAITLAND

INKUBATOR
BOOKS

Published by Inkubator Books
www.inkubatorbooks.com

Copyright © 2022 by Iain Maitland

ISBN (eBook) 978-1-83756-022-6
ISBN (Paperback) 978-1-83756-023-3
ISBN (Hardback) 978-1-83756-024-0

Iain Maitland has asserted his right to be identified as the
author of this work.

PRAISE FOR IAIN MAITLAND'S BOOKS

The Perfect Husband

"Heartrending and macabre, *The Perfect Husband* delves deep inside a decidedly imperfect mind." Barbara Nadel

The Wickham Market Murder

"A well-crafted murder mystery, weaving a family saga with engaging protagonists and a clever twist." Thomas Waugh

"If you like TV shows such as *Murdoch Mysteries*, *Midsomer Murders* or *Father Brown*, this book is a perfect one to read. The characters and writing are described well, and it feels very easy to read, to get into and follow." Steph Louise On Instagram

"I really enjoyed the plot and the pace, it was easy to follow, and I was fascinated to see how they might solve this case without clear-cut evidence. What was even better is that the story really highlighted justice, or rather injustice at times, and how difficult it would be to solve some cases." David's Book Blurg

"... the dramatic climax. It's a shocker. I really enjoyed this book and hope to see our intrepid duo again soon." Lynda's Book Reviews and News

"I won't say too much, but it's engaging and gripping right to the end. The pacing is perfectly matched to the story; it speeds headlong like a high-speed train from the first page until you are closing the last." Chicks, Rogues and Scandals

The Girl Downstairs

"No one does uncanny like Iain Maitland. *The Girl Downstairs*, a tale of poignant grief, explodes into unimaginable horror." Barbara Nadel

"*The Girl Downstairs* is a very well-written book, so well that I've finished it and am wanting more. I need more! This is one of those books that sits with you for a while after you read it. It definitely plays with your head! Excellent read!" The Book Booth

"I did enjoy this book. I really wasn't expecting that. Read in one sitting. Brilliant." Sue Loves to Read

"The themes in *The Girl Downstairs* are those that are crucial to today's society. Homelessness, identity, the need for love and shelter, family, addiction, mental health and assumptions and expectations are so sensitively presented. Iain Maitland forces his reader to confront aspects of life we'd rather ignore so that I genuinely feel altered by reading *The Girl Downstairs*." Linda's Book Bag

The Scribbler

"One seriously weird killer and an engaging cop-partnership dynamic. Exciting." *Sunday Times*

"I feel like I have just made one of the greatest discoveries on earth ... What a mind this author has ... a fantastic ... dark, gripping, creepy and tense read." A Lover of Books Blog

"*The Scribbler* is a slow-burning, tense and downright creepy thriller." Suze Reviews

"A creepy read with an explosive ending, I was engrossed from start to finish." Jera's Jamboree

"Brilliantly creepy." *Scots Magazine*

"*The Scribbler* is well-paced, engaging and punctuated by ... unexpected humour, leading to a compelling and incredibly satisfying crime read. Highly recommended." Raven Crime Reads

Mr Todd's Reckoning

"Splendidly creepy." Geoffrey Wansell, *Daily Mail*

"Iain Maitland has pulled off a masterstroke. Combining the ingenuity of an Agatha Christie, the horror of Rillington Place and the wit of the best of British, the story keeps you on your toes, fills you with dread and makes you laugh out loud." Martin Carr, AbbottVision

"Maitland conjures madness from the inside, looking out ... a brave book." Jeff Noon, Spectator

"Truly scary ... a fabulous dive into the mind of a classic, self-justifying psychopath ... A fantastic book." Barbara Nadel

"Iain Maitland's Mr Todd lures us into his moral abyss. The banality of evil ... drip feeds us its shockingly tense story of unending horror ... Riveting, terrifying." Paul Ritter

"Superbly crafted ... spellbinding and gripping ... brilliantly observed ... The setting of an ordinary two-bedroomed bungalow in suburbia is genius ..." Linda Hill, Linda's Book Blog

Sweet William

"A breathless journey through fear and love that explores how interdependent those two extreme emotions are." Ewan Morrison

"A dark, rocket-paced thriller." Jon Wise, *Sunday Sport*

"Taut, darkly humorous and heartbreaking, with an unforgettable narrator, *Sweet William* packs a real emotional punch." Lisa Gray, *Daily Record*

"A compassionate novel imbued with a deep knowledge of mental health issues ... Tense and insightful ... A heart-stopping thriller with a powerful denouement." Paul Burke, Nudge Books

Out of the Madhouse

"An excellent exploration of the phenomenology of mental illness and its wider impact." Joshua Fletcher, psychotherapist

"I love this book; profoundly moving, beautifully written ... incredibly important ... wonderfully hopeful." James Withey, Founder, The Recovery Letters project

"Confronts the shocking bleakness of mental illness head on." Charlie Mortimer, author, *Dear Lupin*

"The overriding ingredients ... are the warmth of his connections, ... and the power of communication." Dr Nihara Krause, Stem4 Founder & CEO

Dear Michael, Love Dad

"A wonderfully entertaining and moving book, with lessons for every parent." *Daily Mail*

"A moving read – honest, funny and sad." *Woman and Home*

"Raising the issue of men's mental health is important, and *Dear Michael, Love Dad* is to be praised for that ... [a] loving and well-meant mix of letters and commentary." *Daily Express*

"By turns acidly funny, exasperating and poignant, painting a moving portrait both of mental illness and of a father in denial. But paternal love ... shines through." Caroline Sanderson, *Sunday Express*

For Adam.

PROLOGUE

We sit, side by side, in bed, our backs against the padded headboard, him to the left, my "perfect husband" as he likes to be known, me to the right, his "wife", of sorts anyway. Common-law wife as it used to be called in England. Living together but not married.

He is wearing a black tee shirt and black boxer shorts. I am in the Disney *Frozen* pyjamas he bought me at Easter. I think, at thirty-seven, I am too old to be wearing these, but I like the colours. And the pyjamas are warm. And he likes me to wear what he buys for me.

It is 6.35 a.m. on Wednesday, 26 May, and it is a surprisingly chilly morning after a week or two of warmer weather. I have just been downstairs to turn on the heating and to make two mugs of tea. We are now sipping our teas quietly.

It is his birthday today.

Robert James Wilkinson. He prefers "Rob". He dislikes the formality of Robert. Bob is the name of an idiot, so he says. And Bobby is the name of a stupid child, apparently. Robbie is a yappy and annoying Scottie dog. So, Rob it is.

He is forty years old.

He has transformed my life since we met at a barbeque at Harry's house, on the other side of our horseshoe-shaped close of five detached houses, just nine months ago.

Up until then, my solitary life amounted to little more than working in EYFS, early years, teaching four- and five-year olds at a local primary school during the days, and mulling over lesson plans for the following weeks in the evenings and at weekends.

I filled the rest of my time, and the long, endless holidays, with reading and crocheting and occasional get-togethers for coffee or lunch with work colleagues. All alone, I had grown old before my time. I knew it. I smiled in public, but inside, my heart was breaking.

He sits there expectantly by my side.

He believes I have a card and a present to give him after drinking our tea. Something special tucked by my side of the bed.

I do – and I think they will make him very happy.

Harry introduced us as I was standing near the barbeque, waiting to refill my glass with white wine. Here," Harry said, gesturing towards the short and stocky man dressed in a fresh white shirt, navy knee-length shorts and boating shoes next to him. "This is Rob, my investment guru. You and he will get along." He winked at Robert, and I had a sense that they'd just been talking about me.

We shook hands, both of us smiling and laughing, and we chatted about the weather, Harry's new pond, and, well, all sorts of nonsense. He gazed steadily at me, whenever I glanced at him, and seemed interested in everything I said. By the end of the afternoon, early evening really, I had fallen in love.

I thought he was handsome in an old-fashioned, tidy sort of way. With his gelled blond hair and ready smile, I felt an instant attraction. I loved his lilting voice, and, at that first meeting, I wanted to just shut my eyes and listen to him talking away. Most of all, though, I loved his gentleness and his old-time good manners that reminded me of my dear, late parents, especially my darling father.

He puts his empty mug on the carpet next to his side of the bed.

Yawns and stretches as though it is just another day.

I sip at my tea, feeling the card and the present by my side.

I told him about my life. How I lived at home with my parents after qualifying as a teacher and that they passed away not so very long ago. I sold up, moved here and put the rest of the money in the bank. He told me his father turned him out of the family home when he was twenty-one, just before his mother died. There is an older brother, but they have not seen each other for years.

He is an investment adviser, working for himself, putting investors' money into schemes that pay more than forty per cent a year through his clever investing. Harry has been getting four per cent a month for the past ten months or so.

Since Robert and I became a proper couple, when he moved in six months ago, he has been investing my rainy-day money. Now and then, he shows me computer printouts and tells me I will be a millionaire in five years' time.

I put my mug on the bedside cabinet.

Lift up the card and the present. I lay them between us.

This is an unforgettable moment in our lives.

He takes them and looks at me as if to say, "Which one do I open first?" I smile and lift my hands as though to reply, "Either, it's up to you." They are, in their own ways, the same thing. A life-changing announcement.

He picks up the present, unwraps the bow, tears open the shiny blue-pink paper, and takes out a plain white cardboard box. He opens that and looks at a tiny pair of white baby bootees.

He stops, and there is a silence as neither of us breathes. And then he drops his head. I think he is close to sobbing. I am weeping.

I really hope this will be a happy day today. A day when he does not take out the notebook with my name, Laura, written in block capitals on the front cover.

PART I

THE HAPPY COUPLE

1

Robert seems stunned by the news of my pregnancy. He opens the card, "Happy Birthday Daddy!" and looks at it intently for a while, front, inside and back, and then puts the card, on its side, and the present on the bedside cabinet. He stares into space for what seems an age. I do not know what to say or do.

In truth, I thought I was too old to fall pregnant, and I have not taken any precautions, and, lately, I have not really needed to anyway. I think he assumes I am on the pill. Early on, he said he did not like wearing anything, and I said I'd sort it out. I never got round to it somehow. We had not talked about having children. But I have always wanted at least one, and deep down, if I am honest, I am so thrilled by it, yet just as scared, too.

He gets up out of his side of the bed, seeming distracted, and mumbles something like, "Best get on ... be late for work." I am not sure how to respond to that. I guess if you get to forty and have never had children, you never expect to. I think he is still in shock and will warm to the idea when he gets used to it.

He busies around, going to the bathroom and back, taking longer than usual, getting ready for the day. Even though he works in the box room, the smallest bedroom at the front of the house, he likes to dress for work. "Smart casual" he calls it.

I make breakfast – a big fried Birthday Breakfast like Mother used to make for Father and me on our birthdays – and stand in the kitchen waiting for him. I put on my brightest smile. He comes through, barely glancing at me or the piled-high plates, and makes himself a black coffee. He says he is in a hurry, has calls to make, no time to waste. Trades to do ASAP.

I am angry, bewildered too, but turn most of his breakfast into two sandwiches, one bacon, one sausage, which I leave on a plate outside the box-room door. I gently pull down the handle of the door to go in and wish him a happy birthday again and then kiss his cheek, but I can hear him talking nineteen-to-the-dozen on his mobile phone, so I slip away. I leave a few bits of cut-up bacon on a small plate on the patio in the back garden for Ginger, a thin cat that comes calling now and then. He always looks hungry and meows loudly and lets me stroke him whenever I see him. He does not appear today, so I leave for work.

It is a happy day at school with all the little children. It is sunny, and we go outside at morning break, lunch and afternoon break, which is always nice. The classroom can be hot and stuffy. I eat my packed lunch sitting on a bench, watching the children running around playing the latest games. The boys seem to be chasing a bouncy ball. The girls sit and fiddle with each other's hair. Various children come running up to say "hello" one after the other. There are few moments to yourself at school other than hurried visits to the toilets.

I have a good friend at my school, Sharon, who has been my teaching assistant for about five years now. She is in her late forties and has three grown-up children and two grand-children. I tell her at the end of our lunch break that I am pregnant. I'm not sure if I am laughing or crying, a mix of both, really. She hugs me long and hard and seems thrilled by my news.

As I stand by the door at the end of the day, seeing the little ones off to their parents, Sharon hurries up to me and says we must go into town for a celebratory coffee and cupcakes. Her face is shiny with excitement. I'd love to, but I say I need to get back for Robert, that he'll be expecting me by four o'clock. We agree to do it another time.

When I get back home, just before four, I was going to suggest to Robert that, as it is his birthday, he might finish early and we could go to the cinema in Ipswich and then have a meal somewhere nearby afterwards. But his door is still shut, and listening in, I can hear he is on his mobile phone. He seems angry, is not shouting exactly, but certainly sounding loud and forceful. "Soon," he keeps saying. "I told you. Very soon." I come downstairs and make mugs of tea, waiting for him to come down too.

But he does not. I potter about the kitchen for a while, noting that he has put the sandwiches I left for him, untouched, in the flip-top bin, at the top for me to see. I then sit in the living room, where, by angling the slats of the big venetian blind, I can see out into the close. After that, the close being so quiet today, I go into the conservatory and gaze into the garden to see what birds are there. A noisy blackbird is often in the tree at the bottom of the garden, although it does not appear today. I note the bacon has gone from the patio, and I am pleased my ginger friend has had something to eat. The plate has gone too; Robert must have seen and put it in the dishwasher.

He comes downstairs just before six, as I am unloading the dishwasher and putting everything away in the cupboards. He seems distracted and edgy. Sweaty too, which is not like him. "Business?" I ask cautiously, but he shakes his head.

"You wouldn't understand," he answers. He makes himself a glass of orange squash and gulps it down in three or four mouthfuls. I have a card and a present from me – not from our baby – on the side, and I gesture towards them. "Later," he says. "I must have a shower. I've been working hard."

The evening does not go well, as he is out of sorts. He does not give an explanation, and I do not ask. I think it is something to do with his investments, but cannot say for sure. He agrees to go out, as there is "nothing to do here". We sit through a Stephen King movie, which is not to my tastes, but Robert seems to enjoy it well enough. Afterwards, he says he is too tired to go to a nice restaurant, so we have a McDonald's surrounded by loud and aggressive teenagers making mooing noises at each other. I don't know why. Robert looks like he wants to kill them. We head home soon enough.

It has been, if I am honest, a horrible evening where he largely ignored me. I do not say anything, partly because it is his birthday, but mostly because I do not want to make things worse in any way. Back home, I give him my present, an expensive electric razor and a nice little card with a heart on the front and All My Love inside.

I say the razor will give him "the closest shave ever"; part of the promotional message, I think. He looks at it as though I have handed him a lump of dog mess I've picked up from the pavement and just says, "What, you don't think I shave properly?" And I have just about had enough at this point. He has never said a word about the baby at all. Not one word.

He goes upstairs to bed first, saying it has been a long day and he'd had to be especially clever with his investments – "to beat the market every time", as he puts it. I wait for him to finish in the bathroom. And then I follow him upstairs. Normally, I hurry along, as he says he cannot get to sleep when I am "crashing about with the lights on". But tonight I am fed up with it all – I am both angry and sad – so I have a bath. I lie here, thinking back over our time together, taking an age and not worrying what I might face later. His disapproval. Maybe his wrath.

WE WERE HAPPY FOR A WHILE. Ecstatic, really. All my dreams were coming true.

At least we were happy for two or three months after we first met. Our whirlwind romance.

And then things changed after he moved in with me. Looking back, I know the exact moment.

His investing work kept him on the road, forever moving. He lived in London ... and Manchester ... and Edinburgh; he had homes, apartments, in half a dozen cities, a property portfolio he called it, and he would live in whichever one was empty, improving it, he said, before re-letting it and moving on. Offices too – London and Edinburgh and more – where he'd meet his clients, do his presentations, go through all of his charts and gobbledegook, and arrange investments into his FX fund or arbitrage fund, whatever it was.

I fell in love with him that first evening, this handsome, successful man. I have never been good at banter, but it all seemed so easy, so natural, between us in Harry's garden. He was attentive to me, listening to what I had to say about my life and work and my parents, selling the family home and moving here. He shared his life story with me, too. I remember turning and gesturing over the way at one point. "Number three," I said. "The one with the red door. All mine," I added proudly. And he replied, with feeling, "All yours. I'll remember that." And he smiled at me. And that shy smile, and the twinkly look in his eyes, was the moment I fell in love.

At the end of the evening, he walked me to my front door. We stood there and looked at each other, and he inclined his head to one side, and I did the same, but the other way, and he stepped forward, and I did as well. And we kissed. For ever such a while. And we stopped and looked again at each other. I would have invited him in for coffee and maybe more. In truth, there was no maybe about it. But he was the perfect gentleman and simply asked for my mobile phone number, and I gave him that and my email, my address too, and he noted it all in his phone. And then he was gone, and I did not know if I would hear from him again.

He telephoned me later the next evening. And we talked happily, about this and that, long into the night.

And we spoke each morning and every evening, with text messages in between, from then on. Never more than a few hours apart. Even at Christmas, when he had to go to New York on business and I sat here on my own, we stayed in regular touch.

I think, looking back, that was when I was at my happiest. The anticipation of all my hopes and dreams being fulfilled.

Arriving back from school late one Friday afternoon in the New Year – worried that I had not heard anything since the Wednesday evening – I found him slumped in the front seat of an old car, a lime green Ford Fiesta, on my driveway. He looked as though he had been in a fight. I invited him in, and he told me what had happened.

He had been attacked and robbed by a gang of men outside his upmarket Edinburgh home – he did not know who they were – and he'd feared for his life, that they would come back again and kill him. His words were garbled, but I got the sense that he had been investing money for them, and they weren't happy with their returns. "A blip in the market," he said. "That's all, things would have come back up in a week or two."

He had borrowed a friend's car – he could not get to his brand-new Audi – and come to me. "My sanctuary," he said and added, "My love." Then finally, "My life." My spirit soared. He had a bath whilst I made up the bed in the spare bedroom at the front of the house, and then I went down to make something for us to eat. He changed into some fresh clothes from a rucksack he'd filled hurriedly before leaving Edinburgh. Then he came downstairs.

We ate together in the little conservatory with its patio table and two chairs at one end. And we drank a bottle of red wine between us. I was so happy. Afterwards, we watched something or other on the television – including my favourite old Agatha Christie movie, *Murder on the Orient Express* – and, towards the end, we fell into silence; both of us nervous, but excited, about what was to come.

He went upstairs first, to use the bathroom and then to bed in the front bedroom. I had made it look as nice as I could, moving a vase of fresh flowers from the kitchen and putting it on the chest of drawers by the wall. I followed him upstairs ten minutes later, went to the bathroom, and then lay in my bed in the back bedroom wondering whether I should knock on his door to check if he was well and had everything he needed. But, as I hesitated, he knocked on my bedroom door, and I sat up and said, "Come in." He stood there looking at me, and I held his gaze. And then I pulled back the duvet from the other side of the bed and beckoned him forward.

It was wonderful, that first night. And the days and nights that followed. I thought it would last forever. He spent his days on his laptop in the box room upstairs at the front of the house, a makeshift office, making money from trading so cleverly through rising and falling markets. I worked at school with the little children all day. In the evenings, we shut ourselves away in our own world. At night, it was heavenly. Even just having him there, lying beside me.

One Sunday night, the first day of what he called "the wrong time of the month", he suddenly asked me how many men I'd slept with. I laughed it off as a bad joke about my inexpert lovemaking – I "lie there and just pull gurning faces" he'd told me some other time – but there was a long silence, and I was not sure whether he was trying to be funny or not.

So, to avoid the uneasy possibility that he was not, I got up out of bed – he did not say anything – and I went downstairs to fetch and bring back up a half-empty bottle of rosé wine in the fridge and two glasses. To be honest, with the sense of foreboding I had, I should have simply told him to get up and out of my house there and then. I think at that time he might have gone. But I did not. And, for a long time afterwards, I felt that all that followed was my fault.

As I walk into the bedroom after my bath, I expect him to be fast asleep with his back to me. I hope that will be the case.

After today, I do not think I can face it if he rolls over and starts pawing at me, forcing himself upon me.

I slip under the duvet, next to him, him facing one way, me facing the other. I think he is asleep, and I hope that I can get to sleep quickly.

"I've had a rotten day," he says suddenly in a strangely self-pitying voice. "A horrible birthday."

I am not sure how to reply. "Serves you bloody well right" comes to mind, but that is the last thing I'd say. I know where anything like that will lead. And fast.

"I'm so sorry," I answer. It seems the safest thing to say. It sometimes works. It really depends if he blames me for everything or not.

"The markets still keep going the wrong way. I've got to turn that right round in the morning."

Nothing is ever his fault, of course. There is always someone or something else to blame. I know not to ask him to tell me more about it or whether I can help in any way. He'll only come back at me with a putdown.

There is a silence.

It stretches on and on.

He is expecting me to say something.

"What will you do?" I ask at last.

"Like you'd understand any of it," he replies.

Another silence.

On and on it goes.

As always, it is me who has to soothe the situation.

"You're going to be a daddy. What a wonderful daddy you will be."

He says nothing.

"We'll be a happy little family," I add.

More silence.

I had thought having a baby might turn things around for us. I think that's why I've stayed. I see now how stupid I am to believe a baby might make things better.

"I thought you said you'd sorted out ... your contraception."

If I say I never did sort it out, he'll roll over, his face twisted in anger, accusing me of tricking him.

If I say I did, he might want to see the packet, checking if I've missed taking one. So he can blame me. But, of course, there is no packet, and he would be even angrier about that.

"I thought I had." It's all I can think of to say.

I expect him to come back at me with a "What's that supposed to mean?" But he does not.

Another silence.

He doesn't want to be a father, I realise that. This pregnancy has made everything worse. I did not think that could be possible.

I wait to hear what he says next.

"When are you ... when is the baby due?" A neutral voice. I am not sure which way this will go.

"November," I say. "The twenty-fifth."

I can hear him – imagine him – counting back from November in his head.

"March. I got pregnant the first week of March." Before he accuses this of being someone else's baby.

I hear him breathing unevenly. He knows the night I mean. I did not want to make love that night.

I also know what he is going to do now. What he always does when he cannot turn the blame on to me and feels he has been beaten.

He mumbles something about not feeling well and being unable to sleep, that he needs to go downstairs to get something to settle his stomach.

Up he gets and off he goes, and I know he will sleep downstairs on the sofa and be in a bad mood in the morning and that it will be all my fault. As per bloody usual.

And it will be another bad day tomorrow when he tries again to beat the markets and most likely fails. I cannot help but feel that something significant is unravelling. I wonder what that might mean for us. More importantly, I do not think that he will ever warm to being a daddy, and I wonder what the consequences of that will be for me and my baby.

2

THURSDAY, 27 MAY

The next morning is just as I expected – as I come downstairs, he pretends to wake and huffs and puffs as though he is in great pain but is trying to disguise it. As if I have somehow forced him to sleep on the sofa. That his terrible agony, as he presents it, is all my fault. As we sit down for tea and toast in the kitchen, he continues grimacing occasionally. I ignore it all, as I know where even the gentlest enquiry might lead.

"You'll have to stay at home, be a proper mother, not one of these women who works and dumps their child on a childminder," he announces. I nod, not sure how to answer. With my savings, I'm lucky enough that I can afford to stop work, and I would love to be a full-time mum at least until my baby goes to school. But I'm not sure I want to stay at home forever, which is what he'd have me do.

"So everything is on me to earn enough to support us," he adds, sounding tense as though I've put him under so much pressure and that this, like everything else, is down to me. I should say that my money is enough for me to not have to work for ten years, so please can he just put it back in an ordinary account. But I don't. He would take it as an insult that I don't believe he could double it, triple it, whatever. And then he is up, in high dudgeon, and off to the box room, all twitching and edgy, to do his trades. I leave something out for Ginger – I just happen to have a tin or two of cat food in a cupboard – and go to work.

I have another lovely morning at school. From the moment I arrive, through lessons and mid-morning break and on to lunch, so many teachers and teaching assistants, and everyone else who sees me, seem to smile at me more than they've ever done before. I am sure it cannot be a coincidence.

It is as if they are all in on my secret but have been told not to say anything to me just yet. Sharon is a terrible chatterbox. She winked at me the first time one of the teachers smiled so brightly – the sweet and gentle Mr Aziz – and I winked back at her. Sharon is such a kind and good-hearted person. I do not mind everyone knowing so soon – I have such a wonderfully warm feeling, as they are all so pleased for me.

I am on playground duties – supervising the children as they run around – for the second half of the lunch break when Charlotte, an older teacher who never had the baby she'd longed for, comes up to me. She doesn't say a word; she simply hugs me tight and smiles through teary eyes, then pats my arm and walks away. It makes me realise how lucky I am. I am going to have the baby I've always dreamed of.

It is later, just after I have finished seeing the small children off to their parents at the end of the day, that one of the job-share teachers, Layla, comes back to the school. She had her baby, a little boy called Johnny, about a year ago and has been working mornings these past few weeks. We get on well enough, but we're not friends, really. I'm quiet and keep to myself. She's the life and soul of the party. I've always been in awe of her self-confidence.

I watch as her red Mini pulls into the school car park. She gets out, looks at me and waves, and then opens the boot and takes out one of those huge IKEA bags. I go across to help her, thinking, for some reason, that she is carrying lots of heavy books for the school library. When I get to her, I see the bag is full of maternity clothes. On top, I recognise one of the sweet floral dresses she used to wear all the time that I liked so much. I stop and do not know what to say. I am so moved by this gesture.

"For you," Layla says, holding the bag out to me. "Sharon told me ... aw, come here." She can see I am tearful, and she embraces me in the biggest hug ever. Stepping back after what seems like minutes, I am surrounded by so many other staff, Juanitta, Mrs Winterton, Frances, Mandy and even starchy old Mrs Smith, who all want to smile and hug and pat me on the back and ask me so many questions about my baby, when it is due, and so on.

I seem to be there for ages with everyone making a fuss of me. I don't think I've ever felt so elated and so part of everything. I've always been a solitary sort of person, who just kind of got on with things. I keep telling them how happy I am that I am having a baby, and I cannot believe it is happening to me after all this time. And they seem to know and understand what I mean, and they all keep saying they are "thrilled" for me and "so excited" and that it is "a dream come true". And it is, and I cry so many happy tears.

Eventually, with my handbag and what I call my "bits and pieces" bag over my shoulder, I pick up the big IKEA bag to leave and walk home. Everyone fusses around some more, saying it is too heavy and I should be careful, but I tell them it is much lighter than it looks, and I say my farewells, and there are more hugs and kisses and tears all round, mostly from me. They then stand there and wave me off as I walk through the school gates and along the high road back towards the close. I don't think I have ever felt so loved, at least, not for years. My heart is bursting with happiness.

There is a bench on the high road, about halfway between the school and the close, and I sit there to rest a while, the bag proving to be a little heavier than I first thought. I rummage through all these beautiful clothes, and, item by item, my mood, which was so high, starts to falter and fall. These clothes are just too bright and gorgeous for me.

And then I look at my watch and see it is 4.35 p.m., and I am going to be home later than I've ever been since Robert moved in. I know what that will mean for me. I wonder what his reaction will be when I come through the door with all these lovely clothes. He'll hate the idea of charity. But there is so much more to it than that, though. I sit here a while longer, thinking things over.

I AM A PLAIN WOMAN, tall and thin like my father. I know that, and I am comfortable with it. "You've got the basics," my mother used to say to me as a young woman, whatever the basics were. "You'll have to make do with that." It was not meant unkindly. It is just that my mother was a practical sort of woman. We had, at home when I was young, a painting above the fireplace of a strong and beautiful, exotic-looking woman with dark hair and eyes and a burnt orange roll-neck jumper. I loved that painting and wished I was her. I still have it, the painting, above my fireplace at home.

I have never been one of the girls, worrying about my hair and my make-up and the latest fashions. I had, for many years, brown, shoulder-length hair cut every six weeks. I use a Boots No 7 face powder and lipstick – and mascara when I go out in the evening. I wear sensible clothes and shoes, which I've always bought from Marks & Spencer in Ipswich. I sometimes imagine my father's voice in my head when wearing something new. He would often say I looked "clean and tidy" and "that should be good enough for anyone". And it still is. For me, anyway.

When I was younger, I was bullied at school because of my looks. A dusty old teacher once called me Olive Oyl, and that became a nickname amongst those who liked me. "Skull-Face" was what some of the others called me. But I knew Father and Mother loved me in their own way, and they were always telling me how good I was at things, arts and crafts mainly. So, although there were times – many times, in truth – when I wished I were shorter and prettier and less ungainly, I eventually kind of grew into my skin and was used to it.

And then Robert moved in. I don't think he has ever said anything complimentary about my appearance since; I have been told by other men that I have nice eyes, for example. He has never made a positive comment, not even an encouraging noise when I returned from the hairdresser's early on.

He said, in those early days, that a top I was wearing was rather revealing, especially when I was leaning forward "showing everything". I made the mistake of laughing and saying there was not that much to see. Then I added that, besides, I was wearing a sensible Marks & Spencer bra. His mood soured for the rest of the day.

The next morning, he asked me to let him get the post when it arrived from now on, because he was expecting something for me. This – getting the post every day and, after looking it over, handing me anything that was addressed to me – is something he has done ever since.

What he got for me was a dress from a catalogue that

you'd find in amongst the Sunday newspapers. A catalogue that seemed to be targeted at old and infirm people living in homes, selling glasses with attached lights, non-slip lap trays so you can eat in front of the television, and fluffy slippers for both feet at the same time.

It was a dress that might have been appropriate for someone forty years older than me – a plain, light blue cloth thing that covered every part of me almost from top to toe. It wasn't a hazmat suit, but it wasn't far off it.

I did not know what to say. I knew by then that if I laughed or outright rejected it, his mood would darken and that could last the rest of the day. He was already mercurial, and I did not want to spoil everything with a careless remark.

I tried it on, going upstairs to the bathroom to look in the full-length mirror. I looked myself up and down, buttoned up to my neck and down my arms to my hands, and truth be told, I think it should have gone down to my ankles, but my legs are longer than average, so it was shorter than that; neither one thing nor the other.

I changed back into what I was wearing before and went downstairs. I looked at his expectant face, as if he thought I was going to say how much I liked it, that it was lovely and how pleased I was; thank you so much. Instead, I said it would have been perfect, but the catalogue company wasn't very good with their sizings, and it was short in the leg, and even though I wear modesty shorts, I was worried it might show more than I wanted to. I'd return it for him. I knew, even then, he must not be seen to be at fault.

I suggested we sit down together online and look at different clothes for me as it was "about time I updated my wardrobe". I soon realised, as we scrolled through the pages of various websites, what he wanted me to wear. Plain, simple clothes that covered any part of me a man might find remotely attractive. My very own sackcloth and ashes collection.

I know now how foolish I have been, as I seem to have become some sort of dreary old drudge in my appearance. I did it because I wanted to please him and to make him happy. I also recognised – from comments about men "gawping", as he put it, down my top – that he was lacking in self-esteem and felt insecure. I wanted to boost his confidence.

In bed, in terms of what I wore, he liked me to wear pyjamas and nightdresses that were aimed at younger women, teenagers even. Winnie the Pooh. Disney princesses. He never said, and I never asked why, but I now suspect that he wants to see me in the bedroom as though I were young and innocent and with a man for the first time. But perhaps I overthink things. Maybe he just likes Tigger.

The fact is, I now only wear what Robert would like me to wear. Anything I am thinking of buying, I show to him first with a casual, "What do you think?" I await his approval. Anything pretty, he'll reply, "It's not really you, is it?" and then point to the attractive model wearing it as though adding, "You don't look like her, do you?" I can't help but wonder what will happen as my body changes through pregnancy and what he will be like with me then.

I GET HOME, eventually, carrying my handbag and the bits and pieces bag and the IKEA bag full of maternity clothes. It crossed my mind, I am ashamed to say, that I could have left the IKEA bag somewhere, not taken it home, and I believe I would have done so if there were somewhere I could have hidden it well.

He is sitting there, on the sofa in the living room, a mug of coffee on the armrest, as I come through the door. I can see from his face that he has worked himself up into a fury. I am not sure if it is because the day's trading has gone badly again or whether it is because I am late. Either way, I know where this is going.

"Take your fucking time," he says matter-of-factly. "I made you a milky coffee." He nods over to the armchair by the windowsill, where the mug is sitting. "It'll be cold by now ... have a skin on it." He sighs as though I have committed a terrible crime, caused such great offence.

I leave the IKEA bag in the hallway, thinking I can maybe slip it into the garage out of sight later. But he spots it. And, as he then glances at me, I can see he knows that I realise he has seen it. I wonder if he might not mention it straightaway, leaving everything unspoken with the tension building to a flashpoint over something and nothing later on. But he goes straight on in.

"What's that?" he asks.

"Just a few maternity clothes ... from a woman at work." I don't say "friend". He does not really like me to have friends. Just him. Not-so-lovely him.

"You've told people already?" A raised voice of mock surprise. Like I've given away a state secret.

I shrug and put my hands on my tummy as if to say, "They guessed ... what could I do?"

"And you got the begging bowl out."

"She gave them to me ... I couldn't refuse ... it would cause offence."

A silence.

I say, "I'm sorry." The phrase sticks in my throat. I am ashamed of myself for saying it. But sometimes it helps. Not always.

Another long silence.

"Bring it here," he says. "The bag. Let me look."

He watches me go and get it, lift it, bring it back, put it by his feet.

He rifles through, smirking to himself at what he sees. But, really, he wants me to see he is mocking me.

He pulls out a dress that is bright and short and pretty – perfect for Layla, but as he would say, not me at all.

"Here," he says, handing me the dress. "Put this on."

I do not want to stand there undressing in front of him. I rather think he will look at my body, my tummy, in disgust.

I do not want to go upstairs and try it on in front of the full-length mirror in the bathroom. "What are you doing?" he'll call up after me. "I've seen it all before ... what there is of it."

I do not want to put the dress on at all; it is for someone curvy like Layla, not a lamp post like me.

I want to say no, but cannot bring myself to say it out loud. I know what the consequences will be.

"I'll get rid of it all." That's what I say. "I don't know what she was thinking." I feel a surge of guilt, as though I am betraying Layla, my baby-to-be too.

I don't look at him. I have to contain my thoughts. Guilt. Resentment towards him. Anger mostly; growing anger, if I am honest. I had believed – at least hoped – that having a baby might turn things round between us. How wrong I was. If anything, it has already made things worse.

He looks through the rest of the bag, a "dear oh dear" expression on his face that he knows I will see and that will make me feel humiliated. That I am a woman so plain – so ugly – that I could not possibly wear anything nice.

He is about to say something about the beautiful clothes in the bag and how I look and how people will laugh at me if I wear them and how he is only thinking of what is best for me.

But then the doorbell ding-a-ling-lings, followed by a knockety-knock at the front door.

He says, "Get rid of these stupid things."

And I go across and pick up the bag and take it through the kitchen into the utility room and on to the garage, where I leave it just inside the door. All I can see is Layla's smiling face and how happy everyone was for me. I feel such impotent fury burning inside me.

I stand there in the garage, listening to Robert having a conversation on the front doorstep. I think it is with Harry from over the way; I recognise his East London accent. I cannot hear what they are saying, but I suspect it is related to Harry's investments with Robert. Harry seems upset, his voice raised and slightly whiny, and Robert seems to be placating him. Robert is completely different outside of the house with everyone else. He is a charmer, of course. Nobody would ever believe what he is really like behind closed doors.

I stand here aimlessly. I do not know why there is a garage here. People don't put cars in garages anymore. My house has a driveway that takes two cars. I have never put my car, a white Nissan Micra, in the garage. I have always worried that I would park too far to one side and not be able to get out the door. That I'd then reverse and scrape all down one side of the car. And so the garage is empty other than shelves of half-full pots of paint and weed killer and lawn restorer against the back wall and a big shelf with some storage space beneath for a toolbox, a pile of spare bricks and roof tiles, a lawnmower, a broom and a rake and a tub of car engine oil and a wheelbarrow.

And then I walk into the living room just as Robert comes back indoors.

"I suppose you heard all that, didn't you?" he says in quite a nasty voice. I shake my head. "Harry wants his money, the interest payments, by the end of the month. The stupid old bastard won't wait," he adds.

He doesn't expect a reply; instead he goes straight up to the box room, to do his trades and move all the money about.

He does not come down until almost eight o'clock, leaving me to struggle to keep our dinner nice and hot. We eat in silence. He is in such a foul mood I dare not speak. He then goes back upstairs to the box room, barely a word to me. I read one of Father's old books about churches for the rest of the evening and go to bed about ten thirty. I hear him walking around later, slamming doors as loud as he can, and then he sleeps downstairs again.

3

Today is my last day at school before the half-term holiday – a week off; although, in truth, I normally spend at least some of the days preparing lesson plans for the next half-term through to the long summer holidays. I will try to busy my way through the week ahead.

Breakfast is another tense affair, even though I made him a cooked breakfast, which he usually enjoys. As he finishes, I take a piece of bacon he's left and cut it up and put it on a plate out the back door for the ginger cat. I then tell Robert that a baby scan has been booked in for Tuesday and how lovely it would be if we could go along together. "It's to check the baby is well."

He seems calm but distracted, asks the time (three o'clock) and the place (Ipswich Hospital), and does not seem disagreeable to this. He is not exactly excited, but I take his question as a positive sign or, at least, not a negative one.

"We'll go, then?" I ask. "Our first chance to see our baby."

And he nods his agreement as he gets up to go to work upstairs. I leave for work more hopeful than I have been since I revealed my pregnancy to him on his birthday.

My day at school is so lovely. Everyone now seems to know about the baby, and there are smiles and hugs galore. Even the head, Mr Shearman, who can be rather dour, comes up to me and seems very pleased. "A dream come true for you," he says, and I wonder if everybody knows how long I've yearned for this.

All the female teachers and teaching assistants I am friendly with say we must have lunch in town next week. "Or Ipswich, that new Italian place that's opened by the waterfront," Sharon adds. "And then some shopping for baby clothes. Make a day of it."

I say that would be wonderful, but I cannot this holiday ... maybe we could do something in the summer. "Robert's going to surprise me. A few days away! I don't know where yet." I make this sound as believable as I can. I do not know what else I can say or do. He does not like me to go out with my friends. He sulked for ages when I went for lunch with them just before Easter. And he was very sour the next time, a week later when we went for morning coffee. I have not done it since, to keep the peace with Robert. I just make endless excuses as varied as I can to my friends.

As I walk home after school, words of love and best wishes and warm congratulations in my ears, my mood sinks again. I sit on the bench halfway between school and my home, and I ponder over my life. How I have it in me to be happy at school, but sad at home. Of course, it is Robert that makes the difference. I hope again that maybe the baby will change things for the better for us.

I am not looking forward to this half-term holiday. In fact, I dread it. When I am working Monday to Friday and doing a little preparation for the next week on Saturday and Sunday and he is up in the box room, trading and making money for his investors, the time passes well enough. I can make the best of it, such as it is.

A week at home and I will be on edge all the time, waiting for the next explosion. I do not know which way he will go with the baby. I had thought that sorting out a baby scan without his knowledge might have angered him. He likes to be in control of things. Me, really. And now the baby too. That worries me. But he let it go about the scan and seemed agreeable enough. Perhaps he will warm to the idea. I wonder if he will continue to sleep downstairs, a clear sign that he remains unhappy, or if he will return upstairs. And whether, if he comes back to the bedroom, he will bring out the notebook again.

LOOKING BACK, the first real warning sign came that night when Robert asked how many men I had slept with. I managed to avoid the question then. But he returned to it the next night and the one after, and eventually, to reassure him, I told him more about my life, or at least a version of it.

I was an only child, and Father and Mother, my elderly but loving parents, raised me to be a good person who would be kind to others and play an active role in the community in the village of Trimley St Martin near the seaside town and port of Felixstowe in Suffolk. I went away to university in Nottingham to do a degree and qualify as a teacher, and then I returned to teach at the primary school down the road. I moved back into the family home in Grimston Lane. It seemed the natural thing to do. But now I think it was a mistake.

I had various boyfriends when I was younger, two serious ones at university and even a fiancé in my first year back, a fellow teacher from the primary school. We broke up – he wanted to travel and teach overseas in Japan of all places. I did not want to leave my home town. He left the school at the end of the term, and that was that. For a long time after, I still hoped to meet the love of my life, a kind-hearted man to spend my life with and have a family. I ached for it.

Working in a primary school and living at home through my twenties and into my thirties made that harder than I'd thought it would be. And I am shy and, if I am honest, a little too tall and plain. And I am not very good at conversing with adults. Men, I mean. Flirting with men. There were moments over the years at Christmas events and the like, but they all came to nothing.

In my early thirties, I'd planned to move out, to give myself one last chance, but my mother fell ill and was diagnosed with pancreatic cancer, so I stayed to look after her. She died within three months. I then looked after my darling father, who was ten years older than Mother and in his eighties, as he suffered from Alzheimer's and then prostate cancer, which crept its way around and spread through his body until it was too late. He passed away at home, nursed by me, and I was thankful for that.

Grieving, alone and depressed, I somehow acted on his dying wish and made a fresh start – selling the family home and buying myself this three-bed detached house in a close on a housing estate in the neighbouring village of Trimley St Mary. I put the rest of my inheritance in the bank for a rainy day. I had everything in a practical sense – a nice job, a lovely house, money tucked away – but there was a massive hole in my life where love and affection should have been: a husband and, in due course, children, with me at the heart of our family.

I told Robert that I had had two serious boyfriends in my life, both at university. I did not mention my ex-fiancé. I don't know why. I think I wanted to keep that to myself. Maybe I still have feelings for him. Robert did not react well to what I'd said. Everything went from bad to worse from there.

"TWO MEN ... AND YOU'RE THIRTY-SEVEN." He made a snorting noise. I was not sure if that meant he did not believe me or if he was mocking me; that I was so plain, so unappealing, that no one else would want me. He badgered away, worrying at all of it until, at last, we had covered everything from my first boyfriend, of sorts, at school through to a drunken kiss with a friendly waiter after a Christmas dinner with work friends. Even now, I do not understand how I let myself get into this situation; I believe I wanted to placate him, make him happy, win his love. He always pushed me for more.

It got worse. He would go back over, time and again, the who-what-when-where of each and every one of the men, boys really, whom I had been with in some way. And he would get angry if I said something different, got a fact wrong, and he would make me repeat myself. I tried to stay calm to ease his frustration. Over the weeks, we progressed, if that is the right word for all of this, into a situation where he got out a notebook, and I had to write it all down. I cringe at the thought of it. I am ashamed of myself for letting it happen.

One night, towards the end of the Easter school holiday, we were sitting up in bed, him with his laptop, me rereading Agatha Christie's *Death on the Nile* on my Kindle for the umpteenth time. I love my father's old books. He stopped and sighed and shut his laptop, putting it under his side of the bed. I knew what was coming next. I had done for some time. The long-suffering sigh was the giveaway.

He took the A4 orange notebook with "Laura" written on the front of it from his bedside cabinet. The pen must have been running out of ink when he wrote it, as he had to go over each letter several times. That would have made him angry. He likes everything just so.

There were coloured Post-its sticking up neatly from amongst the pages. He had written "David" and "John" on them. He flicked through the notebook. There were other notes, from schoolday crushes onwards, from the front to the back.

He opened the notebook, licking his thumb now and then as he perused the pages by "David" and "John". We had talked through both of them recently. I gave the same answers as I did on previous occasions. He was satisfied with what I said.

I could see he was going right back to the beginning, before my first proper boyfriend, to those days at school and summer holidays in the fields and Christmas discos and to what he called "gropings and fondlings". I hoped I could go over them without saying anything different or new that he might seize upon.

"Derek," he said. An old-fashioned name even then. He laughed as he repeated the two syllables slowly in a mocking voice. D'uh. Rick. It was not a nice laugh.

I felt myself tensing.

"Tell me about D'uh. Rick," he said, his voice calm and mannered now.

I had to say what I said last time but without repeating it word for word as if I had rehearsed it.

I swallowed hard and spoke. "Derek was the first boy to kiss me ... he came up to me ... I was standing with two friends against the wall ... we had the last dance at the Christmas disco at school. 'Last Christmas' by Wham!"

I waited. He liked to lead these conversations. If I rushed through it, all neat and tidy and well prepared, he would have got angry. As though I were cheating him out of his pleasure.

"He asked you for the last dance?"

"Yes."

"You fancied him?"

"It seemed rude not to accept. My parents knew his parents."

He made another huffing noise; it sounded derisive.

"And then what?"

"We danced. We just kind of had our hands on each other's waists. And I then stumbled over his feet and ..."

"Did he do it on purpose?"

"Um, I think so ... so he held me close, and I felt uncomfortable as he pressed himself against me."

"You did not struggle or push him away or shout at him?"

I hesitated, remembering what it was I said last time. "It was so crowded and loud, and everyone was squashed in together."

"So you didn't mind him pressed up against you ... his thing against you." He sounded disgusted.

I knew the moment was in the balance. That I needed to get through it quickly, satisfying him, keeping him happy. I didn't want him getting angry.

"He kissed me. I didn't know what to do. I was sixteen. I don't like that, I said to him ... and then he grabbed my left boob, and I pushed him away ... and then the music ended, and he disappeared into the crowd, and I did not speak to him ever again."

He looked down at the notebook, reading over what I'd said last time. He tutted, and I wondered if I had said something wrong, something different to the time before.

"He grabbed your boob, and then you pushed him away?"

I nodded.

"Straightaway? Or did he have a feel first?"

"Straightaway."

"Did you push him away or his hand away?"

I could not remember exactly what I'd said the time before.

"I kind of pushed his hand away as I went to push him on the chest."

He sighed.

He turned the notebook and pointed to a note I had written some time earlier. "I pushed him on the chest."

"So what was it?" he asked in a reasonable tone, as if this were a perfectly normal thing for him to be checking.

"I pushed him on the chest, knocking his hand away in doing so."

He sighed again.

He reached across to the drawer of the bedside table. Took out a pen. He started correcting the notes.

Derek was the first boy to kiss me all those years ago. He came up to me and asked me for the last dance. I had waited all evening, hoping he would. He held me tight, and I liked it. And we kissed. On and on while George Michael sang. And he walked me home, and we both fumbled with each other, and I missed my ten-thirty curfew. But Derek stood there in the porch and apologised to Father and Mother, and they thanked him for bringing me to the door, and all was well.

It is true that we did not speak to each other again. Christmas came and went. So did the New Year. When we returned to school, I hoped – was expecting – that he would ask me out and that we would be boyfriend and girlfriend. At that young age, I thought we would live happily after. But he did not seem to be in the usual places at break and lunch times. Later, I saw him with another girl, Steph, who was livelier and shapelier than me. And I was disappointed but not as heartbroken as I might have expected.

But I could not tell Robert any of this. That I'd wanted Derek to ask me to dance. That I'd loved everything about that evening and those first moments in the trees and fields down by my home in Grimston Lane. For Robert would have seen it as seedy and told me that I was a slutty young girl. But it was not. And neither was I. I'd enjoyed every moment of it.

And then Robert, having corrected his notes and sighed once more, put the pen and notebook back in the drawer. I knew what was coming next. That he would turn off the light, wait a moment or two, and then turn towards me. And then he would roll on top of me, pulling my pyjama top up.

But that night, he did not. He turned out the bedside light, and as I waited there, expecting to feel his hand on my breast, he spoke in a tight and reasoned voice, saying, "Don't ever fucking lie to me again." I went to say, "No ... I'm sorry," but I knew he might think that "no" meant I was defying him. So I was going to just say "sorry" and was first thinking how to make my voice sound just so.

But then he hit me with his fist, striking the side of my head, my skull. I lay there, stunned into silence, as he got up out of the bed.

"All right?" he said. Then again, as I did not reply, "All right?" in a stronger voice.

"All right," I replied, trying not to cry. I lay there listening to him urinating loudly into the toilet, the bathroom door wide open. He then came back and climbed into bed and turned his back on me as if nothing had happened. I lay there, stifling sobs, until he was snoring. As I lay there for hours, I felt a sense of shame, but was not sure why.

BY THE TIME I get home from school this Friday afternoon, all the love and warmth and kindness I felt from everyone around me has gone. Instead, I now feel sick. I have that same old fearful feeling inside me as I walk up the path, a sense that something bad will happen tonight.

There he is, sitting on the sofa in the living room with a mug of coffee on the armrest. I can feel the tension and hear it in his voice as he greets me. "Don't answer the door if it goes," he instructs. "It might be Harry. He's being a twat. Just ignore it. Pretend we're not in." I do not mention that we have two cars on the driveway, so it is obvious we are here.

I assume Robert still owes Harry money, and that it has not yet been paid. And this means he will be bristling all evening, and I will have to tiptoe around him so that he does not lose his temper. It should not be like this. None of it. These should be the happiest days of my life.

I go into the kitchen to make myself a cup of tea, and I see it through the window.

The ginger cat lying stretched out in the middle of the lawn.

I breathe in sharply, knowing from the position of its body that it is dead.

I stop for a moment, upset. I am not really a pet person, as we never had any when I was young. But I had grown rather fond of Ginger. I fed him something every day; I have done for weeks since he first appeared one morning meowing loudly.

Robert walks up behind me, puts his empty mug in the sink and then looks out of the window. He does not say anything.

"It's Ginger," I tell him. "He's dead." My voice cracks a little, but I go on. "He was feral, I think, ever such a thin thing. I suppose he must have been older than he looked."

I wonder if Robert is about to say that he is sorry the cat is dead and that I should go back into the living room whilst he buries it down amongst the bushes at the bottom of the garden.

But he does not. He says nothing.

Instead, I get the feeling that he is watching me.

I turn, and he gives me such a strange look.

I take a tea towel from a drawer and a bin bag from under the sink. I find a trowel in the garage, and then I walk down to the bottom of the garden and slowly dig a hole between the bushes. I find myself fighting back tears.

I go up to Ginger and look down at the poor animal. It is clearly dead, its legs all stiff. I have never seen a dead cat. I go to pick it up, wrapping it in a tea towel.

I sob as I bury the little thing. Then go into the garage to find a brick or tile to cover the muddy earth where he now lies.

I say a prayer, The Lord's Prayer, after I have placed a brick on the grave. It's all I can think of to do.

When I go back indoors and wash my hands at the kitchen sink, Robert seems more cheerful. He slips his mobile phone in his pocket as if he has just ended a conversation. He does not mention Ginger. Instead, he says he is going to be "on the road" this evening, that he's "meeting new investors" tonight and tomorrow and that "new investors are the lifeblood of investment schemes ... got to keep them coming in!" I nod and smile and ask him what time he will leave and be back.

He answers me in a pleasant enough way. "Eight tonight until late tomorrow night ... I'll stay in a Travel Lodge somewhere overnight." He does not say where, and I do not ask. I say I will this evening look at things online for the baby, including nursery equipment. And that tomorrow I might go out to the out-of-town supermarkets to look at baby clothes. He nods his agreement.

As he goes upstairs to pack a change of clothes into his rucksack, I ask him if he'd like me to make a sandwich to take with him. He looks back at me and smiles, such an odd sort of smile, and says, word for word, "I'll have a bacon sandwich, please ... I won't have to share it with that fucking cat anymore." And I turn away, with tears in my eyes, as I realise suddenly that this monster somehow killed the cat.

And he did it because he does not want me to love or care for anything but him.

4

SATURDAY, 29 MAY

I have always thought this close was a nice, contented place. And all day today, while the sun was shining and I have been busying about on my own with baby things, I think it is.

Robert came back in a foul mood late in the evening and went straight to bed without a word. I do not think his trip went well at all. There will be worse to come because of that.

At night, as it is now, moving towards Sunday morning, the close has a different feel to me. A place of darkness, shadows and danger somehow.

I have started waking up in the night since he started sleeping downstairs. I lie here working things through in my head. I then have trouble getting back to sleep. I turn one way and the other. Neither are comfortable positions. I lie on my back, imagining my baby growing inside me. But that, for some reason, is the most uncomfortable. My back hurts.

I walk along the landing into the bathroom, where I sit on the toilet and wee. I pour myself some cold water from the tap into the toothbrush mug, just an inch or two to wet my parched lips. I walk slowly back along the landing with it. I stop and listen for him downstairs. He is snoring now, not loudly, but enough for me to know he is in a deep sleep. If I ask him in the morning how he's slept, he will, of course, pull a face and say "on and off" in his bravest, most long-suffering voice.

I go into the room at the front of the house, what will be my baby's room. There are dark blue, full-length curtains, the walls are a pale grey, and there is a slightly darker, fluffy grey carpet. I like the feel of it between my toes. I had the room recarpeted at the end of last year, as the old carpet was flat and thin. We have still not yet talked properly about the baby, and I hope that the scan on Tuesday will see him coming round more to the idea. I think I would like to change the old curtains to something more child-like, maybe light and patterned, and to paint this room in a pale yellow or green – boy or girl – colour. I don't want to wait and paint it blue or pink.

I walk across to the window, just to look out, to think about things, as I sip at my water.

All the street lights are turned off at midnight and come back on at dusk the next day. The council cut back on these things before the pandemic.

The moonlight allows me to see across the close, and I gaze over at the other houses. Harry's son is standing there, looking back at me from number five.

Number five is lived in by Harry and his son, Alex. Harry is a widower in his early eighties. A busy bee of a man, he moved here with his son from East London when his wife, Helen, died. "A fresh start," he once said to me. "Near the sea." He is a member of various local societies and on all sorts of committees, filling his hours with good deeds. A busybody, some might say. But I have always liked him. Alex, on the other hand, is a dishevelled and wild-eyed man in his forties. He has spent time in prison for burglary, but is now out and unemployed and spends all day looking out of his bedroom window. I do not like Alex; he unnerves me.

The blind to his bedroom window has been pulled up. I am not sure if he did that as he saw me enter my front bedroom – so that I could see him – or whether he did it earlier and has been like this for some time. He is standing upright and watching me. He is stripped to the waist, possibly naked. I cannot be sure from this distance. I am not sure what to make of it.

I feel instinctively that I should step back, out of sight, leave what will be my baby's room. But part of me thinks I should not have to do that. This is my home. And another part of me does not wish to cause offence, if he is standing there, as I am, suffering from insomnia. He may simply have taken his top off. I am dressed, as I always am at night, in my pyjamas.

I am about to turn, to wander away as if I have not noticed him, when he raises his left arm and waves at me. I wave back, without thought, being polite, not realising that he may take this as some form of encouragement. I stand for a moment, thinking, expecting, that he will turn and go after my friendly gesture. But he stands there, looking down now at whatever he is doing out of sight of me. And then he looks up at me, and I know what it is he is doing. And I walk away.

When my mood dips, as it always does at night, I think this close is an oppressive, claustrophobic place; everyone all around, knowing each other's business, watching each other.

Harry banging on my front door, without so much as a by-your-leave. Bringing trouble to my house.

And now Alex, whom I saw as a sad, rather sorrowful man, has shown himself to be more than that. An unpleasant, sexually active man. And that makes me feel both uncomfortable and disgusted at the thought that he might somehow take this further.

———————

I GO BACK TO BED, my sleepless mind twisting this way and that in torment. I know as I look back again over our relationship, I should have ended it – goodness knows how – that first time he hit me. But I remembered my sad and lonely life before him. And I thought then he had some good qualities; everyone seemed to like him in the close. I remember Mrs Knox from next door at number two, usually so circumspect, saying how lucky I was to have "such a nice man". Sarah from over the way at number one said much the same thing another time. He invested my money so well. And I hoped to change those parts of him that were not so nice.

But the fact is, he was, and still is, a controlling man. It took me a long time to recognise it was him, not me, who was at fault. After that first physical assault, he carried on as if nothing had happened. He went about his business. He continued to work upstairs in the box room every weekday. Other than going to work and doing humdrum tasks – getting the weekly shop, going for petrol, picking up milk and bread – he did not like me going out, seeing friends, even talking to the neighbours. He preferred me to stay at home, to attend to his needs, to be blunt. But he did not like me to make a noise, vacuuming, tidying up, going in and out of rooms.

"Walk round banging a wooden spoon in a saucepan, why don't you?" he would open the door and shout downstairs.

I thought he was joking the first time he said it, but, on another occasion when I was vacuuming outside the box-room door, he wrenched it open so hard that the handle almost came off in his hand, and I could see from his face how furious he was.

I recall watching a film together a few nights after he first hit me, towards the end of the Easter school holidays, *Harry Met Sally*, with Billy Crystal and Meg Ryan. I had long learned by then not to respond to any of his questions about whether I found this man or that man attractive on the television. I had to anticipate his questions and somehow avoid them. "But you must find someone attractive!" he exclaimed at one point.

I did not know what to say. Damned if I do. Damned if I don't. I thought for a while, sensing how stressed he was becoming in the silence, and then said, "I find you attractive. But it's not just about looks, not really, it's about the whole thing." I gabbled on. "The whole person. I fell in love with you because of everything about you."

That seemed to placate him. I reached out and held his hand as we watched the film, and he did not pull it away as he sometimes does when he is upset. He then went on to tell me towards the end that he found Meg Ryan attractive, her face, her hair, everything, although, less gallantly he added, "She must be bloody ancient now." With my tall and thin "birdlike appearance" – as someone once said – I could not have looked less like Meg Ryan.

But I did like her short blond bob. It looked so much nicer than my brown, shoulder-length hairstyle that I'd had forever and a day. Her hair made her look sassy; mine just made me look dreary.

And so, one afternoon before going back to school after the Easter holiday, and having told Robert that I was off to the hairdresser's and would be back at five o'clock so he would not worry, I had my hair cut short with streaks of blond put in it.

I have to say I looked quite different and it made me feel somehow younger and better-looking.

My hairdresser Alice said it looked "wonderful" and it

"takes years off you!" which I think was meant to be a compliment. It did not sound like it. She has the biggest bottom I have ever seen on anyone. It looks as though it has been grafted to her body by Dr Frankenstein. I have never said anything about it though.

Robert did not like my new hairstyle. He was drinking a coffee in the kitchen and turned as he heard me coming in the front door and through. His mouth dropped open, and he swore, "Fucking hell," but not in a "that looks great" kind of way – more of a "what the hell have you done?" He hesitated and then laughed at me, long and loud, as if I simply looked stupid.

He spoke little for the rest of the afternoon and evening. Just glanced at me as I brought our evening meal to the table in the corner of the kitchen and smiled to himself; his intent to belittle me was unmistakable. I felt myself burning with embarrassment and anger inside. Then later, as we watched a TV programme on Sky about UAPs, which fascinate him and about which he has various interdimensional theories, he kept glancing at me theatrically and finally said, "What on earth were you thinking?"

I shrugged, fearing to answer him but determined not to cry.

"You'll have to do something about it," he said, as though I were some hideously deformed creature. "Everyone will laugh at you. I'm just thinking of you."

I couldn't bring myself to say it did not look that bad. Just different. And I liked it as well. Instead, I said I'd go upstairs and wash and colour it back, that I could wear a hat to school whilst it grew out, but he said I didn't suit a hat, and he spent the rest of the evening in a sullen silence. In bed, he turned his back to me and went straight to sleep. And I was so angry with him.

That, I think, was the moment I decided I had had

enough. I could live with many things, but the constant drip-drip-drip of derision and endlessly belittling me wore me down to the point where I could not take it anymore.

But I had no idea how to break up with him. He was there in my house, in charge, in control of me. He had my money, which he was, I believed, increasing every month. I rehearsed over and over in my mind how I might ask him to leave but was too fearful of what he would say and do in response.

And then, a few days later, having missed another period – and I have been regular as clockwork since I was a teenager – I bought a pregnancy test from the pharmacy over at the supermarket at Warren Heath. That evening I shut myself away in the bathroom, and a few minutes later, I was stunned to see that thin blue line.

I sat there on the toilet for ages, a mix of utter joy and terror filling my heart and mind. I cried to myself for a while. Then took the test downstairs and pushed it and the packaging deep down into the kitchen bin. When I got to bed, he was already fast asleep, and I lay there next to him, awake for ages. I decided, finally, for the sake of my baby, to give things one last try.

I AWAKE SUDDENLY and lie here blinking, gathering my thoughts.

I turn slowly, uncomfortably, onto my side and check the time on the clock on the bedside cabinet. It is 2.33 a.m.

He is still asleep, snoring away downstairs. Something else has woken me, and I wonder what it was.

I listen to hear if whatever it was, a side gate opening and slamming in the wind most likely, happens again. But all is quiet. I wonder whether it might have been the noise of a car door, someone arriving back in the close or leaving it. I lie here still, deciding which way to turn to try to get comfortable. I doubt I'm going to fall back to sleep again easily.

There's another noise. The slamming of a gate for sure. Not my gate, though. It's a gate at one of the other houses in the close. I expect it will swing open and crash to again at the next gust of wind. And I'll not be able to ignore it and go back to sleep. I think that, as I am nodding off, it will slam again, waking me up. And I will lie here waiting for the next time, and the next, on and on. I decide to get up and look out of the bedroom window at the front of the house to see which one it is. If it is next door, I will slip on my dressing gown and go out and shut it properly.

I pull back one of the curtains so that I can look across the close. What I see alarms me. To the left of my house, at number two, lives Mrs Knox, a widowed lady in her sixties. She has two sons in their thirties, Mark and Paul, who both still live at home.

The elder son, Mark, has had mental health issues and works on and off; mostly off. He always seems very angry. Shaven-headed and with a goatee beard, he scares me with his intense stares. The younger son, Paul, has special needs, and he sorts out the trolleys at a local supermarket. He is what Father would have called a simple soul. Others would be less charitable.

I chat to Mrs Knox sometimes, and she is friendly enough if rather stiff-backed and mannered. Formal, that's the word. I think her life may be rather sad what with her sons always and forever at home. She seems to be at their beck and call.

The two Knox boys, Mark and Paul, are on the other side of the close, by Harry's house. One of them, the slower one, is standing watch, looking around the close for curtains to twitch, lights to go on, neighbours to appear. I step back. He does not seem to have noticed me over here. The other one is throwing something, maybe stones from the gravel driveway, up at Alex's window.

I can see Alex at his window. He is dressed and standing up and moving, jerkily, from side to side as though he is dancing to music. There are coloured lights flashing on and off behind him in his room. He must have earphones on so Harry is not woken by the music. It is a strangely unsettling feeling, seeing this act unfolding, as though I have intruded in some other dark reality.

The two Knox boys start miming his jerky movements but in an exaggerated, mocking way. They stop now and then to gesture up at him, although he does not seem to respond and just keeps dancing in that odd way of his. All of this – the dancing, the mocking, the gestures – is done silently; at least, I cannot hear any shouts, those catcalls full of obscenities that you might expect to hear. I am privy to some sort of odd relationship I never knew existed. I wonder why Harry's son stands at the window moving around like this and why the Knox boys are watching and joining in in this strange way.

One of the Knox boys, that older, angrier one, makes ever more exaggerated dance moves and more violent gestures as Alex dances on regardless. It is this apparent insouciance that seems to annoy the Knox boy the most. I wonder why this is. Perhaps they were once friends. Maybe something more than that, even. I don't know. There is something personal in this, I'm sure.

I watch on until at last, as Alex continues dancing, the older Knox boy picks up an ornamental rock from the edge of Harry's driveway, steps forward and throws it as hard as he can towards the upstairs window. But he misjudges the weight of it and misses; this infuriates him more, as he picks up more stones from the driveway and hurls them upwards, some hitting, others missing the window. Alex dances on. The younger Knox boy eventually drags the older one away.

I slip back to bed, lying on my back, pulling the duvet up to my chin.

This close is not the happy, idyllic place I had imagined.

It's not the safe haven it might seem to be.

There is wickedness here, depravity and evil. What I have seen tonight frightens me more than I can say.

5

We are having breakfast, and things between us are on a knife edge. He seems ready to blow. Most likely, it is because he did not get the money he expected yesterday. But it could be about anything, really. Him just being him. I am waiting to see which way he goes. Things are not so good when we spend long periods together. The day stretches out ahead of us. I'm dreading it.

I suggest carefully that we might go shopping for the baby clothes and nursery items I saw in Ipswich on Saturday. "Not yet," he replies, as though distracted. "Later, when ... you know, we're sure." I'm not certain what he means by that. It could be "we're sure of the sex". But the implication, I think, is that I might lose the baby, and that horrifies me. I don't know why he'd think such an awful thing.

I sit quietly for a few moments, regaining my composure, and then suggest seeing a film in Ipswich. "That new Tom Cruise is out," I say. I am about to add, "You'd like that." But I do not in case he wouldn't and takes offence at my assumption and snaps back that he's always hated Tom Cruise films.

"We could walk along the waterfront after, have something to eat." He shakes his head. It's going to be one of those days.

There's a knock at the door. A "bang, bang, open up" kind of knocking.

"Christ's sake," he mutters, throwing his serviette on the table as he gets up. "I get no fucking peace from that stupid man." I assume he means Harry.

He is moving to the door in such a fury that I think he may assault Harry, so I am up too and following him.

Robert pulls the door open.

I stand to the side in the living room, and I can see Harry on the doorstep.

He looks nervous.

"I've told you," Robert says in an angry voice. "There's been a mistake, that's all. End of the month. I said, didn't I? How many times ..."

I can hear Harry talking, the slightly whiney tone of his voice, but not the exact words.

"Here," Robert shouts at him. "Laura will tell you. Laura, come here." He turns and steps into the living room, pulling me out into the hallway. I can feel each of his fingers pressed into the flesh of my upper arm.

"Laura is in charge of the books and making payments." He looks at me for confirmation, and I stare back at him. I nod involuntarily and wish I hadn't. "She got in a pickle, and it's taking me ages to sort it all out. But I've told you ... you'll have it tomorrow by midnight, the thirty-first of May."

"It's not just me, Rob, is it?" Harry speaks more confidently in a self-righteous voice. He turns and gestures towards other houses in the close. "You've others to pay as well, you know ... what are you going to do about them?"

Robert stands there, and I can see he is so angry; he's standing there literally shaking with fury. I know that what he really wants to do is to lash out at Harry and send him sprawling on his back on the path. And then bang Harry's head against the ground again and again until he feels satisfied that he's won the argument.

Harry carries on blithely, obliviously. He turns to me and says, "What do you think, Laura, is this right and proper ... is this what was promised?" He speaks as though I have made assurances to him about his investments. Maybe he assumes Robert and I work together.

I do not know what to say to him. I know better than to contradict Robert in private. I would not dare to do it in public. But I do not wish to be rude to Harry, to tell him it's nothing to do with me and to go away and mind his own business about other people's affairs.

I shake my head – too dismissively, I think – and turn away. It is the only thing I can do. I go back into the kitchen and stand there, now shaking too, listening to the rest of the conversation.

"End of the month, Harry. End of the month," Robert shouts, really, really loudly, and before Harry can reply, Robert slams the door in his face.

"What was all that about?" I say, without thinking, as he storms through into the kitchen. But then I wish I hadn't spoken.

"What do you think?" he yells, so close to my face I can smell his breath. "What do you fucking think?" And then he pushes me on my chest, just jabs out with the palm of his hand, and I tumble back and land on the floor.

I look up at him. He stands there panting, gathering his breath and his thoughts.

"Don't ever, ever, get the door again."

If I weren't frightened, I would laugh at the idiocy of the comment. But I don't. I just crouch there, knowing that if I get to my feet now, he will see it as defiance and knock me back down.

Off he goes, this horrible, cowardly man, back to his box
room. To do his trades, if that is possible on a Sunday, or to
move money about from one account to the other, presumably to pay off Harry and the other neighbours by tomorrow
night. I honestly don't know. I have a sudden stab of fear that
the money owed can't be paid and that Robert might use my
money to pay them off. I can't imagine where this might end.

I LIE on the sofa for a while whilst he works upstairs. I can
feel my unhappiness spreading through my body and
making me feel physically ill. I go back over our relationship.
I cannot help it. I torment myself.

I sleepwalked through the next stage after he hit me that
first time. It was my own fault. I let it happen.

He always wanted to go over my "former lovers", as he put
it, again and again. The endless details of everything. He
never asked why. Not that I could have said, "Because I
wanted to." Or simply, "I enjoyed it."

He asked me how many men I had slept with, as he put it,
early on. I do not think that should be asked; it is information
that should be shared by mutual choice not demanded. I
shrugged it off that first night, but he kept coming back to it
until I eventually said two, that was all. I did not include my
ex-fiancé, Noel, for some reason. I don't quite know why.
Some sort of sixth sense, perhaps. The thought that I had
once pledged to spend my life with one man, to have his children, would have angered Robert beyond words. He would
never have let that one go.

And so, as we went back and forth over everything from
school fumblings to parent-teacher association dinners and
kisses, it all got written down, and I was tested on it again and
again. He focused most on the two lovers I had spoken of. He

wanted to know all about them. I said that they were at the same university as me but doing different degrees. David was from Middlesbrough and studying engineering. John came from Arnold in Nottingham itself and was studying history.

We all went jogging in the mornings, through some university club, and that was how we met. I was with David first, my funny boy, but he left at the end of the first year to join the family engineering firm, and I did not see him again. Then I had a relationship with oh-so-serious John, which lasted most of the second year and into the third up to Christmas. He met a girl back home, and he broke things off with me in the New Year.

Robert and I went over David and John so many times. He would ask me questions this way and that. Always seeking to catch me out. Waiting for me to hesitate and stumble. I humoured him at first, made light of it, a joke, but there was so much anger just below the surface. I soon learned to take his questioning seriously.

Editing what happened in my head, remembering what was in the notes so I could repeat it when he tested me later.

I thought, deep down, he was insecure, had low self-esteem, needed to feel more confident – so I let this ... this thing ... begin, and it grew into something monstrous.

He would reach for the notebook and look through it, turning each page and reading through it, making the odd tutting noise, and then he would ask me to talk again about David or John or whoever. If I got the order of what he called "sexual happenings" wrong or the details muddled up, he would ask me to go over things again, speaking in a carefully modulated, ever-so-patient voice. And we would do this, on and on, until I got my story right.

Eventually he focused most often on the time after university when I was back at home and looking after my parents. He could not believe that, in those long years, I had not had a relationship at all. But I did not wish to talk about my ex-fiancé. And I did not want to tell him about work dos and nights out with colleagues when I had kissed men, and a little more, because I did not want him to think I was desperate ... or promiscuous ... or whatever. I told him about two easy-to-remember moments where I implied they forced themselves on me. He preferred to hear that than the truth. That I wanted them. And more.

I do not understand – I cannot explain – how this all came to pass. I think, in part, I felt sorry for him in the early days. He did not seem, behind the façade of calm and confidence, to be at ease in his own skin. I do not know why. He was handsome and personable, if a little sensitive about his height; at five feet five inches he was five inches shorter than me. He alluded to a hard childhood. He suggested he had never felt at ease with women until he met me. I wanted to help him, support him, encourage him to become the better person I was sure he could be.

And then he hit me again. I suppose, looking back, it was obvious that he would. And that it would become a regular thing.

He lashed out in anger when I got an answer wrong. I got muddled and upset easily. I should have somehow ended it then. But I did not.

And that seemed to act as a green light for him to get even nastier.

He started to beat me. Where it would not show. Hard and increasingly often. And I had to carry on afterwards as if I were happy. I had to smile, making sure that I showed my teeth.

I'm NOW SITTING in the kitchen, having lunch on my own. Just a cheese and pickle sandwich, a glass of milk and a strawberry yoghurt. I'm looking out at the patio and the lawn, a long rectangle, slightly overgrown, with flowerbeds full of rose bushes to either side and ever-growing laurel bushes by the fence at the end. I can see the spot where I laid Ginger to rest, but I try not to think about him, as it makes me feel sad and angry too. There are fields and trees beyond the fence, but there has been so much house-building here lately that I expect a new development will be built right up against it in the not-too-distant future. I worry my house may soon be overlooked by a block of apartments.

I spent the later part of the morning cleaning downstairs, dusting and polishing as quietly as I could. I did not use the vacuum cleaner, as I could not face him storming down snarling at me to turn it off because he was trying to have an "important conversation" on his mobile phone.

I went to the box-room door and knocked gently when it was all quiet, asking if he'd come down for lunch with me. "No," he shouted back. I then asked if he'd like me to bring him something to eat. "I'm busy," he shouted again at the top of his voice. I expect I will spend the afternoon finding something else quiet to do, weeding in the garden, most probably. It needs doing.

There is a cheerful knock on the frosted panel of glass on the front door. A rat-a-tat-tat.

A long silence. I can imagine him upstairs holding his breath and screaming inside.

Then the doorbell goes, pressed not once, but twice. I recall the Amazon delivery driver, a young Asian man with a ready smile, who always announces his arrival that way. I like him. He always winks at me although he probably shouldn't these days. I wink back.

Just now, though, I do not move. I dare not go to the door. He does not want me to.

I hope they, whoever they are, will just go away.

I wait, hoping it is the smiling Amazon man and he will put the parcel on the doorstep and leave.

I can hear Robert upstairs; I'm imagining him cursing and pushing his chair back and opening the box-room door. Listening.

And then the doorbell goes again, not once, not twice, but three times. Whoever it is seems to be in a happy mood.

I hear Robert stomping down the stairs, beside himself with fury, assuming this is Harry on the doorstep.

I move into the living room in case I need to try to placate Robert. The thought of a brawl outside the front of the house is alarming. He brushes by me, wild-eyed.

He pulls open the door and shouts, literally shouts, "Now what?" as he does so.

Sharon is on the doorstep carrying what looks like a basket full of goodies.

She is open-mouthed, her face full of shock at this sudden and unexpected verbal assault.

I step forward, just behind Robert, and she sees me and tries to compose herself.

There is a silence.

I think we are all embarrassed beyond words.

The moments pass.

And then Robert is composing himself, too, running his fingers through his hair and switching on his cheesy smile. To me he still looks ill at ease and sweaty.

"We've had these young rascals keep knocking ..." he says as lightly as he can, "... selling dusters and brushes ... supposedly for charity ... they take it in turns to keep coming back and winding us up. Seven times today!"

"We think they may be looking places up and down ...

burglars ..." I add. I'm not sure how convincing this sounds. "It's why we've not gone away on holiday this week ... as I'd said we were planning."

Robert glances at me and nods.

Sharon stands there and says, "Yes, I've read about them ... in the *Evening Star* ... it's, ah ..." Her words fade away, and I wonder if any of us think any of this story rings true.

"I meant to say ... before you left on Friday, that Angela has been promoted ... temporarily ... to replace Tracey until summer." Sharon stumbles over her words as I look at her, wondering who these people are she is talking about.

"If you wanted to ask Angela anything?" she adds.

And then it becomes clear to me. "Ask for Angela" is a safety initiative for people who feel unsafe or threatened – they can alert others simply by asking for Angela. This is Sharon's clumsy, improvised attempt to help me.

I'm not sure that Robert knows about this initiative. But he is fine-tuned to anything out of the ordinary, and if he suspects we are talking in some sort of code, he will react badly, shutting the door on her and turning towards me as we step back into the living room.

I gaze at Sharon, her wide, hopeful face encouraging me to say "yes". But I don't know what she'll do if I did, nor how Robert would respond. I have a terrible image in my head of her desperately pulling me outside by my arm and shouting at him, with him responding by punching her to the ground and kicking her repeatedly in the head. Once his façade has been exposed, he would have no reason to keep up the act.

I look her in the eye and say, "No." And, to add emphasis, I go on, "I have nothing to ask Angela at all." I dip my head down so neither of them can see the mixed emotions of shame and embarrassment in my face. I could not bear to bring Sharon into this, nor be the subject of pitying gossip by work colleagues. I don't want anyone to know what I'm going through. I have to sort it out myself. And I will. I'm sure of it.

Then Sharon, in her hustling, bustling way, moves straight on and thrusts the basket towards Robert and me, kind of midway between us. "I've had this since yesterday and was just passing and thought I'd drive in to see if you were here ... anyway ... it's a gift from all of us!" she says brightly as if to say, "No matter about Angela, my mistake."

I look at him, and he keeps smiling at her, but, to me, he appears glassy-eyed and uncomfortable. He pushes the basket towards me.

I take it from him and look it over. It is full of baby clothes, such a good mix of pastel colours and sizes from "newborn" to "0–6 months", some nappies too and even an old-fashioned rattle. Such kindness. I am touched by the gesture.

I thank her profusely. She moves her body slightly in my direction as if expecting me to hug her. But I do not. I am conscious of Robert watching me. And then, regaining his composure, he brings everything to a close. "We'd invite you in," he says, "but, ah, instead of going away, we're getting ready to decorate ... the place is such a mess ... but thank you for all these lovely presents ... please thank everyone for us."

That clearly signals this conversation is at an end. Sharon looks at me and smiles uncertainly. I think she was expecting to at least come in and have a cup of tea and a natter for half an hour. But I could not ask her, knowing Robert would be smouldering away upstairs. I smile back. "We'll have a catch-up when we're back ... Monday week." I add, "We can sort something out." I'm implying a coffee up the town but without saying that; Robert would not be happy if I did.

Sharon lurches forward, her arms around me, patting my back. "If you ever need me," she whispers in my ear, as though Robert cannot hear, "you've got my number." And she glances at Robert and smiles at him in a flustered way; then she is backing away from the doorstep. Robert glances at me as she leaves, and it is not a nice look at all. I sense he has picked up my "We can sort something out" comment and read more into it than I meant.

The moments in the living room after she has left are painfully awkward and make me feel sick and close to tears. "You work with her?" he asks. I nod my reply. "Christ," he replies. "The state of it." I say nothing. Sharon is plump and can look sweaty, but she is just the nicest, sweetest soul. I cannot bring myself to say anything derogatory about my friend just to placate him. "Don't have her round again," he instructs. Still I say nothing. He glares at me, and I finally nod back.

He rifles through the basket, pulling clothes aside to see what's below. He pulls out a little jumper with its price label still attached. "Like we'd want this." It is from Primark and inexpensive, but it is cute and snuggly. I am touched at the thought that it was probably bought by someone who does not have much money. I like it and am grateful. He throws it back down on top of the basket and turns and goes upstairs. I spend some time looking through all the things and put some of them out on the coffee table for him to see later.

The rest of the day I spend quietly. I start reading a new book, a Ruth Rendell, Mother's favourite author, and a free newspaper that is pushed through the letter box. I text Sharon to thank her and to put her mind at rest. I end with "mad busy week getting the bedroom ready for baby! See you again on Monday the seventh!!" I then decide that the two exclamation marks seem too forced to be genuinely jolly, so I delete them. I leave a similar message of thanks to the teachers' WhatsApp group and feel tearful reading through the replies. I have to keep all these lovely people at arm's length because of Robert.

He comes down just after six o'clock, and I make us something to eat. He sits there waiting, all nerves at the kitchen table, drinking red wine, as I put ready-made meals, lasagne for two, in the microwave and heat through some peas and carrots on the stove. I come and go, showing him some of the presents I had laid out on the coffee table. "This is nice," I say, showing him a top. "This one is pretty ... and so soft," with another. I hold it towards him, and he touches the material. He looks into the distance with such a strange expression on his face. It's one I cannot read.

Later, having eaten with me chatting away as brightly as I can, we sit and watch Netflix on the television. He flicks through, back and forth, over and again, saying how much there is to see but so little to actually watch. Eventually, he settles on a UFO documentary, which he watches in silence. I cannot make him out this evening, really I can't. Eventually, after catching the end of the news on Sky, I yawn and stretch and go upstairs. Perhaps tonight he will follow me. But he does not. I think he is still angry. But then, one way or the other, he always is.

6

I am having another restless night. Lying in bed, thinking things over, going to the bathroom, looking out the front and back windows and listening to him snoring downstairs. It is quiet and peaceful outside, but I do not feel like that inside, in my heart and mind.

And then I am suddenly awake and slightly confused. I must have fallen asleep, overslept, and can now hear him downstairs moving about the kitchen, making breakfast. The red illuminated numbers of the alarm clock on the bedside cabinet show it is 8.11 a.m., more than an hour later than I'd usually get up.

I dress quickly, searching unsuccessfully for my mobile phone, which must have slipped down the side of the bed. I hurry downstairs, as I think he might be making breakfast for us. I want this to be a happy day, building towards the baby scan tomorrow. One last chance for us. For all three of us.

He sits there at the kitchen table, a mug to one side, a plate of scrambled eggs on toast in front of him. He cuts the toast and pushes scrambled egg onto it before shovelling it into his mouth. He swallows and takes a large swig of black coffee. He has not made breakfast for me.

He looks up at me; neither a warm nor a cold look. "I'm in a hurry," he says briskly. "I've got a meeting in Cambridge ... to sort the money out. I should be back early evening."

I nod and say, "Okay." I then move towards the kettle to make myself a mug of tea.

"Tomorrow, isn't it, the baby scan?" he asks and then goes on, "I'll come to that."

I turn and smile at him and say, "Thank you." He seems, if not exactly warm and loving, at least calmer and less aggressive than he has been lately. I hope he will get the money "sorted" today, whatever that means exactly.

As I squeeze and remove the tea bag and add milk to my mug – thinking I will go and sit opposite him until he gets up and goes – I notice my mobile phone face down on the floor over near the charger by the bread bin.

I pick it up and see there is a crack all the way across the screen. I feel a surge of anger. I occasionally leave my phone on the work surface here overnight on charge but am sure I took it upstairs with me last night.

I look across at him as I turn on the mobile phone. He is staring into space, finishing his coffee. I have a strong sense that he is sitting there waiting to see what I will do.

I suspect he waited until I was asleep, then came up in the night and took my mobile phone and threw it on the floor in the kitchen and stamped on it. A crazy thought. Perhaps I am becoming paranoid. The phone turns on. It has 90% charge left on it.

I show him the phone, the cracked screen. "I thought I'd taken it upstairs with me last night," I say in a baffled voice.

I look at him. He looks back at me.

There is a silence.

I know better than to cross him.

He says, as if shrugging, "First I've seen it ... when you picked it up."

I nod. "Okay." I don't believe him. Not a word.

This is about me having friends.

It is about him needing control over all aspects of my life.

He pauses and then adds, "If you let me have your phone ... the pin for it too ... I'll get it fixed for you in Cambridge."

He puts out his hand.

I hesitate. If I give it to him, he will go through everything in it. If I don't, he will turn sour very quickly.

I give him the phone. "It's 1811."

He takes it and slips it matter-of-factly into his pocket as though it is of no consequence, this favour he is doing.

He finishes his scrambled eggs on toast, takes a last mouthful of coffee and then goes on talking. "It's probably a good time to change all your social media passwords ... something you should do regularly ... we can do it together if you like ... tonight."

He pauses, about to get up and take his mug and plate to the sink. "What social media do you have?" His voice sounds no more than polite and curious, as if this is a casual enquiry, just something to say.

I hesitate. I can see where this is going. He does not want me on social media, talking to people, friends, "behind his back" as he would regard it. If the passwords are all changed this evening – by us, him really – he will forever be going in and checking up on whatever exchanges I have.

"Twitter?" he asks. I shake my head. "Instagram?" Another shake. "Facebook?" I nod and say, "Yes, I set it up ages ago ... but I can't remember when I last used it." "Anything else?" I shake my head. There is a WhatsApp group for the teachers and teaching assistants, but I am not sure he would think of that, and I'm not going to tell him. If he finds it on the phone, I'll say I forgot.

"I'm looking forward to the baby scan tomorrow," he says agreeably enough now that he has got what he wanted. He puts his empty mug and plate in the bowl in the kitchen sink. He turns and comes close to smiling at me. "See how the baby is." There is more to come, I think.

I nod, unsure. He is in a better mood today – most likely because he is seeing someone about money, but also because he is getting his own way with me. He has my mobile phone. He will have access to everything. And from tonight, he will be able to go into my Facebook account. That's enough to keep him cheerful for the time being.

"How are you feeling anyway?" he asks as if in passing, standing in the kitchen doorway, about to leave. The first caring question he's asked me in ages.

"Okay, thank you," I reply automatically. He looks at me, expecting more. I add, "A bit tired." And then I wish I hadn't as I see the expression change on his face – not exactly delight, more like grim satisfaction.

"Yes, you look it ... more than a bit. We should have a little chat later about you working on ... if you want to call it a day at the end of the summer term ... or now ... that may be better for you ... if you're feeling so tired already."

Of course, "little chat" is a euphemism. It means him telling me what to do and me agreeing just to keep the peace. To appease him. To stop him getting angry – his face up close to mine, snarling, pushing me over, maybe more, if I disagree with anything he says. Even if I answer him in the wrong tone of voice.

"Have a nice day," I say as cheerfully as I can.

He smiles, more to himself than to me, as he goes.

I wonder what tonight will bring. I don't doubt it will be another step towards his complete control. By the end of this week, he'll have me trapped at home, no friends, no contact with the outside world, no escape at work; I'll be his prisoner. I'm facing utter subjugation.

And then it strikes me. Is this the life I want for me and my baby?

MY MOOD SOMEHOW LIFTS, being here on my own at home. I find myself having a surprisingly enjoyable day. I vacuum. I turn music up louder than I normally would. Emptying the dishwasher, I take two saucepans and clang them together, simply because I can.

I become unexpectedly happy. I make some cupcakes. It is something that I will do with my baby when she is older. *She.* I don't know why, but I think – I sense – that I am having a little girl. And the thought of that fills me with such joy.

I am going to do everything I can to make things work with Robert. I am sure he will get the money he wants today. Perhaps that is what is lifting my spirits. He will be cheerful. Nicer to me. Tomorrow, we will see our baby for the first time. Things will start getting better. I believe it. I have to.

I weed the front lawn late morning, and I see Sarah and Lucy from over the way at number one. Sarah is a thin blonde woman in her late forties. She always seems to be in a hurry. She works in a care home in Felixstowe. Her lookalike daughter, Lucy, works there too, part-time. She is doing her A Levels and going away to university next autumn. They are both smiley when they see me.

There is an older brother, Daniel I think he is called, and he is training to be an architect or a surveyor or something like that in London. I have lived here now for almost three years, and I have only seen him at Christmastime and have never spoken to him. They all seem nice and friendly. I do not know what happened to the father. No one has ever mentioned him.

Sarah and Lucy come across on their way out into town. I wonder if they will mention money and Robert and investments, but they do not. I am relieved.

As I stand up to speak to them, I put my hands on my tummy without thinking. Sarah notices and smiles at me. I smile back. She asks, "Are you?" tentatively, and I smile shyly and say, "Yes."

She says, "Congratulations, that's wonderful news! When is baby due?"

"November," I reply. "We don't know what it is yet." There are more smiles all round, and as they leave, Lucy reaches out and touches my tummy. I laugh. I do not mind. It is a kind gesture.

Later, after lunch, I come back out the front to wipe the windows. Harry is over the way, tending to his flower beds. His front lawn is always pristine. Grass just so. Flowers colourful and all in a row. Weeds never to be seen. I suddenly wish I had a big old tomcat that would go and do its business right in the middle of his lawn. A centrepiece display for him.

I have my back to Harry as I wipe the windowsills, but I can see him in the reflection of the glass. He looks across, clearly umming and aahing whether to come over or not. As I am finishing, he gets up and walks towards me, a trowel in his hand.

I watch him every step of the way, and as he reaches me, I turn, look at him, up and down, and go inside before he can speak. I am not normally rude, but I just don't want to have to listen to his moans and groans. As I stand in the living room watching him walking back, I have second thoughts, wondering if he were simply going to be friendly and pass the time of day with me, somehow easing the tensions between us.

In the afternoon, towards teatime, I am out the front one last time, vacuuming my car. It is a job I have been meaning to do for ages. And I vacuum now because I know if I do it when Robert is here, the coming and going, the noise, the whole fiddling about and fussiness of it, will annoy him immensely.

I wave cheerfully as I see Mrs Knox – no sign of the two odd boys – driving back from wherever she has been. She waves politely but hurries indoors. She once said she had to get the boys' tea on the table for six o'clock. I laughed, thinking it was a joke, but, from the look on her face, it wasn't. I'm not sure they can fend for themselves much beyond beans on toast. They'd probably burn the house down.

I then see what I call the "lovely tattooed couple" arriving back from work. They live at number four to my – our – right. Nick and Amy are tattooists in nearby Felixstowe, and both dress in black, ripped clothes. She has tattooed arms and legs, full of all sorts of Disney character faces, and he has intricate patterns up his neck and by his ears, Chinese symbols, mostly. They have a son, four-year-old Noah, who is dressed traditionally with his blond hair neatly brushed to the side. He's such a gorgeous little boy; I always want to hug him. I think he may be coming to the school, possibly my class, in September. I hope so.

I watch as they get Noah out of his car seat, and he runs ahead towards their house.

Amy turns towards me and shrugs as if to say, "We'd come across and chat ... but ... Noah's in a hurry!"

I laugh and wave back. It's been such a nice, ordinary kind of day.

And then, early evening, he is back, a good hour or so before I expected. I am standing here in the kitchen as he arrives, not sure what to do for dinner.

"All good?" I ask without thinking as he storms towards me and then barges by to get a drink of water from the tap.

"No," he shouts. "It's fucking well not."

I don't know what to say to that. I have a terrible sinking feeling inside. I want to ask him what that means for Harry and everyone. And for my money, too, my rainy-day money. The money for my baby. If it will all be okay.

I stumble over words of sympathy and then change the subject by asking if he has my phone. That enrages him – that I should mention something so mundane at a time like this. He takes my phone out of his pocket and hurls it across the kitchen, where it hits the washing machine and lies there spinning on the floor.

Then he turns to me. He looks at me. I know what is coming next. He hits me around the side of my head with his clenched fists until I fall to the floor. I fall more quickly than I might because then it will be over sooner. He beats me. He does it mostly about my head even though it must hurt his fists more. He does not want to leave marks that can be seen. When he has beaten me enough to make himself feel better, he goes upstairs to carry on as if nothing has happened. I am expected to do the same.

I AM LYING in bed in the front bedroom, trying not to think about Robert. I have not seen him since what happened in the kitchen. It is now gone midnight.

My mind is going this way and that, ever restless. My head throbs with pain. I'm not going to fall asleep easily. I will just have to wait until I am exhausted.

I wonder how it is that I have got myself into this mess; more than that, this horror of a relationship. But, in truth, I know why. I see it all plain as day.

I was so lonely. I could see my empty life stretching out before me. There were moments – those long, dark nights with the rain lashing against the window at four a.m. – that I thought of taking my own life. As I lay there, with a handful of tablets in my hand and a bottle of whiskey on the bedside cabinet, only the thought of Father and Mother and a sense of shame stopped me from doing it.

Everyone around me seemed to be in relationships, happy, loving, laughing all the time. Women, so much younger than me, were having babies. I knew I never would. That I would spend my life hugging children at school, always the same age, whilst I grew ever older. Working on and on until some feisty young mother complained to the head about me: "That sad old hag who keeps putting her arm around my child." And, to avoid the fuss over my desperate but innocent gestures, I would take early retirement and sit staring out into the garden all day.

I just wanted someone, anyone really, for myself. A man who would like me, be interested in my thoughts and feelings and who would care for me as I would for them. I had no interest in looks or status or money or prospects. I dreamed of a kind and gentle man whom I could share my life with enjoying simple, easy pleasures: reading, walking, sitting in the sunshine holding hands. I thought I would never have it. Any of it.

And then Robert turned up and seemed to offer everything. I grabbed at it greedily in utter desperation. I pinned on him my hopes of complete happiness.

I even dreamed of having a baby although I never expected that dream would come true.

Early on, before he moved in, when he was what Father might have called "wooing" me, everything was perfect. The texts, the emails, the telephone conversations – all full of love and tenderness – made me feel that I could have everything I had ever wanted. On reflection, I expected too much. I had an image of him in my head – an image of perfection – that I shaped into what I wanted him to be.

He was not that man, but I did not discover it until he moved in. He was pleasant enough at first – not the man of my dreams, but not the monster he would become – and I was happy. To be honest, I was thrilled that I had a man of my own. I overlooked his foibles and worked hard to make him happy too; I recognised that he had many issues just below the surface.

As time passed, he changed, or at least I saw him more clearly as the person he was. If I am honest, I am sure he came and talked to me at that barbeque because Harry told him all my business, that I owned the house and had a similar sum put by. Once he had moved in and had control of my money, he no longer needed to keep up the pretence. That's when he showed his true colours.

There was a moment when I thought I would leave him. But I did not know how I could do it, not easily.

What with him living here in the house. Him having invested all my savings.

But I knew that I would somehow. But then I found out I was pregnant. I decided to give him one last chance. And another. And another.

I thought fatherhood, the expectation of it, would change him, make him happier and a better person. That something deep down inside him would open up and blossom into something wonderful. I saw in my head how we would be, the three of us, just like Father, Mother and I were when I was young. A happy, self-contained little family. That is all I have ever wanted. I would do anything to have it in my life.

But my pregnancy has made no difference at all. I thought at first that he was stunned by the news, that it would take some time for it to sink in. But he has shown little or no interest – just briefly this morning when he mentioned coming to the baby scan. He has not talked "boy or girl?" or baby names or decorating the bedroom, nothing. There is no sense of breathless excitement, no tears of joy at becoming a daddy.

Now here I am, damaged beyond repair, and wondering what will happen next. If I do not somehow break this cycle, I am sure it will just go on and on. He will beat me whenever he feels bad about himself. In time, he will bully and torment and belittle my beautiful, gawky, awkward-looking daughter. He may beat her too. I cannot allow any of that to happen. I have to protect my baby. More than that, I have to give her a wonderful, contented life.

I will give him tomorrow, the baby scan, to make amends. One final chance.

Otherwise, somehow, I will leave him. I have no choice. I will do it this week.

I think, and the thought stuns me, that otherwise, he will eventually kill me and my baby.

7

TUESDAY, 1 JUNE

I am soaking in the bath before going to bed, my hands on my tummy. It is both a protective and a comforting gesture.

I am hoping one day soon that my baby will kick. To say, "Hello, Mummy." I'll say, "I love you," in a whisper. So he does not hear me. I don't think he'd want me to say that to anyone but him.

Now, without my baby, I do not know what I would do. He crushes my spirits and makes me feel worthless. But at the same time, I stay – I stay alive – because of the baby.

Late this afternoon, we went for a scan at the hospital in Ipswich. It is free on the NHS, and it was what you might call a "flat scan". You can buy black-and-white photographs, and he paid for one. There are other places locally where we could have gone private – it is not that expensive, really, for such a magical moment – and we could have a 3D scan and see the baby, living and breathing, much more clearly, right in front of us. I did not suggest this, though. He does not like me to ask for things. To get above myself, as he puts it. To act as if

I am better than everyone else. The suggestion would have made him angry and spoilt the occasion.

He was just perfect, in his way, as we arrived at the hospital. He parked the car easily, finding a space that he could drive right into without other cars on or over the adjacent white lines. He gets frustrated if he has to drive round and round anywhere, especially if he is behind hesitant, elderly drivers. He shouts at them in frustration. "Take your time – I've nothing better to do." He was charm itself at the reception desk, with a cheery "Good morning" and smiles galore. He was attentive to the sonographer, joking as she smeared gel on my tummy and saying how clever she was to check all the baby's "bits and bobs". He was a charmer all right.

He did not put his arm around me or hold my hand or make any show of affection. He hardly looked in my direction, let alone spoke to me. It was only later when I carefully broached the subject of the baby's sex that he even acknowledged my presence and said jovially that "we" did not want to know so "don't zoom in down there, please!" I would have liked to have known but did not wish to sour his mood. I did though, unwittingly, later, when I bumped into a woman, someone I knew from school years ago, in a corridor on the way out. We had a brief chat, I could feel Robert was on edge, and she asked if we'd chosen any names. As Robert stood there in silence, I rattled through various boys' and girls' names I liked. One boy's name was meant to be Jonah, but I accidentally said John, my ex-boyfriend's name, and I could feel him tense and stiffen. He barely said a word after we had left to come home.

Having a bath is just about the only happy time I have now. It's time for me and my baby to be together. Bonding.

If he is at his laptop and I am anywhere else in the house, he summons me, expecting me to be there immediately. To fetch him this. To take that away. To uncover the source of the tap-tap-tapping he can hear in the house and to stop it.

He sat without speaking as we drove home. I sat next to him, studying the scan of the baby. I tried two or three times to jolly him out of his mood, to cheer him up, by pointing out features of the photograph. He did not speak. I worried then where the rest of the day and evening might go. When his mood darkens, he tends to go quiet and then quieter still with me until, eventually, he explodes.

Back at home, he said he had some market analysis to do for tomorrow's trades and went off to the box room with his laptop. I asked him what he would like for dinner and if he would be coming down at, say, eight o'clock. I suggested we could perhaps talk about the names he might like for a boy or a girl. But he was already up the stairs and away as I finished my sentence. I took him up a sandwich and a glass of cold beer, just as he likes them, for a teatime snack, but I saw later that he'd left them untouched.

As the clock in the living room moved towards nine p.m., and I sat there on the sofa, the TV turned down, crocheting a lemon and white jacket for the baby, he came in and sat in one of the armchairs. He had a tray with a bowl of tomato soup and three or four slices of buttered, white bread. It struck me quite suddenly that he had not had the "hot meal" he felt he should have every evening, and it was possible that, if I then said something out of turn, that bowl of hot soup might be hurled towards me. I got up, made my excuses and came upstairs for a bath. To give him time to cool down, hopefully.

It takes a while, but I start to relax and think that, maybe, the moment has passed.

The bathroom door slams open, and he comes striding in, his face contorting in fury. "All I've fucking done for you."

In that split second, I do not know whether to protect my baby, cover my nakedness, or try to defend myself.

"You pathetic, ugly bitch."

He is across the room, his hands on my face, pushing my head down into the water.

———

I LIE HERE in the bath, ten minutes or so after his attack, my heart breaking. I know I have to do it.

I have to end the relationship with him.

But how? He is the father of my baby. And he scares me to death.

I have been a dutiful wife to him in every way. I put him and his needs and wants before all else. I have placated him. Jollied him along. Been conciliatory. And still he has so much anger inside him, taking offence at anything and everything, his rage building up and up until he blows up over next to nothing.

He does not, and I do not understand why, lose complete control, shouting and swearing and throwing things about and knocking things over. I could perhaps understand that. Instead, it is as though he channels all of his fury into a sharp focus and then attacks me. As I lie there afterwards, in the bath tonight, on the kitchen floor yesterday, he stops suddenly and seems to compose himself before walking away.

Then he is normal again, just going about his day-to-day business. It is as though nothing has happened – no brutality, no humiliation – and we are expected to carry on as we were before. If I am crying, either in pain or through shame, he will sometimes look at me as if irritated. And I try to "behave myself", as he occasionally puts it, to stop crying, or at least to find something to do out of his sight so that the cycle of anger does not begin again.

Tonight, as he stood over me, I could not "behave myself" or "pull myself together" or even "stop fucking sniffling". And he stormed out of the bathroom, pulling the door almost off its hinges as he slammed it shut.

I was in such shock and in real pain. Crying quietly to myself, I could not seem to stop.

He waits outside whilst I "sort myself out". I know I have spent too long here after the attack for his liking. I held a cold flannel against my forehead and then lowered it and sobbed into it. He knocked so loudly then that I stopped and said I'd be "out in a minute".

I do not know how to end it. I have so little experience of relationships. I think, with a normal relationship, one that was not so intense and controlling, one partner could simply ask the other to go, and they would have the decency to leave. This is my house – my home, although it feels tainted and soiled forever now – so he has to go.

I wish I had a family member who could be here when I told him, "I want you to leave. Please pack and go now." I feel sick at the thought of saying those words to him, and how he will react. He'll tell me that I am so ungrateful. Selfish. That I care only about myself. And he will beat me, in time with his words, until I apologise for saying such an upsetting thing to him.

I have considered going to the police, telling them what has been happening, perhaps even requesting that an officer is here when I ask him – no, tell him – to leave. But Robert is smooth and charming and will slip and slide this way and that and say I have not been well, that I am mentally ill, "schizophrenic" he will add quietly, and will offer to bring in the neighbours to say how unstable I have seemed to them.

Then, when the police officer has gone, Robert will follow me upstairs, shut the door and beat me relentlessly.

At last, I get up out of the bath, dry myself as best I can and wrap my dressing gown around me. I open the door, and he is still there, waiting. He steps back and looks me up and down. I am trying not to cry. I do not look happy enough for him. I don't show my teeth when he asks me to smile.

It seems to trigger something in him again. He steps forward and punches me hard, twice, to either side of my head, behind my hairline. And then he goes to hit me on my stomach. My baby, I think as I turn away and fall to the floor.

"Sort your-fucking-self out," he says as he steps over me. "And make me something to eat ..."

I lie here half on the landing, half in the bathroom, knowing what I now have to do. I have to cook him a proper meal. One he'll approve of.

———————

HE SITS in an armchair in the living room, watching one of his stupid UFO programmes on the television.

The sound is louder than it needs to be. Every time there is background music, it is louder still.

His hands grip the sides of the chair. He is motionless, as though he is relaxed. He is coiled tight though, ready to explode at my next transgression.

I stand across from him, dressed now, my wet hair brushed to the side but still dripping; I do not have time to dry it.

I look at the painting of the strong and beautiful woman above the fireplace and remember how I used to imagine I was her. And now I have come to this.

"What would you like to eat?" I ask as neutrally as I can so I do not risk incurring his wrath again.

He turns his head and looks me up and down as though I disgust him. I stand as tall as I can, my shoulders back like the woman in the painting. I do not smile in case it angers him.

He does not say anything. He thinks I have somehow betrayed him by not looking my best. Not that it would be good enough for him. Nothing ever is.

"I've a nice minute steak ... I can do that with some of those skinny fries you like ... and some mushrooms."

I hate the wheedling tone in my voice. And that I have been reduced to this pitiful state, as though I am begging. The strong and beautiful woman in the painting would have been too proud to beg.

He nods and turns away, dismissing me.

Then he picks up the remote control.

He changes channels, one to another, faster and faster.

I am in the kitchen, taking a frying pan from a cupboard, a tray leaning against the side of the fridge, a plate from another cupboard, a knife and fork from a drawer. I then put a sharp knife and a chopping board alongside them on the work surface. My hands won't stop shaking.

I do not know if he wants his meal on a tray on his lap or if he'd prefer to eat at the kitchen table. I dare not ask him. "What do you think?" he'll snarl. And he'll hit me if I get it wrong.

There is a mark, a leftover smear of something on the plate. I cannot give this one to him. I put it in the dishwasher, reaching for another from the cupboard. It clatters as I put it on the work surface.

"Hurry up," he shouts.

I imagine him sitting there stewing in his own fury.

I hear him switching channels. Again and again.

Some sort of rap music. He turns up the sound. Then a

football commentator jabbering away excitedly in Spanish. On he goes with the remote control. Click. Click. Click.

The minute steak is there in the fridge, ready to be cooked. Medium rare is what he likes. I've yet to do it exactly right.

The packet of skinny fries that I can cook in the microwave is empty. The only ones left are the thicker ones, which need to go in the proper oven.

There are no mushrooms. Only the big fat tomatoes I slice onto my salads. They will take ages to do. He hates them anyway; he only likes vine tomatoes.

I'm drenched in sweat. I don't have time for any of this.

"Fuck's sake," he says at the top of his voice. His patience is at breaking point.

He changes channels again. So many that it's just a blur of shouts and endless, inane noises. Click. Click. Click.

As he clicks, he turns up the sound until it feels as though the walls are shaking.

I am close to utter despair. I put the steak on the chopping board, ready to cut round the edges. That's what he says should be done. So I do it.

I have a wooden meat hammer, so I fetch it from a kitchen drawer. I don't think minute steak needs to be tenderised, but he says it does.

I have no idea what to do with this steak. I wonder if I could make a sandwich with it. But the bread is not fresh, and he only likes fresh bread. I could fry some onions, but he says they leave a nasty taste. So I stand, hopelessly, feeling unbearably desperate, at a loss to know what to do.

The television has been switched off. I still have the noise of it ringing in my ears.

I'm taking too long making him something to eat. All is quiet. The silence unnerves me. I don't know what he will do next.

I TURN INSTINCTIVELY, the knife in my hand, steak on the chopping board, on the work surface, as he storms through the kitchen door.

He comes at me like a madman. All the imagined indignities and boiling anger of the day in his twisted face.

I think, in this instant, that I and my baby are going to die by his hands. Here in the kitchen. On the floor.

Raising his hands to my throat, he launches himself at me. It happens so fast. As his hands tighten on my neck, the knife is in his stomach. He makes an odd "oo-oof" sound, an almost comical noise as though all the air has been let out of him. I expect him to fall back onto the floor. I will call an ambulance, the police as well, and somehow this nightmare will be at a terrible end. If need be, I will get a restraining order. Even that may not be enough to keep him away; I may have to leave here, to disappear.

But he does not fall to the floor. He does not even step back. He just stands there for a moment, a pained expression on his face, and then he puts his hands to my neck and squeezes.

I stab him again. The knife in his stomach. Again and again. The tighter his grip on my throat, the more I stab him over and over. I know if I pass out, and he is still conscious, he will kill me. And as I lay on the floor, he will stamp on my stomach time and again and kill my baby.

That thought, the murder of my precious, innocent baby, drives me on. But his hands are strong and relentless and I can feel myself unable to breathe. My head is spinning. I am disorientated. But I keep on stabbing. He has to fall down dead before I pass out. It is the only chance my baby and I have to live.

I am about to black out. Starved of breath, I can feel myself going.

I stab him one last time, with all that's left of my strength, desperately twisting and turning the knife this way and that inside him.

He squeals and squeals in agony and then falls at my feet as I stagger and collapse to the floor by his side.

I think, as I lie here, noticing a blob of what looks like grease on the middle of the ceiling, that I may have passed out for a minute or two, perhaps longer. It takes a moment for my thoughts to flood in. I am alive, and I am breathing, and my throat does not hurt too much. I have survived his monstrous attack. My hands go to my tummy, rolling across it and around, to make sure that my baby is well. I feel, instinctively, that she is.

But I can also feel him close to me, where he dropped, his face turned towards me. He is watching me, and I am paralysed with fear. I cannot move my face to look at him, nor do I have the strength to get up onto my feet. I think suddenly of the knife that clattered and spun away as I fell sideways to the floor. I move my hands slowly, this way and that, searching for it so that when he gathers the strength to lift himself up and come at me one final time, I will be ready.

I read somewhere once that the only certain way of killing someone with a knife is to sever the windpipe or an artery or something in the throat. I forget which. I cannot bear the thought of it, though. I do not know if I can bring myself to do it or whether I even have the strength. And I cannot see the knife. It is over there somewhere, and I am too exhausted, too shocked, to move. I sob once, then twice, and it all pours out of me, that my life has come to this. I turn my head, ready to shout at him in defiance, imagining him getting to his feet to kill me and my baby.

But he lies there still, his eyes staring into space. His

mouth hangs open and is lined with blood. His chest and stomach are a bloody mess.

He is dead. I have killed him. I am a murderer.

As I fall back into unconsciousness, I wonder what I should do. If I call the police and they see me untouched and him with so many stab wounds, I cannot help but think I will go to prison and my baby will be taken into care. I will never hold my baby in my arms. I will not see her grow up. I will never be able to tell her how much I love her. I might as well be dead.

PART II

NO PLACE LIKE HOME

8

I have been here on the kitchen floor for hours, sometimes awake, more often not, most likely passing in and out of consciousness.

The kitchen and the hallway lights are on, but it is now dark outside. All is quiet. Other than the whirls and gurgles and sudden thump-thump-thumps from his body. I never realised a corpse could be so noisy.

I have my hands around my tummy. Protecting my baby. Even though, with Robert dead, we are now safe.

At some point, I will have to decide what to do. I have been working through the choices in my head. I know I should call the police and tell them exactly what happened. And why. How he has made my life a misery for so long. But they will look at my neck and probably see little more than bruising – him fighting for his life, they'd think – and will examine his body and see a dozen or so stab wounds. And they will ask why I stabbed him so many times – as if I were in a frenzy – and why I did not call an ambulance straight-away, some two or three hours ago. When he might have had a chance of survival.

I will be taken into custody for further questioning, and
two detectives will ask me about his death. "His murder",
they will call it. And I will say it was all so fast, that I just
happened to have a knife in my hand when he came at me
and that he ran on to the knife. One of them, the nicer of the
two, will repeat my words, "It just happened," in an unnatu-
rally neutral voice, and the other, the nasty one, will say, "So
he ran on to the knife?" and then pause and add sardonically,
"Twelve times?"

They will look at each other, and I'll know what they are
thinking. That I am a madwoman. I will say he was a monster
and that he controlled me and tortured me mentally. A
doctor will examine me and find nothing much other than a
few marks at my neck where, they would say, he battled
desperately to stop me stabbing him to death. They will ask
for examples of what he did. I will talk about the notebook,
and they will look at that and see it is in my own hand. They
will think it is just my own twisted account of teenage boys'
hands inside my bra and between my legs. I will say he
controlled my money, but they will check the account and
most likely see I have more money than ever because of his
trading skills. And they will talk to the neighbours, who will
say he was a nice man, an ordinary and decent man.

I turn and look at him, the moonlight through the kitchen
window on his face. He is dead and cold now. Snot hangs
from his nose.

The whole scene looks exactly like the police will claim it
was – the slaughter of an innocent man by an evil woman.

I have an idea of what I can do – all I can do, really – even
though the thought is horrific.

If I go to the police, I will be charged with his murder, and
I will spend time locked up in prison awaiting my trial. A
year, maybe more. I will have my baby in the prison hospital,
and she will be taken away from me and put into care. If I am

found guilty, I will be sentenced to ten years or more. If, by some miracle, I walk free, perhaps with a suspended sentence, my baby will still be in care, out there somewhere with foster parents. And I do not know whether I will get my baby back or if I will ever see her again. I cannot bear the thought.

So, come what may, I will not – I cannot – tell the police. I won't risk losing my baby nor spending the rest of my life in agony, wondering where she is and what she is doing and whether she is happy or not and if she is being loved the way I'd love her. I would never know if she were nearby or far away and whether I might pass her in the street years later after my release and not realise it. I would not know if she ever thought of me. She might not even know I ever existed. And so, sobbing at these heart-rending imaginings, I formulate my terrible plan.

I am bigger than he is – he was – and even though I am pregnant, I think I can move him, drag his body somewhere and hide him. The thought appals me, not only moving him but burying him somewhere he will never be found. A place where I can keep an eye on things. The back garden, perhaps. I can clean up in here. With bleach and disinfectant and hot water, and a mop and a vacuum cleaner, going over everything again and again. I will have to pack his clothes and belongings and dispose of them. The car too. There is so much to think about, to weigh up. It is something I will have to live with for the rest of my life.

But it is either that or losing my baby. A stark choice. Truth is, there is no choice. My baby is all that matters to me.

I sit up slowly, my back resting against a kitchen cabinet. I will do what I need to do now, working through the rest of the night to clear everything up.

I get onto my feet, steeling myself. And then, in the still of the night, there is a banging on the front door.

I FREEZE, rigid with fear.

Whoever is there will have seen the lights on. Will think I – we – are still up and awake downstairs, maybe watching television. That we will come to the front door.

I cannot answer the door. I have his blood all over my face and hands and body.

I stand here, looking through the open kitchen door into the hallway and out towards the front door. I can see the shape of a person through the frosted glass panel. I wonder, when I do not open the door, if they will peer through the glass and see me, or at least the shape of me, with him lying there motionless at my feet. The hallway and the kitchen are both lit up, and I do not know, looking from the dark outside to the light inside, how clearly we will be seen.

Very clearly, I think. I have only seconds to decide what to do. Whoever is there banged hard on the front door. They did not press the ding-a-ling-ling bell or rat-a-tat gently with a knuckle on the glass. It was a demand. An urgent and pressing demand. "I want to speak to you now!" And if the door is not answered in the next few seconds, they will bang again even harder, maybe even shout out, "Answer the door!" And if there is no response, they will then peer through the frosted glass and see me – us – in full view. Maybe whoever it is will not bang again on the door but will simply look through that glass. Any second now.

I cannot move, even though I know I should. Fear keeps me where I am. I need to move to the kitchen door and shut it. But I think that movement, and the change in light, will be seen by whoever it is outside. And they will shout, loudly demanding that I open the front door. I could just move towards the door and speak through it, saying it is late and, please, we are going to bed and whatever it is can wait until the morning. But I can't bring myself to do that. I cannot seem to do anything. I stand here, shaking, waiting to be seen.

Bang, bang, bang.

There it goes again.

Louder this time, ever more insistent. I wonder if something awful has happened, a car crash or even a fire in the close.

"Rob? Rob?" It is Harry's voice, and the anger in it is unmistakeable. "I need to speak to you!"

This will be about Harry's investments. I know that pretty much all of Harry's life savings are invested in the schemes. That the interest payments Harry has been getting each month have supplemented his state pension. Without these payments, Harry will struggle to survive financially.

And I know last month's payment was not made. Robert made out that I had forgotten to do the transfer, had done something to mess up his system. And Harry, I think, agreed to wait whilst he untangled it and would, I guess, take a double payment and a little extra interest to make up for it this month.

I know that money was due to be paid today. Presumably Harry has not been paid as promised. I realise that Harry will have demanded the payment be transferred by midnight – and it is now gone midnight. That is why he is here at the door, banging furiously.

Bang, bang, bang. On and on he goes. "Rob! ... Rob! ... Rob!"

I pluck up the courage to inch my way out of sight. Perhaps even to push the kitchen door closed.

Then he moves, and I can see Harry's snow white hair, his nose pressed against the frosted glass.

He is looking straight at me. Through the glass panel into the hallway and the open kitchen door. To me, standing here, with a corpse at my feet. And I look back, frozen as I am with fear, knowing that if he can see me, if he can make out two bodies, one standing, one lying, that this is all over. That he will shout, "What the hell?" and hurry back home as fast as he can to dial 999.

With mounting horror, I wonder whether I can go after him and prevent him, explaining what has happened, and begging him not to call the police. And, as he shakes my hand off his arm and presses on, whether I can somehow stop him by stabbing him with a knife. I know I cannot do that. No matter what, I can't kill another human being. The thought sickens me.

So I look back at Harry, unmoving, as he looks towards me. I have a feeling that, if I do not move, I have a chance. That Harry, with his fading eyes and his bifocal glasses, may not be well enough to really see what is in front of him. That I might just be one more blurry shape. He moves his head this way. I stay the same. He moves his head that way. I remain the same.

Then, with a curse and a petulant kick at the door, he is gone, his fear and anger to fester some more.

I slip down to the floor, my body giving way on me.

I gather my thoughts. I have to hide Robert – his body – before Harry, and others, come back in the morning.

————

IT IS NOW THE MORNING, and I am lying in the single bed in what will be my baby's room at the front of the house. My hands are on my tummy, instinctively protecting her. It has been a long night, and I am exhausted.

There was so much cleaning to do over and again. I have lost count of the number of times I have showered. And put clothes and bedding and towels and anything else he has touched in the washing machine. Then sat in the bath, scrubbing myself raw.

Now I am here, thinking what to do with his clothes that I have packed back into his rucksack and two carrier bags and left by the front door. I have put his watch and his bunch of keys and his mobile phone and his laptop on the desk he worked at in the box room. I will look at these later and decide what to do with them. It's hard to think straight now. My mind flits, terrified, here and there.

I have dealt with his body although it broke my heart to do it. I was sick several times, dry-heaving on the last two occasions. More from the horror of it than the physical exertion, although that was tough enough. I was slow and careful, trying not to strain myself, ever mindful of my baby. I know that murderers – for that is what I have become – sometimes cut up their victims to dispose of them. The thought of it had me on my knees, sobbing and retching. I could not do anything like that.

There were not that many places I could put him. His body. "The body" is how I must think of him. I could not risk dragging him out to the car on the driveway in case Alex or the Knox boys, or anyone else looking out, saw me. Even if I drove to Rendlesham Forest to hide the body, I might be seen by dog walkers or the police sitting in a car in a lay-by. I could leave the body in a shadowy corner of a copse in woodland somewhere, but I would forever live with the fear of imminent discovery.

I've had to keep his body here. Intact. Wrapped up in as many layers of plastic as I could find. And as far away from me as possible. Downstairs, my home has a hallway and a cloakroom, a living room and a dining room and a kitchen, a utility room and a big cupboard under the stairs. There is an attached garage with a work unit at the back, accessed through the utility room.

Upstairs, there are three bedrooms, a bathroom, a shower and pull-down steps into a large and empty boarded-out loft. In the garage, I found the wrappings from a recently bought carpet for this, my baby's bedroom. Beneath the kitchen sink, there were bin bags and rolls of black tape. Under the stairs were bubble wrap and a roll of leftover underlay for the next bedroom to be recarpeted.

So I put cellophane and bin bags all around the body. Taped it ten or twelve times with the tape. It looked like a wrapped-up roll of carpet when I'd finished. Sort of. If you only glanced at it from afar.

Then I dragged it. Pull-pause, pull-pause; so much effort, such agony, from the kitchen through the utility room to the garage. Mopping and wiping and washing away the trail of blood afterwards.

And so, I hid the body, at least for now. It took some doing. I found the strength from somewhere.

By two forty in the morning, I was done. Body hidden. I'd cleaned and bleached the kitchen as best I could. Scrubbed my skin endlessly. Put loads in the washing machine and the dryer. And then, as I got into old pyjamas to sleep in my baby's bedroom, it struck me. I'd need to have a story prepared about him and why he was no longer here. Gone away, I'd say. I woke up in the morning, this morning, and he had disappeared. No, I had no idea where. Harry and anyone else who wanted to speak to Robert would now have to leave me alone in peace. To have my baby.

I realised then – I was not thinking straight at all – that his car, that beaten-up old Fiesta, was still there on the drive-way. He would have driven away in it. And so it needed to go. Now. I got out of bed and pulled on some dark clothes, then I stood, with the front door slightly open, looking out across the close, watching for Alex at the window. Or the Knox boys.

All was still; no one seemed to be watching. I held my breath as I walked to his car, got in and drove slowly away.

I took the car and parked it at the nearest railway station, Trimley St Mary, a run-down sort of place where there are no CCTV cameras. There are cameras, I am sure, at the next station along at Felixstowe. As I got out of the car, I realised I had not worn gloves, and the thought of my fingerprints everywhere alarmed me. I wiped everything over with the edge of my sleeve. No one was about, so far as I could see, on the fifteen-minute walk back to my home. As I hurried up the driveway and put the key in the front door, I felt a huge surge of relief. But then, just as I went to step inside, something made me turn and look over my shoulder. To my horror, I caught sight of Alex at his window, staring out.

I jerk awake in the single bed, realising I've been nodding on and off, my hands still in their protective, cradling position.

Something has woken me. I sit up.

"Rob? Rob? It's Harry. I need to speak to you now!" Dear God, he is back already, shouting through the letterbox.

I INVITE HIM IN. I have no choice. I have to face him sooner or later. It might as well be now. If I ignore him, I will worry even more about what he's doing out there. I need to know.

I wonder if this is just about his investments. If that's not enough in itself. Or whether Alex has said he saw me walking back in the early hours. Maybe he even saw me drive off in the car. How do I explain that? Truth is, I cannot do so easily.

Harry stumbles and almost barges by me as I open the front door. He marches into the living room, probably assuming Robert will be there, tapping away on his laptop.

Harry turns to me, a step or two behind, as he sees the

living room is empty. I am in my pyjamas, no make-up, looking exhausted. So many thoughts race through my head. Whether there's a splatter of blood on one of my ear lobes. If the stench of death is in the air. Whether the smell of bleach is so strong, so overpowering, that he notices and is puzzled by it. Have I missed something obvious, a giveaway sign of the horrific thing I have done?

But he is angry and emotional – his eyes are wild – and he does not seem to really see me. "Where is Rob?" he says loudly, almost shouting, and he moves slightly as though he is going to push by me and go back to the stairs, up them two at a time, looking for him. I move to my left to block the way – I do not want Harry running round the house, seeing the double bed stripped bare and me having slept in the baby's room. Looking at things he should not see. That he may puzzle over later.

"Sit down," I say, gesturing towards an armchair. This is the hand I stabbed Robert with. I wonder if there might be blood splattered on the underside of my arm that I cannot see.

Harry slumps into the armchair, and I sit on the sofa opposite, covering one arm with the other. He is sweating and twitching and does not look as though he has had a good night's sleep. There is a mark on his shirt front; food that he has eaten for breakfast that he has spilled down himself. His hair has not been brushed. He is normally so fastidious but is now dishevelled. It is as though he could not wait to get across here as the clock turned to nine. As if nothing else mattered. I suppose if, as he imagines, he has lost his life savings and is ruined, nothing else does at the moment.

"Where's Rob?" he says again, his voice now more desperate than angry. He has, I notice, a sickly pallor as though he might suddenly lurch forwards and collapse to the floor.

"I don't know," I reply. I have no idea what to say. If I tell Harry he has left me, disappeared, he may go straight to the police. I don't want them here today, poking about. I will crack. It may be better to tell Harry a white lie.

"He left in the night. His mother ... his mother's friend ... was taken ill. He's gone to help." I went to say "his mother", but suddenly realised Harry may know she is long dead.

Harry sits there shaking and then suddenly leans forward and takes me into his confidence. He tells me, spluttering and gasping, what I already know, or at least suspected – that he put all of his life savings, "Everything I saved over forty years," into two of Robert's schemes, arbitrage and currencies trading. That he was expecting to be paid four per cent a month. For the first nine or ten months he had been. That he has not been paid last month – "Rob said that was your fault" – and he has not been paid this month's money either. And he needs it – his voice squeaks as if he's in pain – to live on, and he is worried all of his capital has gone.

"But you know all this, don't you?" he asks angrily, looking at me as if it is all my fault. And I reply as firmly as I can, although I am shaking inside, "I don't know anything about any of it. It's nothing to do with me." Harry holds my gaze, and I can see all sorts of thoughts are racing through his mind. He's uncertain. Whether he can sweet-talk me into helping him. Whether he should bully and threaten me into doing something.

"At all," I insist. I don't want to get drawn into this. And I don't want Harry here. I want him gone. I need time to think. About what this means. How I should handle it. Maybe Robert was taking in money from all sorts of people. Paying the early ones their interest with the later ones' capital. Until there were no later ones and the money dried up. There's a name for these scams, but I can't recall it for now. I think he came here to hide out. To lie low. And I am afraid that my rainy-day money has gone too. I stand up and tell Harry I will let him know just as soon as Robert contacts me. Harry scowls and huffs, but, as I stand firm, eventually he gets up on his feet.

As Harry leaves, he glances at and seems to notice the rucksack and two carrier bags of clothes by the front door. He looks at me with a puzzled expression, but I do not say anything, and he goes.

I wish, suddenly, that I had said to Harry that Robert had left me, disappeared into the night. Gone forever. And I would deal with the consequences, the police, whatever. I will have to one day, for sure.

As it is, Harry will now keep coming back. Next time, he will ask about the rucksack and bags of clothes. At some stage, Alex will tell him about me coming home in the early hours. Maybe more if he saw me driving the old Ford Fiesta away. I wonder what will happen then.

9

TUESDAY, 1 JUNE, THE DAYTIME

After a cursory breakfast of porridge and tea, which I struggled to eat and drink without choking, I am at my laptop at the kitchen table.

I have not used this laptop for ages. I have my mobile phone for pretty much everything these days, including banking matters. But, thanks to Robert, the screen is cracked, and, anyway, I want to see things more clearly on this bigger screen.

Harry has scared me, all this talk of not being paid and losing all his investment money. I want to see that my money is safe. The thought of it not being there worries me more than I can say.

I start by checking my day-to-day affairs. I log in to my bank and my current account with my username and password – always the same ones, a mixture of Mother's and Father's initials and the dates of their births. I check the balance, which is much as I expected, and then trawl through the past month's transactions and double-check the direct debits and standing orders. All is just as it should be, and I sit back and sigh with relief, suddenly realising I am sweating and have been holding my breath. I sign off, relieved.

"Ponzi scheme." That's the name I've been looking for. I fear that is what Robert has been running with Harry's and other people's money.

I google it. "A fraudulent investing scam ... offering high rates of return ... and little risk to investors ... returns for earlier investors paid with money from later investors ... when there are no new investors and there isn't enough money left ... the scam unravels." I remember how Robert said he always needed new investors.

That, I think – no, I know in my heart – is what he has been doing. And it's now unravelling fast. Harry has been here. Others will follow; no doubt about that. It is only a matter of time.

I walk to a drawer by the kitchen sink. I dig out my notebook listing the various accounts where I've been keeping my savings. All were earning a pitiful rate of interest. Inflation eating my money away. That's why I gave Robert access to all of them early on when I was happy and trusted him. I signed whatever he put in front of me without thinking. So that I, too, could earn four per cent a month. He showed me printouts now and then at the beginning, revealing how rich I was becoming. I never really took much notice, happy that my money was growing; confident that it would be enough to set my baby – by then a young woman – off on a mortgage-free life when she reached twenty-one or so, after university.

I sit down again at the laptop, entering the username and password for the first account. They are not recognised.

I do the same for the second, third and fourth accounts. None of my details work anymore. I try them time and again, with rising anxiety, making sure I have not mis-typed any of them. And then, after so many attempts, I am locked out.

I sit back. I can feel myself sweating and breathing irregularly. I used half of my inheritance to buy this three-bed detached house. The other half I saved. That has now vanished.

I FEEL SICK, physically sick, going over to the sink and dry-heaving into it. My money has gone. Why else would all the passwords have been changed?

I will now have to manage on the salary going into my current account. When my baby is born, I will not be able to stop work for long. I will have to keep working and pay for a childminder who earns almost the same as me. I will be on my own and don't know how I will cope.

But I will manage somehow. I will have to. Father and Mother taught me to be thrifty. And to be humble and not to think I was better than anyone else and deserved more. Not that I do. I know I have been fortunate to have so much money in the bank, but it came at a price. I would have rather not had it; I would give anything for Father and Mother to still be with me. But I am angry that he has cheated me. I have been comfortable, financially secure, but now my life will be a struggle.

I have a sudden thought, a flash of hope. Of course, Robert will have moved all my money out of these low-paying boring accounts and put them together in a proper, fast-growing investment fund of my own. He did, after all, show me those forms and charts and suchlike, revealing how much I now had. He could not have done that – "Here, take a look at these!" – if the money was not there, to be seen accumulating rapidly, demonstrating to me how clever he was. He would not have risked me studying what he presented to me if those were false. And would he really have cheated me, the woman he was going to spend his life with?

I only wish I had read the paperwork and seen what he had put and where. I hurry to the box room where he worked each day, tap-tapping away on his laptop, moving money from this trade to that, making a few per cent here and a few per cent there. "It all adds up," he once said, proud of himself.

As I was frantically tidying round in the night, after putting his clothes and rucksack by the front door, I'd moved his laptop and his watch and his mobile phone and his keys to the desk to keep everything in one place. So here it all is in front of me on the desk, with drawers to either side and a printer below.

I open the drawers, perhaps expecting to see files for each of the investors, including one with "Laura Curtis" on it. But after opening and closing the six drawers, all I have found is a half-eaten packet of Polo mints and an unopened box of tissues. That's it. Everything – his business, his life, his secrets – is most likely on his mobile phone and his laptop.

I turn them on one after the other and sit there, spending twenty minutes or so entering every conceivable password I think he might have used, all without success. As I turn them back off, feeling defeated, I wonder, if I take the mobile phone and the laptop to a computer man in Ipswich who knows about such things, and I say I have forgotten the pass-words, whether he may be able to open them, letting me into the secrets.

As I sit back in the chair, my left foot catches the lid of the printer, and I realise this is both a printer and a scanner too. I had never given it much thought.

I lift up the lid, and I see there is something there. A blank sheet of paper. I turn it over to see what is on the other side.

It is a scan of his driver's licence. With his face on it and his date of birth and an address in Norwich, forty or so miles away. He never mentioned Norwich to me, not once, let alone that he lived there. That puzzles me. It worries me too. I sense I have uncovered a dark secret.

I TRY to put my troubled thoughts about my savings and the address in Norwich to one side for a while, as I spend much of the morning cleaning, vacuuming and washing relentlessly, going round and round over everywhere he had been and everything he had ever touched. Not just to remove as much physical evidence as I could, but also to try to obliterate his existence. I felt so frantic.

I kept going back and forth to the garage, checking and rechecking what I had done, opening the door, dragging him through, pushing him under the shelf of the work unit, covering the front with a wheelbarrow and the lawn mower, and then retracing my footsteps out, looking for any mistakes I had made.

At one point, I was crouched over, my hands red raw, a bottle of bleach in one hand, a cloth in the other, having wiped the garage floor for what seemed like the hundredth time, and I saw myself for what I was. I felt, truly, at that moment that I was on the brink of madness, about to tip into insanity.

I stood and looked at the body wrapped in its makeshift cocoon of plastic and bin bags, and I realised that anyone who ever comes in here will see what it is straightaway. I have covered the front of the work unit as best I can, the far end is against the wall, but the side closest to the door is exposed. There is not enough room, between the unit and the door, to put boxes there. I leaned a rake and a broom against it; that is all that I have.

The length of the shelf is some two metres; the body only a little shorter. He – it – the body – is clearly visible,

and anything more than a cursory glance will reveal what
it is.

And I thought there was a smell already, although that
may have been my imagination. I sprayed air freshener all
around and then found myself sobbing again, perhaps at the
ridiculousness of the gesture. I was beside myself with so
many conflicting emotions and was not thinking straight. I
doubt I ever will again.

I lay down on the single bed in the front bedroom for a
long while, two to three hours, trying to still my mind. I was
not successful. My fears overwhelmed me at times. Only the
thought of my baby – keeping her, protecting her, loving her
– kept me going.

Eventually, I decided that I had to get up and get on
with things for my baby's sake and for my own sanity. I had
to be practical and make the best of the situation. I
concluded that I would have to be a recluse. I cannot have
anyone in the house ever. There would always be the fear of
discovery.

I changed my clothes again after that, had a bath and put
on my make-up. I sat there, staring at my face for ages. I have
a look of my father, who bore a resemblance to an elderly
Roald Dahl even as a relatively young man. I think I do too,
although that is the least of my worries right now.

I then went back to thoughts of my savings, spending the
afternoon telephoning the banks and building societies that
had the money spread between them. "Diversify," the inde-
pendent financial adviser I spoke to had said soon after
Father's passing. "The main banks and building societies ...
and not more than £85,000 in each ... so you are covered by
the Financial Services Compensation Scheme." As I could
not access any of the accounts online, I thought I would telephone on my landline in the kitchen and speak to someone
who could reissue them. If I could access the money, or at

least what was left of it, I could make my finances more secure.

The person I spoke to at the first bank, after pressing so many numbers and waiting for so long in the system, made me feel like a criminal. She said she had to go through various security questions before we could have a conversation. I answered them all easily enough, but then there was a long silence, and she asked me to hold the line, and there was an even longer silence that alarmed me as if I had got all the questions wrong. She came back on the line and told me I had failed security and that I should come into a local branch to speak to them.

I put the phone down and rang the next bank, and the same scenario played out. I could hear the man on the other end of the line breathing as I gave my answers to all of his questions. "I'm sorry," he said finally. "You have failed security," echoing the woman at the first bank. By the time I got to the third and fourth, the building societies, I immediately tried to explain what had happened, that I thought the account had been closed and the money had been transferred by my partner, and I wanted to check where; but they both parroted the "security questions" line.

By teatime, I was tired and frustrated. I'd had nothing to eat since this morning's porridge, so I made myself two slices of buttered toast and a mug of tea. I ate them in the living room, looking out through the half-opened blind into the close. I decided I would set a timetable for the rest of this week, looking over my lesson plans for school next week and so on. I would keep going as though nothing had happened. And I would not answer the door to Harry or anyone else. I would lock every window and door before going out. I would get on with things.

The up-and-over garage door at the front worries me. It has a lock, but is unlocked, and I have lost the key. I went through the kitchen drawers to find it but could not. The two conservatory doors do not fit together well – they shut and lock but seem loose, and I am afraid that sustained pressure might force them open. But I tried to tell myself I was worrying over nothing, that I needed to ignore these thoughts preying on my mind.

Then my mind went back to the scan of Robert's driving licence. I wondered why he had done that and left it there. But the address – it sounds like an apartment in Norwich – keeps worrying me more. I googled the address, and it is part of a block of apartments close to the railway station. It makes me think, somehow, that Robert may have had a whole life that I knew nothing about. At some point, I will need to find out more about that.

It is now the night. It has been a long day, the worst of my life. I feel stunned; shocked and ashamed of what I have done. I never imagined I would be capable of this. I was so terrified of him, though. I was so afraid of what he would do to our baby.

And now I am scared and will be forever that his body will be uncovered. That Harry and other investors will be at my door every day. The police, too, if his investment activities turn out to be a scam. Along with others, so many more, whom he owed money to.

I cannot stop thinking about this apartment in Norwich and what I might find there if I visit. I am fearful, not least because I hate the thought of leaving Robert's body here. I need to stand guard over it.

As I approached the evening, I tried to still my mind. I decided I had to try to live as normal a life as I can. For my baby's sake and my own. I have to create a routine for this half-term week. To keep my mind occupied and away from his body and the money and his other secrets. It will be easier next week when I am back at school, working through to the end of the school year in July and then taking time off to have my baby in November. I will be too busy to think, to dwell on the horrors.

I had another bath, did some washing and cleaning, still desperate to get rid of any remaining traces of him, and had mushrooms on toast and a glass of lemonade for my dinner. I left most of the meal, as each mouthful made me feel sick. I then sat and crocheted for the rest of the evening with the television on quietly in the background; I was just trying to be normal. I felt so tense inside. Even stroking my baby through my tummy did not ease my fears. If anything, I felt worse, wondering how I could possibly protect her all her life.

I came upstairs early, just after the news at ten, and lay in bed in my baby's room. I must sort this soon, redecorating it and sleeping here until my baby is born, maybe longer. I cannot sleep in the main bedroom again. I would feel his presence most of all there. As I lie here, in this single bed with its flat pillows and cheap, scratchy duvet, I attempt to still my mind, which just goes over everything constantly, making me feel as though I am going mad. I try counting sheep and numbers, even reciting The Lord's Prayer, to get me off to sleep; none of it works.

I awake, startled for a second or two as I gather my thoughts. I must have nodded off without realising.

I sit up, wondering what woke me. A noise outside my window, most likely. Or something inside the house. Or someone. Moving about.

I listen, my nerves all on edge. But everything is quiet. Yet something worries me. I pull the pillows up behind me as I lean back against the headboard, waiting for a noise.

I fear, and I know it is madness, that Robert is not dead. I recall my grandmother passing away in our back bedroom when I was young after a long illness, Father telling me later that he put a mirror to her nose and mouth to see if there was still breath in her body. "That's how you check," he'd said. I did not do that with Robert, just assumed that he was dead because he did not move at all.

My mind wanders, recalling newspaper stories where people have been buried alive and have come back from the dead.

As I wrapped underlay and plastic wrapping and whatever I could find around his body, taping it all up, round and round, I never thought to check for any signs of life. I had just killed him. I was distraught. I wanted him gone, his body and all traces of him, just as soon as possible, put somewhere that I would rarely come across him.

And he has lain there, eventually coming round and trying to cry out, to move, to somehow free himself. As I have been troubled and distracted at home all evening, he has slowly pushed and pulled and loosened everything that covered his body. Now, in the early hours of the morning, he has freed himself and is coming for me. I shake my head at this utter nonsense. I tell myself my mind is playing tricks.

But there is a noise. From downstairs. A clear and unmistakeable *clink*. As though a china mug has been put on the work surface in the kitchen. Or perhaps a kitchen knife has been taken from the rack.

I am being foolish. I know I am. Yet I sit here holding my breath, waiting, straining to hear another sound. The next sound. The proof, the absolute proof, that he is downstairs.

If – when – there is another noise, I will know for sure he is there. And I will listen to his footsteps as he comes up the staircase. I cannot move. I am frozen with fear.

I feel, I sense, movement somewhere beyond the room,

along the landing and down to the bottom of the stairs. That's where he is, ready to come up, one step at a time. I cannot hear his foot on the first step. All I can hear is the blood rushing in my ears. If I cannot hear him moving, I know that the bedroom door will eventually, suddenly, swing open, and he will be standing there, this grotesque monster, with a knife in his right hand.

I know that three of the thirteen steps creak. I forget which exactly, but one is at the bottom, another somewhere in the middle and the other close to the top. I listen, waiting, for the first creak. If, when, it goes, I will know for sure he is coming for me, and I will have to move, to get up out of the bed, to defend myself in some way against his attack.

I do not hear a creak. Not at the bottom. Nor in the middle. Not at the top. Seconds pass. A minute. Maybe more. I cannot breathe. I do not know if he is waiting there at the bottom, realising I am here, awake and terrified, or whether he knows which steps creak and has crept up slowly, stepping over them, to reach the top. And he is now at the bedroom door, about to push it ever so slowly open.

This will be the end of me. And my baby. He will not let us live.

It is the thought of my defenceless baby that makes me move.

Up and out of the bed, the alarm clock in my hand, ready to defend us as best I can.

10

B y morning, I had to get out of the house, away from my terrible imaginings; my guilty conscience playing tricks on me all night long. I checked the body, and it is as it was. I then left, locking all the doors, checking them two or three times each. And I am now, two hours or so on, standing outside a big old Edwardian building – converted into three floors of apartments – near the railway station in Norwich some forty miles from where I live.

I drove twenty minutes to Ipswich railway station, torn all the time between going or returning home, and then got on the next train before I could change my mind. If anyone had asked, I would have said I was going to Norwich to do a little shopping, have lunch by the castle, and maybe see a matinee at the Theatre Royal. Just an ordinary day out. I doubt any day will ever be again.

In truth, I have come here with the scan of his driving licence, folded over neatly, showing his photograph and his address as an apartment – number five – in this building, to find out what I can. I don't know where else to start. I have his bunch of keys in my hand. Now I am here, though, I am filled with doubt. Trepidation, too. Perhaps I am touched by madness to be doing this.

The front door of the building opens directly on to the pavement. It is locked. Everyone who lives here must have their own key. I look at his bunch of keys. Two are for my house, the front door and the door at the back of the garage. I try each of the other three Yale keys in turn, all without success.

There are entry system boxes on the wall to the side of the front door. And there are buttons – marked 1, 2, 3, 4, 5, 6 – to press to buzz through to each apartment. I go to press 5 but then think better of it. I do not want to announce my arrival.

I have no idea who is inside number five, if anyone. I really hope it is empty other than basic furnishings and a pile of his files and boxes that I can sort through. To find out more about him and his life, and where the money might be. But there may be someone living there. It could be a woman. His woman. His other woman. Maybe one of many other women.

I stand here, outside, waiting for someone to come or go so that I can pretend I am fumbling for my keys and can take the opportunity to slip inside.

I hope one of these keys will fit the keyhole of number five's front door. And I will walk in as though I have every right to be there.

But the thought of that makes me feel nauseous. I wonder what I am doing – if I am losing my senses – and whether I should simply go home and hide away.

As I hesitate, a postman, whistling to announce his presence, moves alongside me and presses something or other somewhere that I've not seen. The front door buzzes and clicks open. I follow him in.

I'm in a small and run-down hallway, with stairs up to my immediate left, a row of post boxes for each apartment in front of me on the back wall and, on the right wall, a unit containing electricity meters, I think, with piles of post on top of it. There are two front doors to the back at either side: 2 on the door to my left, 3 on the right. There is a staircase leading down to the basement and, I suspect, an apartment 1.

So 5, Robert's apartment, will be on the next floor, to the right. I step onto the stairs as the postman sorts and shuffles and puts letters into the metal post boxes. He ignores me.

I am up the stairs and at the front door of 5 where Robert lives – once lived – in this anonymous building with its white grubby walls and checked carpets and faded white banisters and skirting boards. There is a faint smell of spicey cooking and something else, sweet and sickly, that I cannot place, coming from somewhere in the building.

The postman bangs and clangs and pulls the front door of the building shut with a click as he leaves. All is quiet. I rest my forehead against the door of number 5, listening for the sounds of movements inside. There is nothing to hear. I suddenly, unexpectedly, feel a terrible sense of, I'm not sure how to describe it, melancholy perhaps, even regret. Sorrow, that's the word.

I am fiddling with the keys, the three Yale keys, and I think one of these must fit this lock, and I will then be inside to discover what is in the apartment. I try one after the other, jabbing and rattling each of them, trying to force one of them to turn the lock. None of them do. I push at the door, thumping it in frustration. It is solid and unyielding, and I have no way of getting in.

I hear movement inside, heavy, solid steps moving towards the door, and I step back and wrap my hands around my tummy.

I wonder if it might be a student from the nearby university. I am not sure what I would say to them; maybe I could try to talk my way in to look around and see what might have been left behind in a cupboard.

Or, and the idea sickens me, I wonder if I am about to come face to face with someone like me. A lonely and gullible woman with her hands around her stomach. Or maybe a baby in her arms.

I HEAR the door being unbolted at the top, the jangle of a chain and the handle turning as the door is opened just a crack. The chain remains in place.

The balding head of a middle-aged hobgoblin peers through. He is a sour-faced man with a bare hairy chest and a yellow bath towel around his lower half.

"I was just getting into the shower," he says. "I thought it was ... a friend." Then adds abruptly: "What do you want?"

I have to be quick. Before this surly and gruff man tells me to clear off and shuts the door in my face.

I hesitate, then rub my tummy, a nervous gesture. He sees it and guesses I am pregnant, and then shakes his head as if to say, "Come on, hurry up," but I get the sense he may now be a little less abrupt with me.

I reach into my pocket and hold up the scan of the driving licence towards him so he can see the photograph and the name and the address, this address where he is now living.

"I'm looking for ... Robert Wilkinson ... his driving licence has this address on it."

The man swears under his breath and steps back as if he's about to shut the door. That's that.

"Please ..." I say. "He's the father of my child." I hear the desperation in my voice; it's not how I want to appear.

But it seems to work. He stops and looks back at me; then glances down at my tummy and shakes his head.

He makes what sounds like a well-prepared speech, or at

least he is saying something that he has repeated many times before.

"He lived here; he was the tenant before me. I've been here four or five months, and I'm not sure when he moved out. It had been empty for a while when I moved in. I don't know where he is. Nor does the landlord or the agent. He didn't leave a forwarding address."

I smile and nod, "Go on," as he clearly has more to say. "Please."

"It was ... non-stop for a while, people ringing the doorbell, banging on the door ... debt collectors and bailiffs ... he owed money left, right and centre ... credit cards, gambling companies. And so much post, county court summons, all sorts. I complained to the agents, but they just said to show my ID and rental agreement and say he'd gone away ... run away, more like."

He must see the look of horror on my face, as he slows and softens his words a little.

"It's tailed off lately. You've been the first for a month or so. But I still get some post. I've stopped sending it back. I just leave it down there in the hall and keep my door locked and bolted. One of the debt collectors wasn't very nice."

There is a moment's silence. He looks as though he feels he has said too much.

I don't know what to say. This – all these debts – isn't what I expected to discover and it worries me even more.

I sense he is about to glance down and away, then mumble a goodbye and shut the door on me. I speak quickly.

"Has he ... Robert ... left anything here?"

The man shakes his head.

"Has anyone else called for him ... not debt collectors ... I mean ... family?"

"Someone like you?" he says, looking at my tummy again. "No, just debt collectors."

I hesitate. "Um ... Would he have been friends, do you think, with anyone in any of the other apartments?" I manage to ask.

He shakes his head again. "Not that I know; everyone keeps to themselves. And they come and go. Two or three apartments have changed tenants since I've been here."

"So this is rented, then?" I ask. "He didn't own it?"

"No. As I said, it's a rental property."

"Might he have left some things in storage somewhere?"

The man shrugs and tells me, "It's fully furnished."

"He's not left anything at the back of a cupboard?"

"No," he answers matter-of-factly. "He hasn't."

He's getting restless now, the man. He's answering my questions, but fidgeting, adjusting his towel, and glancing back over his shoulder as though he's left the shower running. It's time to go.

I half-expect him to ask something about Robert. Do I know where he is? ... Do I have a forwarding address? ... Am I? ... is this? ... are you? ... as he looks at my tummy.

But he doesn't ask anything. And I can think of nothing more to say. So we smile vaguely, in an embarrassed kind of way, and he steps back and shuts the door.

And I don't know what to do next.

I AM at the bottom of the stairs in the hallway of the building.

I had thought about tapping on each front door in turn to show the scan of the driving licence to anyone who answered, but I could not face the same sort of conversation over and again.

I stand here, distressed by what the man in the apartment has told me.

The Robert who was presented to me by Harry at his

barbeque – a rich and successful investment adviser ... a guru ... something of a genius – is, I think, as far removed from reality as could be. He is – he was – a man who owed money to all sorts of people, including gambling companies. Debts so big and so bad that debt collectors and county court summons and bailiffs have all been involved.

And I wonder, when he turned up at my home battered and bruised all those months ago, if he came to me as someone offering a refuge from this apartment. That there is no property portfolio. No successful arbitrage scheme. No money-making FX currencies scheme. That the old Ford Fiesta was his and not a friend's. Everything he owned he carried in that rucksack. The money he has taken from Harry and others – and most likely me – is being used to pay earlier investors with the rest feeding a serious gambling habit.

If that money has now all gone, and Harry's actions suggest this is so, there is more horror to come. I wonder if he has been using my address too. I recall how he always had to be first to the post, not wanting me to ever pick it up from the doormat. With credit cards and gambling debts and none of them being repaid, it may only be a matter of time before debt collectors and court summons and bailiffs start coming to my door.

I remember what the man at number five said about the post when I see the piles of envelopes on top of the unit in the hallway. I make my way across to them, full of dread. I need to look – maybe they'll help me uncover more truths about his life.

Some of the envelopes are addressed to "The Occupier" of the various apartments. Others to specific names, tenants who have come and gone and left no forwarding address, leaving a trail of bills behind. I imagine it's commonplace somewhere like this.

There are a dozen or so envelopes with Robert's name, or

variations of it, on them. I wonder if he has other debts, perhaps in a former tenant's name, but I see no other envelopes addressed to number five.

I stand in the hallway of this gloomy place, opening each of the envelopes in turn. I want to be away into the sun and the wind and the fresh air and to forget about this horrible building and its sordid goings-on. To feel clean and wholesome once more. But then it occurs to me again that, with his body wrapped up and hidden away at home, I never will feel that way. This is what life will be like from now on.

As I open all of the envelopes before reading their contents, there are footsteps outside the front door, the twist of a key in the lock, and someone is coming in. I turn my back and look at what's in each envelope. Final demands. Letters from gambling companies and debt collectors. Summons for debts. More of the same. All five-figure sums and more. I wonder how many more there are as I stuff the letters back into the envelopes and leave them on the unit. They make me feel so dirty.

I turn and step aside as an exhausted-looking young woman with a small child in a buggy, shopping bags on either handle, says, "Excuse me, please," and moves to the stairs down to the basement.

I look at her, this unhappy woman. And then at her child, a baby really, no more than a few months old, six at most. I look at his round, chubby face and his little tartan hat and coat. He smiles at me, and I notice his eyes. They are round and innocent, but they somehow remind me of Robert's eyes.

As the woman looks back at me, perhaps to ask me to help her down the stairs with her shopping, I find myself pushing by her and pulling at the front door until I am back outside onto the front doorstep. I hurl his bunch of keys across the street in anger and double over and retch on the pavement.

Finally, I pull myself together, then take one last look back up at the apartment on the second floor and see the hobgoblin of a man watching me. I wish I had never come to this horrid place. I hope I never see these people again.

I HAVE BEEN HOME from Norwich for no more than five minutes. That's all. I had to go straight to the bathroom. After that, I thought I'd have a bath. But I just felt physically and mentally exhausted.

So I sat and then stretched out on the sofa in the living room, two cushions behind my head. It occurred to me I had not washed the cushion covers – they still had the sickly smell of Robert's hair gel – so I dropped them on the wooden floor for now and laid my head on the armrest instead.

As I had on the train journey back, I continued going over everything that happened in Norwich. I realised I may have been imagining that the woman and the baby were his former lover and child. My mind is in such torment. But there is little doubt about his debts and what they mean for my money. And what might happen next if he has been using my address to run up even more massive debts.

I am startled from my thoughts by a sudden burst of furious knocking at the front door. It will be Harry; he must have been in his front room, watching and waiting for me to come home.

I groan and get up. I can do without this now, this threatening behaviour. I move towards the front door as he bangs and bangs and bangs again. Such a temper. And this, the endless banging on the door, makes me indignant and angry.

Harry must know Robert is not here; he will have been watching all day. So this banging is for me; he is demanding that I open the door to him. Now! As though I am at his command. I've had enough. I cannot have Harry coming round like this. Pushing by me. Bullying me.

"Robert's not here," I say abruptly as I open the front door. "He's left me."

My words stop him in his tracks. He was about to step forward, brushing me aside as though I don't matter. His words – his threats, whatever they would be, all carefully prepared – now stick in his throat. His mouth opens and closes in a comical manner.

"He's gone," I insist, louder now, before he can answer. "I don't know where he is. You'll have to wait for him to contact you to sort things out. It's nothing to do with me. None of it."

He's taken aback. I watch as he stands there, sweating, with his carefully combed white hair flopping forwards, sticking to his forehead.

"You told me he'd gone to see his mother's –"

"He's left me," I interrupt, all the frustration and rage in me bubbling up so I am almost shouting. "Do you understand that? He's gone. I don't know where."

"He left his clothes in those bags. I saw them. So he'll come –"

"He left them behind," I snap. "Stuff he didn't want. I've thrown them away ... put them in the grey bin for collection."

He stands there, baffled, his mind clearly going this way and that as he tries to make sense of it all.

"You must know where he is, where he's gone." He gestures at my tummy, but does not offer congratulations. "Sarah told me."

I say nothing.

"You know all right," he insists in a sour voice like I'm a crook, not a mum-to-be. "You bloody well know."

I shake my head in disbelief, not speaking, not wanting to get into a slanging match.

"Here," he says, reaching into his pocket for a piece of

paper, which he thrusts at me. I take it automatically. "This is what he owes me. Capital and missed interest. You've got until tomorrow. Otherwise it's the police."

And then he turns, triumphant, and walks away. I notice for the first time that he has a funny walk, almost a waddle. He looks as though his pants are wedged into his bottom.

I glance down to see what is written on the paper. It is a six-figure sum; what a greedy, foolish man he is to have been so taken in by Robert's sweet talk. I feel sick, physically sick. There will be others too, of course. I wonder what Robert did with all the money. If he's gambled it all away, or if he's been siphoning it off somewhere.

These are the thoughts I will struggle with all evening. I will not sleep tonight. This is a living nightmare, and I don't know how it will end. But one thing's for sure: it will not be a happy-ever-after ending.

11

It is coming up to one o'clock in the morning. I am wide awake and worrying in the little bed in the front bedroom. For almost three hours now, I have been twisting and turning; I cannot get comfortable nor relax. It's my baby, but not just that. It's everything really. All of it.

I imagine my baby growing inside me. I will one day feel her first kick. What a wonderful moment that will be. But it makes me feel sad, too; I am on my own now – the only person who can protect my baby is me.

Everything is closing in, and I fear there is much more to come; Harry's threats will turn into action. At some stage, debt collectors will be on the doorstep. And the police, as likely as not. I feel trapped. My home is my prison.

I can sense his presence, Robert's, all the time I am here. It makes me feel ill. I am trying to be as normal as I can, going about my life, thinking about my baby, looking forward to being a mother. But it is impossible. This evening as dusk fell, and I sat struggling through cheese on toast and a glass of orange squash, a cat, a big black cat, strolled along the top of the fence at the bottom of the garden, jumped down and swaggered up the path to the back door of the garage. It sniffed and scratched at the garage door and would only go away when I shooed him off with a cup of cold water thrown in his direction.

I cannot smell Robert – even thinking those words makes me want to gag – but I suspect animals now can and their awareness of the body will only increase as time passes. I nodded off briefly, so exhausted and out of sorts was I, whilst watching the news. I dreamed that rats had somehow got into the garage and were feasting on his body. A dream so vivid, so awful, that as I woke up I swear I could hear them scurrying about. I could not bring myself to go in. It was all I could do to check the door into the garage from the utility room was shut. It was only after confirming that everywhere else was as it should be that I accepted it was just a vivid dream.

But someday soon, the body will start to decompose and smell, especially during the hottest weeks of the summer. Cats and rats and mice will come and try to get to it at night. People passing by, walking their dogs around the close to the alley that takes them out to the fields, will stop and pull a face and wonder what it is. And dogs will drag their owners towards the garage at the end of my driveway. That front garage door is easy to open – up and over – and I daren't get a locksmith in to put on a new lock. One day, some nosey parker will lift it up and walk right on in.

It's not just the smell, and the decomposition that must surely give me away in the summer weeks, but the physical presence of a body so close to me in the house. I think perhaps that I can move it, and if I have the strength and good fortune when neighbours are on holiday, I might be able to bury it in the side passage or the garden.

But one day, a new best friend and I will be having lunch on the patio, our children playing at our feet, when, suddenly, part of the garden will subside in front of us. My new best friend will walk across and look down and see fingers or toes poking out of the soil, and it will all be over. The body will always be there ready to bring everything to a horrifying conclusion.

I can never have anyone round, nor can my daughter. No little playmates for tea. We must be alone. We can never leave. I wonder what will happen when I die and my grown-up daughter inherits the house and maybe decides to extend into the back garden. What she will think of me when the body is discovered.

There is nothing else for it. I will have to move the body somehow, sometime, somewhere. I will open the front garage door late one night, into the early hours, turning the light on, driving my car off the driveway and around and back up, then reversing carefully into the garage. The door back down. Hiding what I am doing. Moving him. I am sure I can have the strength to drag him, stop-start, stop-start, out of the hidey hole and, with a huge effort, somehow pull and push and tip him into the boot of the car. I don't know what I will do from there.

I will have to do it soon, though. It will be harder, so much harder, to move the body as I become six months pregnant, then eight months, until, finally, I give birth. By then, it will be too late. I will not have the physical strength left. The thought of moving his dead body now is horrible enough. It would be unthinkable when it is decaying. I could not do it. The body would have to stay where it is.

So I need to make a plan. The only place I can think of taking him is to Rendlesham Forest, which has trees in all directions for miles and miles around with little paths and thickets and tucked-away places where no one will have ever walked nor ever will. It is about a thirty-minute drive in the car. I can park on the side of the road and go and look around until I find somewhere that I can bury him so deep that he will never be uncovered.

I can then come home and wash and scrub and clean and bleach again and go to work and come home day after day and just be happy, waiting for my baby to be born.

After that, I can put the house on the market, hopefully before the debt collectors and bailiffs and the police arrive. And I can sell it and be gone.

And we, my baby and I, will simply vanish. We can move far away – somewhere like Cornwall or the Yorkshire Dales or even overseas, somewhere where we can live happily ever after.

———

AN HOUR LATER, unable to sleep or even begin to relax at all, I am driving towards Rendlesham Forest. This is a reconnoitre, a scout around to find somewhere to bring the body and hide it tomorrow night. I am beyond exhausted, though, and I am sobbing with despair.

I drove steadily, so as not to attract attention, for half an hour or so, through the villages of Martlesham and Wood-bridge and Melton, until I came towards the forest.

I passed a police car set back in a side lane, keeping my eyes on the road and hoping the police would not follow me. They didn't. But now, half a mile on, a police car – that same police car, I believe – is right behind me.

I keep driving at the speed limit, my head fixed straight ahead, but with my eyes on the mirror so I can see behind, watching the police car. The driver keeps pace with me.

I slow a little, down from thirty to twenty-five miles per hour, inviting the police to overtake me and be on their way to wherever they are going. They may just be on the same road as me at the same time. A coincidence, that's all.

The police car does not go by me, just sits there behind my car, keeping the same pace, maintaining the same distance. As though the police are following me.

I drive back up to thirty and then wish I hadn't. I have shown, by slowing and then speeding up, that I am aware of the police car behind me. That I am troubled by its presence.

The police car is driven back up to thirty, too, so as to stay close to me. It now feels like this is a game of cat and mouse. I have to stop sobbing and think what I am going to do.

I cannot now, as we are on the road into the forest, pull over to the side as planned and hope the police will just drive by and away. They will not; they will want to know why I am going into the forest in the early hours of the morning.

I cannot turn left or right into a side lane, because the police will turn the same way, and I will end up at the bottom of the lane, with fields all around me and a gate in front and nowhere to go. And the police will stop behind me and get out. They will ask me why I am here, and I will have to try to come up with a plausible story. All I can do is follow the road all the way through the forest and out towards the seaside towns of Aldeburgh and Thorpeness and hope that, some-where between here and there, the police will see something to investigate and will lose interest in me and what I am doing.

There are two of them in the police car. I can see them in the mirror. It is a moonlit night, and as the cars flit between the swathes of trees and the light comes and goes, I see there are two men, two policemen, in the car.

One will have turned to the other, when I went by them all those miles back, and wondered out loud what a woman is doing driving towards the forest at three in the morning.

The other, intrigued, will have said, "Let's follow her." And that's what they are doing, one driving and the other using my number plate to find out who I am and where I live and possibly more. I don't know what information the police can access these days. I guess they'll know my name and address from my number plate and that I've driven about twenty miles at three in the morning. They will wonder why.

Then, as we bob and weave our way through the trees into the heart of the forest, the police car pulls out behind my car. The driver does not signal or hoot or flash their lights, but this is it.

The moment when the police car comes alongside mine on this long and lonely road, where nobody but me and them are about. And I will keep my eyes on the road ahead as the police car keeps a steady pace alongside of me.

On and on we will go, side by side, silently, until, finally, my nerve will break, and I will turn my head to the right to look at them. The policeman in the passenger seat will smile grimly at me and gesture sharply that I must pull over and park. They will then ask me what I am doing, why I am here at three in the morning, and I will not know what to say. They will see the guilt and fear in my eyes and want to know more. I won't know what to say and that frightens me.

MY CAR IS PULLED over in a layby in the middle of Rendlesham Forest.

I am standing by the car bonnet. The night is dark and chilly. There are no street lights out here. Only moonlight through the trees.

The two policemen, who have parked their car in front of mine in the layby, approach me.

I expect them to say they waved me down as I was driving erratically. I was not. But that will be the excuse they will use for stopping me.

They are two bored policemen on the night shift out in

the sticks with nothing much to do for hours on end. They just want to fill in time, breathalysing me and searching my car.

To my surprise, they do not. Instead, they stand back from me, almost respectfully, and one of them touches his peaked cap whilst the other clears his throat and asks, "How are you?" as though we are at a dinner party.

Despite everything, it is hard not to laugh at this surreal moment. I had not expected gentleness and sensitivity from the police. They must have been on some sort of mental health course. Most of us in the public sector have had to these days.

I don't doubt they've checked the number plate and know I am Laura Curtis from Trimley St Mary, a half-hour drive away. And I'd assume, in these early hours, that they would believe I am up to no good. Why else would someone drive into the forest in the dead of night?

But from the way they speak to me, I think they believe that I am here because I am ill, mentally unwell; maybe they think I am planning to take my own life. I don't want them to think that; what I fear most right now is a report being filed and later matching up to other notes that may be on the police computer, some clever police officer seeing them and putting two and two together and then coming out to knock on my front door.

Any day now, Harry Wells will report that Robert Wilkinson is missing from an address in Trimley St Mary.

At some stage, the old Fiesta will be found dumped at the railway station. A quick check will reveal that it's registered to Robert Wilkinson.

Meantime, Laura Curtis drives into Rendlesham Forest in the early hours of 3 June from an address in Trimley St Mary, the same address given for Robert Wilkinson by Harry Wells. Something doesn't quite add up.

"I ... have a dog ... a Jack Russell called ... George ... I brought him here at the weekend ... he went off after a rabbit ..." I stop, hesitating, before going on. "He didn't come back ... I spent hours looking ... I've come back to try to find him."

The two policemen stand next to me, looking, as I do, into the trees. I wait for them to say something. The older one asks if I have a tennis ball: "A favourite tennis ball ... dogs can smell for miles in the right conditions." The younger one goes back to the car and returns with an open packet of dog treats. "Long story ..." he says and jokes, "We've not been eating them ... well ..." He looks at the older officer. "I haven't." They smile at each other as I take the packet.

The older officer speaks. "Stay here by your car ... don't go in ... it's more than six square miles in all ... easy to get lost. We don't want to have to send out a search party for you. If your dog's out there somewhere, he'll smell you and the food, and he'll come and find you. Do you have a whistle?"

I shake my head, realising that if I really had a dog, I'd be here with his favourite blanket, ball, treats and a whistle. Not just standing by my car with nothing at all. And then I remember, years ago, how Father showed me to put two fingers in my mouth and make the most piercing whistle.

I haven't done it for years, but I put my fingers in my mouth and whistle – it's sharp and loud and high-pitched. The older policeman pulls a silly face and pretends to cover his ears. "Well, that should do it," he says. They both stand and watch the trees as though a Jack Russell is about to come bounding out.

After a while, they turn to go back to their car. The older one repeats that I should stay by my car. "Don't venture in ..." he tells me, and to drive away if my dog does not appear. "Or if someone else does ... although it's pretty quiet usually," the younger one adds, the implication being that if another car stops near me, I should get in my car and drive off.

The older policeman then adds, reassuringly, that there's plenty out there to eat for a dog. The younger one says that stray dogs usually end up at the Blue Cross at Bourne Hill ... "You should register his details there." And with that, they get into their car.

I stand by my car, waiting for them to go. I would feel foolish whistling for a make-believe dog whilst they are here, although I know I should do just that to keep up the pretence. Otherwise, they may have second thoughts, wondering if they were correct in their initial impression – that they have come across someone who has driven all this way in the middle of the night to take her own life. I turn to wave them goodbye.

They have their heads down, talking, almost certainly about me. I watch them for a moment or two until the older policeman begins looking at his mobile phone, and the younger one is talking to someone, a senior officer perhaps, back at police headquarters in Martlesham.

Then they both glance at me, almost blank-faced, not as friendly as they were. I think I have been reported, that now I am on a list somewhere that will come back to haunt me.

They drive away without a backwards glance, and I suddenly feel very vulnerable. I wish I had never come here. Somehow, some time, this trip will lead to my downfall. I am certain of it.

12

THURSDAY, 3 JUNE, ANOTHER LONG DAY

It's breakfast time, and I'm standing by the living-room window, eating a bowl of cornflakes and watching the lovely tattooed couple going back and forth to their car with bags and notebooks and lunch boxes.

They put a small rucksack and a colourful ball and some books into the boot. I assume these are Noah's and they will drop him somewhere, at a childminder's house or a play-group, before they drive into Felixstowe to work.

My mind has been such a swirl of negative emotions since I returned from the forest and fell into an uneasy, restless sleep. I'm waiting – hoping – for a glimpse of their sweet little boy to cheer myself up.

I realise how lucky I was last night – this morning – in the forest with the two policemen. To talk my way out of a tricky situation with my stuff and nonsense story. As soon as they went on their way and disappeared out of sight on the twisty road through the trees, I drove home, my hands clenched tight on the wheel. I could not help but think I had got away with it – but only for now. I had intended, in those early hours of the morning, to take Robert's body in the boot of the car and bury it somewhere deep in the forest. But I changed my mind at the last minute – I just felt so tired and unable to face the task – and decided on a reconnaissance first to find a hidden place. Thank goodness I did. Even so, I believe the encounter will come back to catch me out when I least expect it.

I dare not go back to the forest again at night, either to scout around and certainly not to bury the body. The thought of being stopped by the police, perhaps a less sympathetic pair of officers, terrifies me. I feel like it – the body – will have to stay in the garage forever. My home is now a hellish place. Uncertainty and danger surround me. The threat of being uncovered for what I am – a murderer – feels ever imminent. I need to find a way for that to change; I can't live with the thought that this is how it always will be.

But in the meantime, I must maintain some sort of routine for these days before I go back to work next week. Keep busy. Occupied. Doing things. To keep my mind off the horror, at least for a few short moments. This sense of doom will never go away, but maybe I can distract myself a little.

I will go to the out-of-town supermarket at Warren Heath to stock up on my groceries and other essentials. Then lunch at home. A visit to the library in Felixstowe to change my books this afternoon.

My attention is caught by Nick and Amy and Noah walking to their car. Amy hugs and kisses the little boy. Nick then lifts him up and takes him round the far side of the car to put him in his seat.

Amy looks across at my house, as if seeing me watching their happy little family. She shouts something across to Nick, "I'll ask her now," and then walks up my path to my front door and rings the bell. My spirit rises.

"Laura," she greets me as I open the door, "how are you?

We're after a big, big favour. As you teach at the school ... and will have Noah from September ... I wonder if you could have him for a couple of hours, midday to two or three on Saturday? We've an important appointment." She pats her tummy, and I can't help but recognise the gesture. I guess it's a baby scan straightaway. I laugh, and before I can stop myself, I'm exclaiming, "Yes!" in a rather too excited voice.

I SPENT the morning at the supermarket, filling a trolley full of essentials and frozen foods. I saw someone I work with – smiley Mr Aziz – but I changed aisles quickly and moved away. Despite the joyful thought of spending an hour or two with Noah on Saturday, my underlying mood is still downbeat and fearful. "Wary" is the word when it comes to friends and colleagues. I need to keep a distance – I don't want to encourage them to my door, expecting to be invited indoors for a cup of tea and a chat.

It is different with Noah. Nick and Amy will drop him off on the doorstep. I will watch television with him and feed him and kick a ball around in the back garden, never letting him out of my sight. Nick and Amy will return a few hours later and pick him up from the doorstep. It will be nice to be a normal person for a while.

I got home and packed everything away in the cupboards and the fridge and the freezer. I made myself lunch, toast and butter is all I can manage with a cup of tea, and I now sit by the living-room window. I love – loved – this close, but it has, other than that dear little family, all turned sour for me here. I pick at my toast, trying not to feel sorry for myself. As I get up and turn to take my mug and plate to the dishwasher, I see something moving out of the corner of my eye.

A police car is coming into the close, one of those yellow

and blue police cars. My heart is in my mouth. I wonder if this has something to do with my visit to Rendlesham Forest. Or Harry. Or something else neither here nor there. It looks like a male police officer is driving the car. A female police officer is glancing out, checking the house numbers. It may be nothing to do with me at all.

The car slows and goes straight by my house. I breathe a sigh of relief. I am worrying too much. Then the car stops, reverses and parks by my driveway. The police officers get out. They are coming to see me. The policeman leads the way; the policewoman is following.

There is a gentle knock-knock on the glass panel of the front door. I put my mug and plate on the windowsill and suddenly feel faint. I put one hand on my tummy to comfort myself, the other on the sill to stay steady.

I don't want to answer the door. But they may look through the window and see me standing there behind the blind. Or they could come around the back through the gate. Perhaps they will even check the garage, lifting the up-and-over door. Even if they do none of these things, they will come back. Again and again. Until I do answer the door.

And so I open the front door. They introduce themselves as "Jack" and "Emma", the community police officers, as informal and relaxed as though they are my friends. "And are you Laura Curtis?"

"I am," I say, and I invite them indoors. I have no choice, but it makes me feel tense with worry. They come through, and I show them to the sofa, where they sit side by side, both of them leaning forward towards me in one of the chairs opposite.

"Congratulations," says the policeman, a man in his thirties with a friendly face and a beard, nodding towards my tummy. I'm not sure how he knows, as I am not yet clearly showing. But I smile and say, "Thank you," although I feel sick inside. It is all I can do to stop myself gagging.

"When is it ...?" The policewoman, in her early twenties with a blond pixie cut and a harder face, stops and rephrases her sentence. "When is baby due?"

I say, "November," and we smile politely enough at each other. She seems vaguely familiar, but I don't know why. It's like that around Felixstowe though; everyone seems to be connected in some way.

I think they might ask me more about my baby, but neither of them does. It is as if the small talk is done and out of the way, a tick off the checklist.

He takes an old-fashioned notepad from his pocket and flicks through it. She sits and looks around and then at me, as if it is a casual thing. I do not think it is. She's checking me out.

There are photographs dotted here and there of Father and Mother and me on the beach, at Christmas, and at other happy times. A large one of the three of us, me in my graduation cap and gown, Mother beaming with pride, my sentimental old father fighting back tears.

And there is the painting of the beautiful, dark eyed woman in her burnt orange top above the fireplace. I look at her now, as I've done so many times over the years, imagining I am as strong as she is.

There are no photographs of Robert and me, not even the baby scan photograph propped up on the fireplace. I wonder if she will notice and what she will make of that.

There is an awkward silence. I try to swallow, but my tongue seems to be stuck to the roof of my mouth. I cough once and then twice, and she offers to get me a glass of water, but I say, "It's okay, thank you." I don't want her nosing about in the kitchen.

And here we go. The small talk is over. The questioning is about to begin. I am to be subject to a politely phrased interrogation.

I do not know how to act. To smile or be downcast. The truth is, I can barely breathe or swallow.

I am wondering if I am fast approaching the moment when they will ask to take a look around, when they will uncover the body in the garage.

THE POLICEMAN BEGINS: "We're looking for a Mr Robert James Wilkinson ... does he live here?"

Simple enough.

I shake my head as if to answer no. I don't know what else to do. Shaking my head and looking down look bad, as though I am guilty of something. So I manage a wan smile and force myself to make eye contact with him.

He waits. She is looking at me too. I feel unsettled, scared maybe. They are waiting for me to say more. To dig myself into a hole. The less I say, the better.

They are here because of Harry, then, who has not waited and has gone instead to the police about his money. He will have told them what's happened and that Robert has fled and, most likely, I am involved in some way. I have to be so careful what I say. I cannot pretend I know nothing.

"He, ah, Robert, we've been together since last autumn ... he moved in a few months back ... I was pregnant ... he, um, upped and left ... Monday overnight ... I woke up Tuesday morning, and he was gone." As I say the last words, something troubles me, but I'm not sure what it is. That I have made a mistake somehow.

Neither of them speaks as if forcing me to keep on talking. "That's about it, really," I add.

"You've not thought to report him missing?" she asks in a strange tone. "File a missing person report with us."

"Um ... well, it's only been two days." I'm not sure what to add to that. I think a moment, then say, "He isn't missing, as such, not missing missing ... he's just packed everything and gone. I ... don't think he wants to be a daddy."

He speaks next. "Did he leave anything behind?"

He knows, he must do. He will have spoken to Harry, who will have gabbled away about everything from me being pregnant to the bags of clothes sitting by the front door.

"Some clothes I suppose he didn't want. I took them down the dump for recycling." I actually put the rucksack and bags, full of nothing but his clothes, at the bottom of the grey general wastebin that's due to be collected tomorrow. I don't want them to know that though. I don't want them searching through. I have a gasping fear there may be a splatter of blood on something in there.

He makes a note in his pad. She asks, "Carr Road Dump?"

And I nod, suddenly worrying that they will go straight there after this and systematically sift through the clothing banks.

Before one of them can ask what type of clothes and how many, I find myself talking. "Yes, just older clothes I guess he didn't want, jeans, cords, checked shirts." I tail off, realising as I finish the words that I've made another mistake. If they go to the dump and search the clothing banks, they'll probably find nothing like that, and if the workers there say it hasn't been emptied for a week or so, they will come back with more questions.

She says, "Did you have an argument the night he left?"

I answer, "No."

They both sit in silence.

And so I add, "We went to bed about eleven. I fell asleep and went straight through to the morning, and he was gone when I woke up." I realise I've made another terrible mistake – Harry was at the front door after that, gone midnight, and saw the lights on. And they may have spoken to Alex, who saw me out and about even later, in the early hours.

He speaks, gesturing towards my tummy. "Do you sleep well?" An innocent, friendly-sounding question. I don't think it is really.

She adds, "You don't have to get up in the night?" Not so friendly.

I don't sleep well, turning one side to the other, and I do have to get up in the night sometimes to go to the bathroom, but I can't now admit to either. "No," I say and then add, "Not just yet." I try to smile, but my top lip sticks to my teeth.

Silence. She looks around. He makes notes in his pad. I can't help but think this silence – stretching out – is designed to unsettle me. If it is, it's working. I am scared to death.

"Do you have a photograph of Robert?" she says, looking towards the windowsill and the fireplace and the mantelpiece and the wall unit.

I shake my head. "No." It sounds odd as I say the words.

"Would you have one or two on your phone?" she presses. I have some on my phone, but I don't want to show it to her.

"No," I answer and then add, "Harry, over the road, will have some. I know he took photographs at the barbeque he held when we first met in the autumn."

I pause, wondering if they will say "Harry who?" or "Which house does this Harry live in?"

But they don't. So they know who Harry is. He'll be where they got their information. I don't know whether I am going to get through this. It depends on how much Harry has told them.

Then he stands up and says, as casual as anything, "Mind if I take a look around?"

HE IS UP, moving through the living room to the dining room and into the kitchen, at my nervous, nodded agreement. His footsteps echo in my head.

And she is speaking to me, asking me a question, repeating it, to distract my attention.

I turn to her, with an acid feeling in my stomach, as I hear him opening drawers oh so carefully in the kitchen.

"Did Robert have any money worries?"

I look at her, trying to focus, but listening to him, and then, after a while, I hear his footsteps going into the utility room. I fear I may have left the door to the garage open and he will go straight through. I brace myself.

"Did he have money worries?" she repeats the question as I look back at her, so distracted by her colleague moving through my house.

I decide to be honest, as much as I can anyway. So I don't have to remember what I said later. Not that any of it matters if the policeman comes running back in from the garage.

"He was an investment adviser. Invested clients' money into foreign exchange and something called arb ... arbit ..." I stumble over the word. "... Arbitrage schemes. He invested Harry's money from over the way. I ... I think he had money worries, yes."

"Were you involved in his business?" A blunt question. I wonder if I should tell her I've lost money too. I decide not to.

"Not at all, no. I'm a primary school teacher ... when it's not the school holidays ... I teach the alphabet and numbers ... early years." I try for a gentle laugh or even a smile, but neither come. My mouth does not seem to work properly. I am listening out towards the utility room and the garage beyond.

"You weren't responsible for doing the books, paying returns, making sure everything added up? You weren't in charge of the money ... in control?"

He is out of the utility room and moving back to the kitchen and then into the conservatory, the hallway, and the cloakroom and under the stairs. Nothing to find there, but still I fear exposure at any moment. I am sweating heavily and can barely concentrate on her. She repeats the question.

I am completely distracted, but I force myself to look at her as steadily as I can. "No." I think of offering her his phone or laptop and also saying that they can check my bank account if they want to. Anything to make them go away and leave me alone. But I hesitate. He would never have left any of those items behind. And I want to see the secrets of the phone and the laptop for myself. "I'd not know where to start," I add.

There is a thump upstairs. As if the policeman has tugged at a drawer of a bedroom cabinet and it has fallen out and hit the carpet. He is digging about and may see the watch and the phone and the laptop, but I do not think he will assume anything other than they are mine. The watch is not a particularly masculine-looking one. The mobile phone is a neutral black one. The laptop is a shiny silver. But I do also have my laptop sitting there in the front bedroom. He may wonder why I have two.

I feel myself sweating more heavily now. My clothes are sticking to my skin. The policewoman must notice. My hair and face feel wet, and I want to lift the hair lying on the back of my neck and rub my neck dry. Instead I sit here, motionless. What a sight I must be.

"Do you have any idea where he might be? Where he might have gone?" She does not seem to notice my discomfort or at least pretends not to.

I think of telling her about the scan of his driving licence, with his photo and the address in Norwich. But I keep quiet. The more I give them, the more they will keep digging. And the more likely I am to make a mistake.

"No, I don't." I then pause and add, "I wish I did. I don't suppose I'll get any help, child maintenance, from him." And then an idea comes to me, to put her on the back foot. "Will you tell me when you find him?"

She looks, for a moment, uncertain, and younger than I thought, not much out of her teens.

I add, "Please ... he's left me in the lurch."

She pulls a face, which sort of implies "I'm sorry, I can't say anything".

We sit there looking at each other, both of us listening to the policeman's footsteps upstairs, going from room to room. I wonder if he has now spotted the second laptop. We are silent for a while as he moves around.

"It's just a formality," she says, raising her eyes to the ceiling.

Not for me, it isn't. I am sick with the thought of the laptop and that I may have missed something else, a smear of blood, an overlooked bloody fingerprint on a drawer or a doorframe, which he might be about to uncover

"You teach my sister's little boy ... Josh Thomas ... I've seen you when I've collected him sometimes." She smiles slightly, as if reaching out to me. I worry that she is trying to somehow soften me up, easing me into saying more, to give something away.

I smile, try to smile, and answer, "Yes, Josh, he's a lovely boy." To be fair, he is very sweet, as most of them are at that age.

"We're just ... you know," she says, stopping to listen again to the footsteps upstairs, and dropping her voice slightly. "If it's money-related ... fraud ... it will be passed up the line to a special unit somewhere. I don't know where."

I nod, an unspoken acknowledgement between us that this – this disappearance – is to do with money.

"You'd need to tell us if he gets in touch, though. Straight-away. At Martlesham. You can do it via the website. Suffolk. Dot. Police. Dot. UK."

I nod again, and we both look away and around the room as if we are not having this conversation.

"We'd not normally deal with anything like this ... missing persons. But we're so short-staffed ... There are so many off. All hands on deck ... I'm a special," she adds, sounding proud of that and smiling a little before going on. "You'd have to file a missing persons report if you wanted someone to ... although I'm not sure if you might need to be a rel ..." She stops as we both hear her colleague coming down the stairs. She glances towards the doorway. I cannot move through fear.

He comes into the living room and nods at the young policewoman as if to say, "All good." Whatever he has seen, he does not think there is anything odd about it. He then writes a few words in his notepad, tears the sheet out and hands it to me. "If you hear from him ..." he instructs, "you need to tell us straightaway."

I look at the sheet of paper as they turn to go. It's the name and telephone number of an officer, a detective I assume, over at Suffolk Police Headquarters at Martlesham. It's escalating already. I guess these officers will report back to the detective shortly.

They glance at me as they leave, and I wonder what they will say back at headquarters. That my story differs from Harry's. That there are no photographs of him and me anywhere. "That's odd," the young woman will say, before adding, "And she was so-oo shifty and sweaty ... guilt all over her face." And the detective will be next to visit, to interrogate me. I doubt I will be able to fool them. I hurry upstairs and, in desperation, take Robert's watch and phone and laptop and push them out of sight under the single bed in the front bedroom.

I WENT into Felixstowe in the afternoon, to change my library books, trying to act normal and not dwell on the police visit and what that might mean for me. I saw Charlotte, a fellow schoolteacher, across the street outside Boots, and I smiled and hurried along, calling out, "I'm running late!" to avoid any conversation. I need to be alone with my thoughts right now.

Back home, I am standing by the living room window, rubbing my tummy and watching the close; I find the gesture strangely comforting. I see Alex, over the way, wheeling the grey bin down the driveway, ready for the refuse collection. At the same time, the two Knox boys come out, and I think perhaps they are going to catch a bus into Felixstowe or Ipswich for a night out somewhere. They walk across to Alex, and there is laughing and joking, and they all then turn and look across at my house. I step back, perturbed. Deep down, I fear these men.

I go over the police visit in my head. The questions they asked and the meaning, the intent, behind them. I replay my answers and compare them endlessly with what I should have said. I recall how I looked and felt – my voice and my sweatiness and my inability to smile or speak in a natural way – and how all those things together must have looked like guilt. I step forward to see into the close again. Alex is walking back into the house, the Knox boys have gone, and the grey bin is at the end of Harry's driveway. My grey bin has Robert's rucksack and bags at the bottom of it.

I think about what's in those bags, and I decide that I

cannot have them going off to the dump in case someone, somewhere, later comes across them. They would be better off hidden away with the body. I make my way out the front to wheel the grey bin along my pathway, through the gate and into the back garden, where no one will see me retrieving his possessions.

As I do so, it hits me that, in my initial state of frantic distress, I never thought of checking the pockets of his clothes for anything.

I recall that he has – had – a wallet, a small, battered bit of black leather that he used to keep in the back pocket of his trousers. I need to find it, to see what is inside. I cannot believe I have never thought of it before – but my mind has been in such a scramble of conflicting ideas and emotions.

I remember an incident once, late at night, early on, as he changed into his pyjamas. He went to the bathroom but then came back and took the wallet out of his trousers and walked away to the bathroom with it. I did not give it much thought then. I do now. It's as if he was saying, "I don't trust you not to look in my wallet." The memory of that makes me now wonder what it hides.

This man, who travelled so light and kept so much of himself concealed from me, had secrets, so many of them, I suspect. I tip everything out of the carrier bags onto the conservatory floor. I feel for the pockets on the front of shirts, putting my fingers inside for anything there, a scrap of paper with a note on it or maybe a credit or a debit card. But there is nothing. I open the rucksack, taking out his jacket and his trousers and his two pairs of shoes, one smart-ish black pair and a new-ish pair of grey trainers.

I put my fingers into his shoes and feel from toe to heel. When I was a teenager, I used to keep a ten-pound note folded up inside a shoe when I went out in case I lost my purse and needed to get a taxi home. I wonder if he might have tucked something away in a similar fashion. He has not. I go through his trousers and their pockets, front and back, and there is nothing there at all. I start to feel a rising sense of despair.

I hold up his jacket, grabbing the material where the inside pockets and the side pockets are. Nothing. As I go to throw the jacket on the floor, angry and frustrated, the bottom of it swings against my leg with a bump. I feel something solid, so I examine the jacket more closely. He has cut the bottom out of an inside pocket and dropped his wallet down and moved it around to the back of the jacket.

Now I have it.

I walk through into the kitchen, where I sit at the table in the corner and put the wallet in front of me.

I empty out the contents. What a treasure trove it is. Full of his secrets.

There is the driving licence that he had scanned. Wilkinson. Robert James. His date of birth, 9 February, forty years ago. His photograph and his signature. And that address, the apartment in Norwich.

There are two debit cards, both with the same bank but for different accounts, one for Mr R. Wilkinson and the other for R. J. Wilkinson. Both valid from two or three years ago. Expiring in a year or two's time. Neither is signed on the back.

There is a Cineworld card, with a number and a photograph and an expiry date that's more than two years old. I'm not sure why he has kept that. I can't think it has any significance.

There are three credit cards, too: a black, a gold and a red one, all from different companies and in variations of my names.

Laura Curtis.

Ms L. Curtis.

Laura E. Curtis.

I take deep breaths. Dear God, what does this mean?

There is also another driving licence. Someone who looks a little like Robert but is two years older.

Andrew Raymond Wilkinson. The brother, it has to be. An address in Lincoln, two or three hours' drive away.

I wonder why Robert has this licence and whether he has somehow stolen his brother's identity. Or it may be that Robert was working with his brother on the scam. If so, the brother may soon come looking for him and the money. That thought fills me with yet more fear.

I pack the clothes away in the rucksack and bags and take them into the garage, where I squeeze them under the shelf between the body and the wall. I think it will be safer for me to keep them here. The thought of them out there in the grey bin worries me too much. I imagine the police coming back into the close and opening the lid, tipping everything out, holding the bags aloft. It feels horribly real, my imagination is running away, but I cannot take the chance.

I put his wallet with his other belongings. I do not think I can do anything with his cards or the credit cards in my name. I do not want to use them to see if they are active or make online searches or landline calls to find out what I can. I think I know. The cards in his name were for his everyday living. Those in mine were for fraudulent use. He must have applied for them online in my name and then opened the post when they arrived. I look at the brother's driving licence from time to time and am not sure what to do with that.

And then I am back at the window again, looking out. It is now getting dark. I see Alex over the way, leaning on the wall by Harry's garage. He is staring across at my house, may have been doing so for ages for all I know. As I stand there, the slats of the blind angled open and with the lights on behind me, Alex raises his arm, his hand flat and towards me as if waving. Then he seems to smile and turns to go back indoors. The gesture – and the thought that he has been waiting there so long for me to see him – unsettles me more than I can say.

13

I t is the early hours of the morning.
I move the alarm clock on the cabinet next to the single bed in the front bedroom so I can see it more clearly. It is 1.05 a.m.

Something woke me. A tapping. There is someone downstairs at the front of the house. I wait for the tap-tapping again.

It is not him, Robert. I checked again after the police visit. It was something I had to do. A compulsion. He, it – the body – is still there, of course, wrapped and taped and hidden away just as I had left it. I looked more closely. Blood, more blood, seems to have seeped out of the body and is pooled there against the cellophane. The sight of it made me think of a butchered animal and that – and the horror of what I have done – made me retch.

My mind keeps coming back to the thought that I will, at some time, have to move him. It. The body. I cannot live with it here for much longer. In time, it will decompose. I know not how and when. I will have to bring myself to google this information. In summer, this first summer, when the weather is hot, I fear that his – its – presence will become obvious to neighbours, who will eventually complain to the council about the smell, claiming it is from the drains, and someone there will investigate. They will keep looking until they find its source.

Time and again I puzzle over how I will move his body and where I will put it. One night, I will have to open the garage door and reverse the car in. Then, somehow, drag and lift and drop the body into the boot. And drive, with a spade, to somewhere he will never be found. I cannot return to Rendlesham Forest after what happened there. But there is Thetford Forest a little further away. Buried deep in that forest, he – it – will lie there undiscovered for years until all that's left of him will be his bones. The thought of ravenous animals uncovering him sickens me. But what else can I do?

There it goes again. The tapping. But a different window this time. At the back of the house, not the front.

Someone is out there, tapping away. First here and then there. Next it will be somewhere else.

It is Harry. Tormenting me. Trying to drive me mad.

I think he imagines I will be cowering in my bed. Frightened of the noises downstairs. That he can move freely about the front of the house and the back and the sides, tap-tap-tapping away on a window and a door and a drainpipe. That I will be scared. I imagine how he will say next time he comes round that he will protect me, this white-haired, silly man, if only I can get his money back for him. He is wrong. I do not need him. I will not be threatened, and I will not be bullied. I will not be softened up in this way. Instead, his actions incense me.

I am at the window of the main bedroom, looking into the garden. I open the window so I can see straight down, expecting to catch him tapping on the conservatory doors. But there is no one there. I come out of the bedroom, along the landing and into the box room. I look out across the close, expecting to see Harry scurrying home. But the close is empty, and other than porch lights here and there, it is shrouded in darkness. I open the front window and look down to the driveway and the path and my own porch. There is nothing – no one – there.

It hits me, as I stand at the window, that Harry may somehow be in the garage. My chest constricts at the thought; I can barely breathe. I usually access the garage through the utility room at the side of the house. But there is a door into the garage from the back garden. I am sure I locked it; I remember checking several times. But I think I automatically put the key under the broken plant pot nearby, and I fear, somehow, he may have found it. And even without a key, there is that unlocked up-and-over door, which offers the easiest access from the front. I walk down the stairs and turn into the kitchen. I pick up a knife for self-protection, maybe more. I don't know. I'm frightened of what Harry will say and do if he makes the discovery.

And then I'm into the utility room, where I stand with my head against the door into the garage. All is quiet. He may have heard my approach. He may now be waiting on the other side of the door. The body that he's pulled out from under the unit by his feet.

I ease the door handle down.

Push the door open. Step into the garage.

I raise the knife instinctively.

I AM BACK, awake but fighting sleep, in my baby's bedroom. Harry was not in the garage. He is toying with me. He will come again. It is now gone two in the morning, and I am going to catch Harry when he returns with his stupid tap-tap-

tapping on the windows. I'm going to put an end to it once and for all.

My mobile phone is on, and when I next first hear the noise, I will go straight to whichever window he is at, front or back, and film him.

I will open the upstairs window and point the phone at him and tell him to go away and leave me alone or I will go to the police and say he is stalking me. I hope my strong words will bring him to his senses.

And there it is. Just as I expected. A noise.

But it's not a loud tap on the window intended to wake me.

It is footsteps – and they are on the wooden floor downstairs.

I sit up, startled, for I had expected noises outside the house: a tap, a knock, a bang. Not this. I wonder if I have nodded off and slept through the opening salvo with my subconscious only waking me as whoever it is – presumably Harry – came indoors. I am livid. How dare he?

I do not fear Harry, not in the way that I was frightened of Robert. Harry is worried about his money. He does not know what he is doing; he is not thinking straight. At heart, he is a benign old man. He is angry now – but I cannot have him doing this, coming into my house, moving about, trying to spook me.

I get up and go downstairs. I will be firm with him, my phone in my hand, as if recording the conversation.

I will tell him to go, go now, I will say with emphasis, and I will not call the police. I think it will be enough.

And so I march downstairs, making plenty of noise as I go, to alert him. I expected him to be in the living room. But he is not. I flick lights on as I go, moving next into the dining room. He is not there either.

I go back into the hallway and open the cloakroom door.

He is not there. I look at the door of the cupboard under the stairs and shake my head; he cannot be in there. I laugh out loud, unexpectedly, at this nonsense; it is, I think, my imagination, all of this, every single thing. My guilty conscience is playing these tricks on me.

I go, at last, down the hallway into the kitchen to make myself a hot chocolate to take back to bed with me. I turn on lights, fill the kettle at the sink, take a mug from the cupboard and a carton of milk from the fridge. I am distracted and clackety-clacking about.

The jar of hot chocolate is virtually empty. I have another jar in a cupboard a step or two away.

I turn and drop the china mug in my hand onto the floor, where it cracks into pieces.

It is not Harry standing there.

It is his son, Alex.

I think he is going to kill me.

"I KNOW WHAT YOU'VE DONE," Alex says, in a rising, accusing voice. He looks at me with what should be a steady gaze. But he twitches and jerks and glances this way and that as if he has taken too much of his medication. I look at him with as steady an expression as I can, even though I am scared of him and what he is saying.

I do not know what Alex knows. It could be that he just saw me coming back in the car that night. Maybe Alex assumes I drove Robert all the way to Ipswich railway station. That I'm his getaway driver. Or perhaps he saw me driving the car away on my own and then arriving back half an hour later, alone. I don't know what he'd make of that. My greatest fear, and it chokes the breath from me, is that Alex has just discovered the body in the garage. He is now going to blackmail me. For money. Or worse. If I do not agree, he will call the police, and my life will be over.

I brush the broken mug to one side with my right foot and move as calmly as I can, still holding my breath, to the cupboard. I open it, take out the jar of chocolate powder and go back to the kettle, opening another cupboard and taking out another china mug. My hands are trembling so much that I cannot open the jar, so I take a glass from the side, next to the knife rack, and fill it with water from the tap. My hands are still shaking. After a sip and a spill of water, I put the glass, clackety-clack, back on the work surface.

"What is it you know, Alex?" I ask, still trying to look steadily at him. My voice cracks.

Alex takes a step towards me, this ramshackle man in his forties who looks much older. He gives me a wolfish smile, something close to a leer as he looks me up and down.

I take a step back, wondering what he sees. What he should see is a close-to-middle-aged pregnant woman, utterly washed out, and with no interest in him like that whatsoever.

He moves to the side, sways really, as if in the early steps of a slow dance, and looks me over again. What he sees, what I fear he sees, is someone who is plainly scared and will do whatever he wants to placate him.

But I will not.

"I know," he says again, in a sing-song voice. "I know." And he twists this way and that in front of me, as if he is going to take me in his arms and dance.

He looks and sounds ridiculous, this beaten-down man acting as though he is a teenager dancing to impress a girl at a school disco. I am sure that he is on strong medication or has taken recreational drugs; maybe both, I don't know. I reach behind me for a knife from the block. I know from Robert just how quickly some men can turn when they don't get their own way.

"How did you get in?" I say, trying to calm my voice. "What are you doing in my house?" Still he twists and turns in front of me, as if he is playing a game. "You shouldn't be here."

I wait for him to stop what he is doing, to end this utter nonsense.

To tell me he came in through the garage and has found the body.

And, as I wait, I move the knife, behind my back, from my left hand to my stronger right hand.

I have to do something if he says he has found the body. I have to protect myself if he lunges at me.

"Does your father know where you are, Alex? Did you tell Harry you were coming here?"

I need to know if anyone knows that Alex is here, or whether he simply came out into the night.

And might possibly just disappear into the night, one of so many sad, insignificant men who vanish and are never seen again.

I bring the knife round and in front of me.

"Answer me, Alex," I say. "You can't just come into my house and do this. I will need to call the police."

He looks at the knife and stops his peculiar dance. He stands still and answers me.

"My dad," he replies, picking his words carefully and saying them slowly, pronouncing each one separately and hesitating between them. "I've been talking to my dad ... he needs ... you have to give him his money back. Within twenty-four hours, one last chance he says." He pauses a while, this man who is clearly mentally ill in some way. He is trying to articulate his words, to make sense, to seem normal.

"I don't have your dad's money, Alex," I reply, dropping the knife to my side. "Robert had it. He's gone off, and I don't know where he is. He's left me and the baby." I gesture towards my tummy. "I'm going to be a mummy." He glances at my stomach and then looks away as if embarrassed. He does not say anything about the baby. I don't think it would occur to him to do so.

Alex stands there, twitching and jerking, as his mind works its way through what I have just said. I still don't know what he knows. It might be everything. It might be nothing. At the moment, I don't think it matters. He just wants the money. I say to him, "Go now, Alex; you shouldn't be doing this. Coming into a woman's home like this, a mother-to-be, and scaring her."

He thinks a while longer, and I pluck up the courage to turn to go, as if to indicate that this conversation is finished. He goes, slowly and reluctantly, to the front door and then stops and turns back.

"Twenty-four hours," he says in a whiney voice just like Harry's. "Twenty-four hours."

And then he is gone. In that moment, I do not know whether to fear him or pity him; both, I think. I fear him, and what he might do next, most though.

14

I am parked along the way from a row of terraced houses in a street on the outskirts of Lincoln, a three-hour drive north of my home. The road is run-down, and I think the houses were probably once owned by the council.

I am not sure why I am here. I think I felt compelled, after the incident with Alex, to get out of the house. I'm sure he does not know anything of note. He just wants the money back in twenty-four hours. I talked him into leaving quietly, but the whole incident left me unnerved all night.

Now I am close to what I think must be Robert's brother's house, according to the address on the driving licence in Robert's wallet. I don't know, now that I am here, quite what I expect to uncover. The truth, I hope, whatever that might be.

I sit here, on the opposite side of the road, in my car, alternating between fiddling with my mobile phone and eating a banana. I sip now and then at a bottle of water and look over towards the row of houses as though I am waiting to pick someone up to take them into town for some shopping. There are people, mostly young women with babies in pushchairs, going up and down to the parade of shops at the top of the road.

A little boy of two or so, his face set in concentration, walks along with his left hand on the buggy, which his young mother tries to steer in a straight line whilst struggling to persuade him to climb back into it. As they get alongside my car, she lifts him up, and he goes stiff-backed and rigid as she attempts to push him down into the seat. He yells, turning it into a high-pitched scream as she finally manages to do so. Then he struggles on as she tries to strap him in place.

As they stand by my car, the woman with her face etched with exhaustion and the little boy having a temper tantrum, I turn away. She will, I believe, look across at me at any moment and assume I am judging her. I have been told I have a snooty face. There was a mother at school last year, in her early twenties, and I tried to give her some suggestions about her little girl, who was finding it hard to make friends. "What the hell do you know about anything?" she'd hissed at me. This young woman, eking out her existence, will be the same, sneering at me in my nice clothes and nice car.

There are no signs of life at the property at the end of the terrace, close to the parade of shops. The one I believe is the brother's home. I don't think anyone is there, but I am readying myself to go and knock and look through the windows, maybe even have a word with a neighbour. To find out what I can.

The driveway at the front does not have a car on it. Just a row of different coloured wheelie bins next to a black bin bag full of rubbish at the side of the house. All the windows are shut.

I've seen comings and goings at the four other properties in the terrace, the ones along towards me. Two old men shuffling out of adjoining front doors, pulling thin coats around themselves and greeting each other, then lighting cigarettes and going on their way. From another, an elderly woman taking two bags of washing to the launderette at the parade of shops. And later, a woman with bright pink hair comes out and trundles towards me on a mobility scooter.

I do not belong here. I do not think I am better than anyone else, far from it. But I know that if I go into the local Co-op or the laundry or the bookies at the row of shops and I ask a question in a polite manner, people around will stop and listen. And teenagers will laugh behind my back, and others will mock me because I speak with a clear and mannered voice. That's all, but I will be seen as odd. I know this, and it makes me uneasy; I feel I am a target.

Father was a good and decent man. He was also a lay preacher. He would stand sometimes in the triangle, a little patch of land in the middle of Felixstowe town centre, on a Sunday morning. And he would share his words of peace and kindness. As a child, I stood there with my mother and listened to him. But Felixstowe is a town full of rough and ready dockers, and there would always be someone who would shout and jeer at him, and he would go red in the face and struggle to be heard over the noise. It was what nowadays would be called banter, not necessarily nasty but boisterous, and Father did not know how to handle it; he just kept going, hesitating and gulping and carrying on in his too-quiet-to-preach voice.

And that seemed to make things worse; it made him an easy target, as others would join in, some calling out unkind words to him. As a child, it made me hot and angry, and I would stand there hoping Father would silence them with a clever response. But he never did. He did not know how. He did not have it in him. One winter, the last time I remember going there, just after there had been snowfall, some teenage boys threw snowballs at him. One must have contained a piece of metal or something, as it felled my father, and he lay there on the ground with his head cut open as the youths ran away laughing. Father was always ... out of place. I am too. I know it. I am ... an oddball ... as they used to say at school. I try my hardest not to be or at least not to show it.

I will do what I have to do here and then go, as quickly as I can. I will not interact with anyone.

I get out of my car and walk across the road towards the brother's house. There are three teenage boys on bicycles up by the shops, and I worry that they have noticed me. One boy moves his bicycle around in my direction.

I walk slowly up the driveway. It is a tidy enough place, and there are flowerpots with pansies in by the side of the doorstep. I have a sense nobody is indoors, so I move to the front window and press my face up against the pane to see inside. And my heart sinks.

I SEE through the front window into a long room with a living area at the front and a dining area at the back, separated by an archway.

A television and a three-piece suite, a coffee table and a sideboard are in the living room, with magazines on the coffee table in three neat piles. There is a picture of a sunset over the wall fire.

Beyond the arch are a circular dining table and four chairs, with what look like papers and notebooks spread across the table. Hanging off the handle of the door at the back, opening out into the garden, is something inside a dry-cleaning wrapper. A just-cleaned police uniform. I swallow hard. I should not be here. I need to go now.

As I am about to turn, I see a reflection in the window-pane. The three teenage boys on their bicycles on the pavement, a few doors along, are standing there, astride their bicycles, just pushing their front wheels against each other's. It is as though they are chatting casually. They have nothing better to do and are just wasting time. But I feel a sudden sense of fear. That they are waiting there for me. When I walk back to the pavement and towards my car, they will ride up to me, one behind and two at either side, and intimidate and jostle me, "Miss, Miss!" and I will struggle to swallow my fear, my hand shaking as I take the keys from my handbag to open the car door.

I realise, as I stand here, seeing their reflections, that my handbag is only over my left shoulder. With my mind on this house, I had forgotten to put it over my head and shoulder and across my body as I usually do. I wonder if one of the teenage boys will bump into me as I get to the car, distracting me, whilst another snatches my bag and throws it to the other riding off into the distance. I do not know what to do. I am sure that they are waiting there for me.

I have always been scared of teenage boys on bicycles. There was a time, when I was a young girl, first walking to high school and back on my own along lonely Grimston Lane, that older boys from school would terrorise me. They would wait, after school, at the top of the high road as the sun was setting and, as I turned to walk down the darkening lane, they would follow me at a distance, making howling noises. I do not know why they picked on me, nor why they made noises like a pack of dogs. They would come slowly closer until I started running, and then closer still, until I got home in tears. This went on for weeks and weeks until I told Father, and he went to the school, and, finally, it stopped.

I tap on the window, sensing there is nobody at home, but wanting to look confident, as though there is and that I am a friend of whoever is indoors, so that the boys will leave and I can hurry back to the car.

But they don't. They just stand there, over their bicycles,

staring at me openly. I can still see their reflections in the windowpane. The jeers and catcalls will start at any moment.

I know I have to overcome my fear, so I move to the side of the house, pretending I am not aware they are there, and go to open the gate to the garden. It is shut, but I reach over the top, find the bolt, slide it back and step inside.

I will wait here, on the path by the side of the house, until they have gone. There is a slight gap between the gate and the frame, and I can see through it. They remain there, waiting for me to come out. I will stand here until they assume I have gone inside, and then they will lose interest and leave to find another victim; these feral children whose parents do not know where they are or what they are doing. I reach into my jacket pocket and take out the driving licence. "Here," I'll say, if the brother suddenly appears. "I found this and wanted to return it to you. I've come through the gate to put it by your back door."

The back garden is neat and tidy, a trimmed and even stretch of grass with a shed at the bottom of the garden. There are piles of slabs, bags of concrete and a mixer by the door. A patio is about to be dug and laid. I walk to the door, holding the driving licence up in my right hand just in case the brother is inside. I do not know what else I will say other than, "I found this." I do not want to engage with the brother, who must be a policeman. The thought makes me feel uneasy, vulnerable really. I'm aware that a conversation may expose me in some way. He might ask questions I cannot answer.

I should not stay here any longer, waiting for the brother to come back home, to see me in his back garden, wanting to know more about the driving licence, where I found it, who I am, whether I know Robert, where he is and so on until I say the wrong thing. But I cannot leave now, opening the gate and running to my car; the teenage boys chasing after me and snatching my bag before cycling away. I move back to the gate, peering through the gap. I breathe a sigh of relief. I am in luck. They have gone.

I move my head this way and that so I can see up the road a little to the left towards the shops and then down to the right and to my car. They are not there. There are a couple of men, older and younger, father and son perhaps, walking along the other side of the road, left to right, carrying a chest of drawers to a van. The father is wearing a black Rolling Stones tee shirt, the son has a white Beatles tee shirt, and they keep stumbling and dropping the chest of drawers and shouting words of blame at each other. A dumb and dumber duo.

I have a clear run. I open the gate, step out, pull it to, and take one step, two steps along the path heading out towards my car. As I do, an old grey car appears to my left, signalling it is turning right. And the brother and I look at each other as he pulls onto the driveway.

HE GETS OUT of the car, this man in his crisp white shirt and sharp black trousers and shiny black shoes. He looks like a taller, older version of Robert. He gazes at me with a neutral expression as though women come out of his back gate all the time.

And I stand there with his driving licence in my hand, shocked into silence. Partly because of the surprise of his arrival. Mostly because of the similarity between him and Robert. They would not be mistaken for twins, but they've a look of each other.

He turns and shuts the car door and then looks back, waiting for me to say something, to explain what I am doing here. "I found this," I say, extending my hand. "Your driving licence."

He takes it and sighs, but to himself, not for my benefit. "I thought I'd lost and replaced that years ago ... so he's still pretending to be me when it suits him." He tucks it into a pocket. He then says, looking at me again with a strange expression on his face, something close to sympathy, perhaps even pity, "You'd better come in. Have a cup of tea."

I thought he would ask me where I'd found the licence, would be suspicious of me, especially walking out from his back gate. But, somehow, it as if he has been expecting me.

I shake my head, as if to say, "No, it's okay, thank you." I am nervous and don't want to stumble or choke on my words, which might arouse suspicions.

Instead, I point towards my car along the road and say, "I've got to go. I'm laa-aate." I don't know how, but I slur the last word, and then I wonder if he will think I am on medication or am drunk and will stop me going to the car.

"Late," I repeat more clearly, and I attempt a smile. My top lip sticks to my teeth.

I wait for him to step aside so I can walk by his car. It would look odd going the other side, the long way round.

He stands there, not deliberately blocking me. It's more that he is thinking what to say next.

"You've come about Robert." A statement, not a question.

I do not answer but can hear myself swallowing nervously. A gulp, really. I shake my head and then nod, confused.

"You're having a baby. His baby." He points to my tummy, and I realise that, although there is no visible sign yet, especially beneath my jacket, my hands and arms wrapped around myself are a giveaway.

I smile, a bleak smile I think, suddenly feeling vulnerable. As though I want to sit down and talk to someone who knows

Robert – knew – and would be sympathetic towards me. To pour my heart out. But I cannot, not with this man.

"He's left you." Not a question that reveals a sense of doubt but a statement as though he knows, has seen this all before. "And you don't know where he is. You thought he might be here. He isn't."

He seems a nice man, thoughtful and kind and wanting to help. But then so did Robert at the start.

"I just found your driving licence in town," I say. "I thought you might need it. I don't know who this ..." And then I stumble on the word Robert, and I wonder for a moment if he is going to step forward and take me in his arms.

I do not know what I would do if he did. I think it would be too much for me. That I would break down and tell him everything. But, of course, I cannot. I have to be strong for my baby.

"I have to go," I say. "I've a doctor's appointment. I'm late." I look at my left wrist, flustered, and realise I am not wearing a watch today.

He steps back so I can pass by. As I do, I can smell him. Joop. Father used to have that aftershave. I bought it for him every Christmas. I loved the smell.

He watches me go to my car, and I drive off towards him rather than attempting a three-point turn to go back the way I came. He waves at me, something close to a salute. I hesitate. And then I wave too.

15

I am curled up on the sofa in the living room, clicking the remote control to find something quiet to watch on Sky, a programme that I might be able to fall asleep to and forget about everything for an hour or so.

I am going to relax as best I can until teatime, then make myself something simple to eat and drink, and I will spend the evening crocheting a blanket for my baby. I have to keep my mind occupied. But I must rest for a little while. I have no energy left after my six-hour round trip to Lincoln. I was disturbed by my meeting with Robert's brother. How he looked. The smell of him. Frightened too, in a way. I must put it all out of my mind.

I am just snoozing off to BBC's *Pride & Prejudice*, which I have seen so many times, when there is knocking at the front door. I feel a sudden surge of anger. I get up and go to the door, ready to send Harry on his way with a few sharp words. But the two police officers are standing there, and I feel a stab of fear.

They say they are sorry to trouble me again but can they

come in and "Have a word?" They make it sound like it is nothing much, neither here nor there.

I invite them in and show them through to the living room, moving the cushions I was resting my head upon. They glance at each other, it seems significant somehow, but I'm not sure why.

They sit down, reintroduce themselves, and we make small talk about the weather for a moment or two; then they get straight to the point. The policeman opens his notebook and reads out a car number plate.

He looks up from the notebook. "Do you recognise that?" he asks. The policewoman watches me closely.

"Yes, it's Robert's car, I believe. A green Fiesta? I'm not sure of the exact model." I clear my throat, adding, "I'm not very good with cars, I'm afraid."

"You remember the plate, though?" the policewoman asks, the implication in her voice that it's odd I can recall the specifics of a number plate.

"C and V were my father's initials." I pause and then say, "And I remember the car is ten years older than mine, which is five years old. The rest of it ... well, I assume it is Robert's ... that's why you are here." I try not to sound too clever.

He nods as if that makes sense. I'm not sure it does.

Then he leans back in the armchair as though he is relaxing and we are going to have a friendly chat.

She does the same. I glance at her. I'm not sure what to think. "When did you last see Robert?" he asks. He knows what I said before. It is in his notebook. I think we are going to go over it all again to see if my story remains the same – or if a change in one small but significant detail will reveal that I am a liar.

"Monday evening. Monday night. Overnight." I don't want to add more than I have to.

"What time was that?" he presses. Again, he has already

had my answer. He is testing me. Just like Robert used to do with his stupid notebook.

I blow air out of the side of my mouth as if I am remembering again.

"Eleven o'clock. We went to bed. I fell asleep. I woke up the next morning and he was gone." But then I remember again that Harry knocked on the door after that. I could kick myself.

They glance at each other. He nods at her, go on, and she leans forward, as though this line of questioning has been rehearsed between them. "Was there anything unusual that happened before you went to bed at eleven?" Then, before I can answer, she goes on as if a thought has just struck her. "How do you know it was eleven, exactly eleven?" She looks at me, but I don't look back. Instead, I look down, not wanting to hold her gaze, appear defiant.

"Um, because we watched the news on Sky to ten thirty and then the weather, as we usually do ... did. I then tidied everything away, washed the cups and plates. Robert locked up. He went upstairs first ... to the bathroom. I had a glass of water and a herbal indigestion tablet, then went to the bathroom, so it must have been about ..."

"Did you have an argument?" she interrupts.

"No," I answer steadily, looking back at her now. He is watching me, too.

"Were the two of you intimate that night?" she says.

I pull a face, surprised that she has asked such a question. "No," I answer as neutrally as I can. She goes to say something, but I add, "I didn't feel comfortable ... indigestion and, um, acid reflux ..." I put my hand on my tummy, perhaps also implying an upset stomach.

"And he was all right with that?" she asks. I glance at her and then at him.

"Yes, of course. You know ... yes." I'm not sure what else to say.

He takes over. "Was he troubled or worried about anything ... did he receive any calls, any texts, that evening that may have upset him?"

I lean back, as if thinking, considering it for the first time. Then I answer, "No ... I mean, I've found out since that he owed money to our neighbours. Harry over the road has come round to say ... he was owed money. So. I suppose ... he's run away from that ... or me ... or ... our baby ... all of it."

I drop my head down. I am not upset, but think they believe I am. I did not phrase that last answer well. It was not quite right.

There is a long pause. I wonder if I should show some interest in the car. I am unsure if that would be a natural thing to do, or if it would seem odd. Then again, perhaps odder not to. A wife would want to know where her husband has gone. I hesitate.

I am about to speak, to ask the question, but I take too long preparing the words in my head, and the moment is lost.

The policeman asks if I woke up in the night and whether Robert was still there. I say no. She asks if that is usual, for me to sleep right through. I reply it was, but that I have had to get up the last few nights. "To have a wee," I add. He asks if I am a heavy sleeper, to sleep through Robert taking his clothes out of the wardrobe when he was leaving. That flusters me, but I say I am. A very heavy sleeper. The question unsettles me. I feel as though he has tested me and caught me out. Just as Robert used to do with his notebook.

He then asks about the next morning, whether Robert left a note. I say he didn't. They look at each other; I cannot interpret the look. I say he simply vanished, and I looked out the window and "the car was gone". As I say this, it seems unlikely that I would do this. I am off balance. Then there is a flurry of questions, have I heard from him since, no; do I expect him to come back, I hope so; do I have any idea where he has gone, no.

And then I go to ask about the car, and where they found it, and what they are going to do to find him, all the questions a loving wife would ask, but, again, I hesitate, trying to express the words in the right order and way.

"That's all ... for now," he tells me. He nods at the policewoman.

They get up to leave, telling me that "the case" – I assume the disappearance, the car, the frauds, all of it – is being passed to a senior officer for review and that she will be in touch. That scares me. Then there is more. As they are at the door, ready to leave, he turns and says, as though he has been holding it back for a final test, as Robert would often do, "His car was found abandoned at Trimley St Mary station ... it wasn't there at midnight according to one neighbour but was there at four a.m. according to another."

I nod, as if to indicate that makes sense to me. I think that is it. But it is not. He asks another question that takes my breath away. "Why would ... Mr Wilkinson ... at two or three a.m. ... drive his car five minutes down the road to a station that has no trains until the next morning and leave it there?"

That stuns me into silence – the realisation of the terrible mistake I have made taking the car there. Finally, I shrug and shake my head and say, whisper almost, "I don't know."

With a last look at each other, they are gone, leaving me with the awful feeling that this is the beginning of the end.

I PACE the living room carpet in torment now, my mind going over the conversation time and again. Their questions. My answers. The looks between them. The sense that I have given myself away over and over. That the two police officers are now at the station, comparing notes with their senior officer.

By nightfall, the police will be back at my door, asking me to accompany them to the station. Other police, perhaps with dogs, will search my home in my absence. And they will go into the garage. After that, I will be arrested, held in custody in prison, and, eventually, my baby will be taken from me, and I will lose her forever.

I wonder, suddenly, if I should make a run for it. Pack a bag, drive to the nearest airport at Stansted, buy as many euros as I can, and take the next flight to Spain or France or Italy. Anywhere. But I do not know what I would do there, or how I would survive, let alone live a happy life. It's madness, of course. The way my mind works sometimes. I would be on the streets when my money ran out. I have no choice but to stay here and to hold my nerve.

There is a knock on the front door. The police, having agreed I was some sort of prime suspect, are back already to take me in for questioning. It is over.

I stand up quickly and feel myself swaying, about to fall down. It's all I can do to steady myself.

They are about to shout, "Open up. Open up!" And break the door down if I hesitate too long.

A face appears at the living-room window, a woman's face. I stare back, trying to make sense of what's happening. This is not the face of the young policewoman I was expecting to see but that of a much older woman. My mind clears. It is Mrs Knox from next door, and she is tapping on the window to get my attention. I put my hand up, an acknowledgement of her presence, and I go to the front door and open it. She is on the doorstep with Sarah from over the way.

A split second of joy as I imagine they are here about my baby, to talk about arranging a baby shower with everyone in the close. Harry and Alex would not come. Not now. But the rest may want to do something nice like that. I could not bear to have it here with Robert's body so close in the garage. But maybe we could do something at one of their houses; I could be happy just for a while.

But, of course, they are not here about my baby. They are not open-faced and cheerful. Instead, they look serious, and they both glance around the close as if they don't want to be seen or overheard. "We've come about Robert," Mrs Knox says, wringing her hands. "About our investments," Sarah adds, and I look at her worried face, and my heart sinks as I invite them in, and we sit down in the living room. There is no small talk. No niceties. No mention of my baby.

I offer them tea and biscuits, but they shake their heads, and Mrs Knox starts talking, Sarah adding comments and corrections as she goes along.

As I sit here, I can see out of the window into the close, and I'm waiting for the arrival of the police cars any moment. I could just scream at Mrs Knox and Sarah as they go round and round and round, not wanting to cause offence, too hesitant to get to the point.

"What does he owe you!" I want to shout.

Still they go on, telling me about Harry introducing Robert to them. And Robert going round to see Mrs Knox later that day. Or was it Sarah first. Robert showed them this. No, it was that. Mrs Knox asked this. No, Sarah says, I asked that. And I smile and nod and wait for them to say what they have to say.

"Where is Robert?" and "Where's our money?"

As I pull sympathetic faces, I am re-running my conversation with the police officers in my head. Someone must have reported Robert's car as abandoned at the railway station. The police, probably the same two officers, checked with the police database and found it was registered to Robert, perhaps at the Norwich address. They then came round to double-check my previous story. They are suspicious of me.

I said the same things again, I am sure. The basic facts. But I gave myself away several times. That I slept right through, not even waking when they believed he was taking his clothes from the wardrobe, seems improbable. And I never asked about the car – where it was found – as a wife would surely do. As I nod and say, "Go on," to Sarah as she tells her side of the story, I am certain the police, from their looks at each other, believe I am guilty of something. That I am at the very least involved in the scam, that I know where Robert is, that we will run away together when everything has quietened down, most likely. Perhaps more than that.

It is the abandoned car that worries me most. I was not thinking straight when I drove it to the railway station. I assumed it would be noticed a week or two later, and the police would believe Robert got a train to Ipswich and then on to London and away. The neighbours, one busybody seeing it wasn't there at midnight and another know-all, coming home from a shift at nearby Felixstowe docks, spotting it there at four a.m. The police are right: it makes no sense at all that Robert took it there at two or three a.m. That will be my downfall.

Mrs Knox and Sarah get to the point at last. Mrs Knox speaks first, an earnest expression on her face. "I invested £20,000 with Robert. My savings. He assured me he would turn it into £30,000 within the year. I was going to give it to the boys when they got jobs so they could use it as deposits for their own places. I haven't said anything to either of them yet. They'd be so angry." She tails off with a reproachful look at me. I am not sure if the reference to the boys being "so angry" is a threat or not. I think it is a veiled one.

Sarah is more nervous and rather hesitant, swallowing twice before speaking. She says that she "invested £15,000 with Robert", which was "money their father left for the children when he went away". I do not ask about that. She looks at me with her sad face as if she is on the brink of tears. They both then sit back in the armchairs and wait for my reply; the expectation is, I think, that I will sort this all out for them.

I speak quickly. "I'm so sorry that you've lost your money." An immediate mistake with that word "lost". Their hopeful expressions change as I go on. "I woke up Tuesday morning, and he had vanished." A sceptical look from Mrs Knox. "I don't know where he is ... I've not heard from him ... the police have been round, and I have been told to call them if he gets in touch."

I'm on the verge of telling them I have lost money too, so much more than them, but I stop myself. They will ask if I have reported that to the police. I have not, and they will wonder why.

I sit, not sure what to do or say next. I put my hand on my tummy and smile at them. I'm not sure why. It is meant to be a placatory smile. I don't think I can bear to face more hurt and upset. I like Mrs Knox and Sarah.

But my smile seems to anger them, Mrs Knox anyway, as if it is inappropriate or I am laughing at them, mocking them. They both get to their feet almost in unison, and I get to mine, still trying to be civil and friendly.

Mrs Knox speaks first in a colder, more abrupt manner. "We had hoped you would give us our money back, Laura ... as you won't, I will go to the police," she announces, and I can hear the rage in her voice. "I will tell them what has happened with Robert and what you have just told us. I will tell Mark and Paul, too, and what it means for them. They will not be happy. I expect they will want to talk to you about it ... to hear what you have to say."

She turns to Sarah, waiting for her to say something before they both leave. Sarah looks as though she is plucking up her courage to speak. She is a timid person, and I expect her to swallow her words and go. She does not.

"I don't believe a word of this, Laura. You have the money. Give it back."

I am, for a moment, speechless. I look from one to the other, these people I thought of as friends, and realise my mouth is hanging open in shock. "I don't have any money," I respond. "He took all my savings, too. I only have my salary each month."

"Shame on you." Mrs Knox spits out the words, her face is flushed, and her mouth is twisted in fury. She reaches out and puts the palm of her hand on my tummy. It feels so intrusive. "How could you do this ... how would you like me to do to your baby what you've done to my dear boys."

I recoil, stepping back and away from her.

Then they are turning and leaving. Sarah stops at the door and glares back at me. "I want that money, every penny of it." She is almost spitting, too, her voice cracking with emotion. "You've not heard the last of this. You need to pay it back."

The door is slammed behind them. They are gone, and I am left to slump down on the sofa, alone and deeply troubled by the encounter.

I STRUGGLED through the rest of the afternoon and into the evening. My mind replays everything Mrs Knox and Sarah said and did. And, all the time, I am expecting the police to arrive.

I made tomatoes on toast and a mug of tea but could not finish either of them. I was choking on the food at times. I just felt so fearful and anxious about everything. Still, I kept up the pretence of normality for a while, working on the blanket for my baby.

The next knock on the front door will be the police, most likely that senior officer who's now investigating the case. I sit here on the living-room sofa, positioned so I can see out into the close, preparing myself for what is to come.

I've taken a decorated wooden box onto my lap. It was made by Father and painted by Mother, an Easter present, given instead of chocolate eggs, when I was eight or nine years old. I have always loved it and have dreamed of giving it to my baby one day. I trace the branches of the still colourful tree on the front with my fingers, taking in all the different birds, little splashes of colour, that are nestling in it. The box still squ-ee-eaks as I lift up the lid. I breathe in the dusty smell that reminds me of my dear, kind parents.

I go through each of the items in it one by one, beginning with a photograph of the three of us on the beach by South-wold Pier when I was a toddler. I'm holding a red bucket and spade. I notice neither Father nor Mother are touching me. They never did, and I did not ever expect them to. They were loving parents, though, in their reserved ways. I then take out a feather and a bookmark made by Mother and a small Bible inscribed inside by Father and a multicoloured pencil with "Laura" in gold lettering on one side. The first and last letters have almost vanished.

There are more treasured mementoes, all neatly tucked into piles. Photographs and postcards and home-made birthday cards – Mother's nature sketches on the front, "To Laura, All Our Love On Your Birthday, Mother & Father, xxx" in Father's careful hand on the inside. All through to university with the last photo of me laughing and throwing my cap in the air at my graduation. I fight back tears, remembering my happy childhood. I wish, in a way, my life had stopped then, after university, before Mother's

cancer and Father's Alzheimer's and all that followed, the loneliness and the sadness and meeting the man I thought I'd spend
my life with. But then, I have my baby. God help us both.

I look up as I see the lights of a car turning into the close.
I cannot make out the type of car it is, but it can only be a
police car coming for me.

It goes by my house and parks along by the tattooed
couple's. That senior officer and her driver will get out and
walk to mine.

I take deep breaths, trying to stay calm as I pack all my
prized possessions back into the box. I dip my head.

I say out loud, "Our Father, who art in heaven, hallowed
be thy name; thy kingdom come; thy will be done; on earth as
it is in heaven."

Habit, I suppose. The familiar words comfort me.

I wait for the knock on the door.

"Give us this day our daily bread. And forgive us our tres-
passes, as we forgive those who trespass against us. And lead
us not into temptation; but deliver us from evil."

I sob and choke on the word "evil", knowing what I have
become.

I gather up my strength as best I can to finish my prayer.
"For thine is the kingdom, the power and the glory, for ever
and ever. Amen."

There is a knock on the front door. I get up and turn
around, take one last look at my life and what I will be
leaving behind. I then go to the door to give myself up.

It is Harry.

"I'm not coming in," he says abruptly as I look beyond
him to see two burly men getting out of that car and going up
the tattooed couple's driveway. "Here, take this." He thrusts a
folder at me, which I take without thinking.

"It's a print-off of the fraud report I've made about Robert
and you. Everything I know about what you've been up to.

I've just emailed it to Suffolk Police and the taxman and Action Fraud and the FCA ... and my solicitor, who will take High Court action against you. You'll get what's coming to you." Then he looks me in the eye and says forcefully, "Bitch," before turning and walking away.

I sit back down, his folder on my lap. I'm struggling with my emotions, but I force myself to open the folder and look at each printout in turn: the home page of the website that Robert must have set up to attract investors, the emails between Robert and Harry up to the moment when Harry transferred his life savings in instalments over two or three months; each transfer and acknowledgement of receipt by Robert printed out here.

And then there are email exchanges between Robert and Harry that feature me. Initial pleasantries between the two after Harry had introduced Robert to me, and vice versa, at the barbeque last summer. A moment that now seems a lifetime ago. I wish I had never gone. But then I do have my baby. I shake my head and go on reading. Emails from Robert to Harry apologising for delays in transferring monthly sums of interest; I, he wrote, wanted to be involved, and it was taking time to "train Laura up".

I find it harder and harder to go on, as more emails refer to me and how I have moved investments here and there, and how he could not access accounts that I had set up, and apologies for the delay. All stuff and nonsense. All lies designed to cover himself when he paid late or not at all. Finally, there is a summary put together by Harry – naming others who he knows invested, including Mrs Knox and Sarah – and stating that Robert has gone ahead and disappeared to set up a new life, perhaps overseas, and how, when he has done that, I will be following him.

"Laura Curtis is a fraudster ..." he concludes. "... Stop her before she makes her getaway."

I go upstairs to the front bedroom and pull out Robert's things from under the bed. I put the file and Robert's wallet and watch and mobile phone and his laptop next to each other on the bed. I sit down by them, trying to calm my mind.

I turn on the mobile phone and the laptop. I need to get into them – these are where all his secrets are. Where Harry's money is. And Mrs Knox's. Sarah's. Everyone's. Mine too. Or at least the evidence of what happened to it all. I think of the credit cards and wonder how much of what Robert did lately has been in my name. There will be more terrible revelations coming. I guess at many pins and passwords for his phone and laptop, all without success. I cannot get into them, so I push them angrily back under the bed. I'll have another go, another time in the morning.

If money is there, somewhere, I could give Harry and everyone theirs back. But I fear it is now too late. I could put the watch and wallet with Robert's body and hand the phone and laptop over to the police, saying I had just found them. But they will wonder why I lied and why he left them behind. Nobody would do that. Suspicion, of what has really happened, will fall on me. I tuck the watch and wallet away next to the phone and the laptop. The net is closing in.

16

He is back in the house. Alex. Downstairs. It is 12.35 a.m.

I am in bed. I have been waiting for him to arrive.

I heard him pushing at the conservatory doors, the long noise as they craa-aacked open.

Thoughts rush through my mind.

He will walk to the hallway and up the stairs.

Push open the bedroom door.

He will say, "It's been twenty-four hours. Have you got the money?"

I don't know what I will say or do.

I could call the police. My mobile phone is on the bedside cabinet. I am outraged that he has come into my home like this. That he believes he can do what he likes.

I am frightened too, if I am honest.

But I cannot call the police. I do not want them here, poking about.

I remember Alex's words from last night. "I know what you have done."

And I recall his long look at me.

He saw me returning home after driving Robert's car to Trimley St Mary railway station.

Perhaps he saw me leaving earlier, taking it there.

Maybe he has put the two incidents together and worked out exactly what it means.

"I know what you have done."

If he does know, really knows, I wonder why he has not already told the police.

He has not told them about what he saw. About his suspicions. Otherwise, they would have taken me in for questioning by now.

Maybe he knows the truth but realises that, if he tells the police, I'll be taken away and Harry will never see his money again.

Blackmail, he'll think. That's his best chance of getting the money back for Harry. And for him, really. That's why he is doing this, after all. It is his inheritance not so many years down the line.

I hear him in the kitchen, moving about. I wonder if he has taken a knife from the rack. Much like the one I have here under my pillow.

He opens the kitchen door as he comes through into the hallway.

He is now standing there, ready to walk up the stairs.

I wonder if anyone knows he is here, realises what he is doing. If Harry has told him to do this.

Alex has left home before. On his travels. Harry told me he once just disappeared into the night and did not come back for months.

And years ago, he was in prison for burglary and theft. No surprises, then, if he were to disappear suddenly again. A thief vanishing into the night.

When he comes at me, demanding the money, right here and now, I have very few choices. I know that.

I cannot give him money because I do not have any, certainly nowhere near the amount Harry invested with Robert.

All I have is my monthly salary. There is little to spare there. Even less when I go on maternity leave, and next to nothing when I have to go back to work and pay for childcare.

I can beg and plead, but I won't do that. I have my pride.

When Alex realises I have no money, he may attack me, force himself upon me. I will not let that happen. I have my knife.

He may say he is going to the police to tell them what he knows. Whether it is that he saw me taking the car away or returning alone, or both, I cannot let him tell the police. They will know what it means.

I hear his footsteps on the stairs, first one and then another creaking under his weight.

I sit up in bed, reaching beneath my pillow.

I listen to his footsteps on the landing up to the bedroom door.

He pushes the door open and stands there, silhouetted in the light from downstairs.

I believe he thinks that by coming here and doing this, I have few choices.

He is correct. In fact, I have only one choice – one solution to this horror.

He has just forced it upon me.

ALEX STEPS INTO THE BEDROOM, and I see him more clearly, this time dressed in black with gloves on and a woolly hat pulled down over his eyebrows and ears.

"Do you have the money?" he says in a raised voice. His head then twitches, and his body twists slightly to the side.

"No," I answer as calmly as I can whilst lifting my knees up under the duvet. It is dark, but I do not want to risk him seeing the knife, the element of surprise then gone. I am ready to talk, to reason with him, to find out more about what he knows.

But it all happens very fast.

He is across the room, pulling the duvet off me and throwing it onto the carpet. The knife goes with it.

He grabs me by my shoulders and drags me to my feet.

I don't have time to think, let alone speak.

He is dragging me across the room by my upper arms towards the door.

I think he is going to throw me down the stairs to break my neck at the bottom.

I pull away as hard as I can and slip from his grip onto my back on the carpet. I go to shout "Stop!"

But he is at me again, hauling me up, wrapping his arms around me and lifting me towards the door.

I cannot move my arms as he stumbles backwards through the doorway, holding on to me tightly.

I can smell the sweat of his body and feel his laboured breath on my face.

I force my forehead down against his face, but he pulls his head back and hits it against mine once, twice, stunning me.

He carries me to the top of the stairs. Then turns. He's about to throw me down.

"My baby," I sob.

He stops and thinks and breathes, then puts me on the carpet.

"Stand up," he says. "Walk down the stairs."

"Wait," I say. "Wait."

But he pulls me around, puts his hands on my shoulders and marches me down the stairs.

I trip once, then twice.

He catches me, stops me from falling. Then he shouts at me, irritated and angry. "Walk. Walk!"

I get to the bottom of the stairs, and my legs go from beneath me. I fall forward onto my elbows and arms.

He stumbles and falls over me, and I twist and turn and manage to get to my feet. My hands are around my tummy.

I head towards the kitchen, but he grabs at my legs and pulls me back; now he's on his feet, and he's wrapping his arms around me again.

Then we are in the kitchen.

The lights are on. My laptop is on the breakfast bar, opened.

A stool is by the breakfast bar.

"Sit there," he says, letting me go. "Transfer the money back now. Or else."

I go to sit down, but then I say, "I need my passwords; they're in my notebook."

Before he can reply or do anything, I am over at a kitchen drawer, opening it, pretending to rummage for a notebook with my left hand. My right hand is at the knife rack.

"What is it you know?" I ask as casually as I can, my back still towards him so he cannot see what I am doing. "About me?"

"I told you. I know what you've done," he replies.

I turn, a notebook in my left hand that he can see. A knife in my right hand behind my back that he cannot.

"What exactly? What is it you know that you can tell the police?"

He laughs. "I know what you've done. And if I tell the

police, they will arrest you and lock you up." He stares at me, wild-eyed.

I take a step towards the bar stool.

"Does anyone ... your father ... know you're here ... now?" Another step towards him.

He laughs again, as though he is in control, toying with me. "No, I can do what I want. I'm forty-two."

One last step and I am at the bar stool. So close.

I put the notebook down beside the laptop. He does not seem to notice.

"Tell me exactly what you know." He does not answer; his eyes are darting everywhere. I wait, giving him one last chance.

He isn't going to say. God help me, what do I do?

I have no choice. I bring my right hand out from behind my back.

"I KNOW YOU'VE COMMITTED FRAUD," he says as I lunge at him with the knife.

He knocks my hand away, and the knife clatters across the kitchen floor.

He seems stunned. I am too, half pulling back as he said his words, revealing he knows nothing really.

There is a split-second silence, neither of us moving.

Then he hits me across the face with the back of his hand.

I fall against the bar stool and then the breakfast bar, just about retaining my balance.

He is across the kitchen, scrambling for the knife.

I move as fast as I can, out of the kitchen into the hallway and towards the front door. I have to get away. He will kill me, I'm sure of it.

I hear him dropping the knife, cursing, struggling to pick it up again from the floor.

I am at the front door, my hands shaking, trying to turn the key in the lock. My fingers can't do it.

I bang on the glass in frustration, then turn to face the hallway, down to the kitchen, where he stands in the doorway, holding the knife.

I am at the staircase, running up to lock myself in the bathroom, to open the window to cry for help as he batters his way in.

I am four or five steps up when he grabs me by my right shoulder and pulls me back, and I stumble round and fall, twisting my ankle.

He drags me up with one hand, his face full of rage.

God help me, I think he is about to stab me. Stab my baby.

I throw myself at him in a desperate attempt to knock him off balance and grab the knife. It works. He falls back against the front door, and the knife tumbles to the wooden floor behind us.

But as I turn, his hands are at my throat, and he is strangling me. I have nothing to protect myself with, but I hit his face with my clenched fists over and over.

I am close to passing out as I try to push my fingers into his eyes, a last, desperate attempt to save my life and my baby's.

But then someone is at the door, banging loudly.

I do not know if it is the police. Or Harry. Or someone passing by who somehow heard or saw our struggle through the glass panel.

I am dying. *Emily*, I think, *Emily*. I would have called my baby Emily, after my dear mother.

PART III

HAPPY EVER AFTER

17

The red numbers on the clock on the bedside cabinet blur and then clear for me.

It is 3.31 a.m. I am in the big bed in the main bedroom at the back of the house where I used to sleep with Robert.

I am beneath a duvet, with pillows and a sheet that seem fresh and clean. There is a faint smell of lemons.

Other than the eerie glow of the red numbers, there is no light. Just darkness and shapes.

The curtains are pulled to, so there is no moonlight coming in through the window.

I can just make out the dressing table, the chair in the corner and the chest of drawers. The bedroom door is shut.

I struggle to make sense of what I am doing here. My mind is still in a fog. I feel uneasy. Something is not right.

As I become fully awake, it all comes roaring back. Alex. The fight in the hallway. The knocking at the door. The last moments before I passed out. I wonder how and why I am alive.

I feel the soreness of my throat, my neck really, where he strangled me. And some pain in my right ankle. Where he wrenched me down the stairs. And I now have to wee. It is a pressing need.

I breathe in sharply. The sudden fear that Alex has brought me up here whilst unconscious, laid me out, done whatever he wanted, and then tied my hands and legs to the bed frame.

I move suddenly, expecting to be bound tight.

But I am not gagged or tied up. I can move my arms and legs.

I believe I am a prisoner here. The door is surely locked. I am at Alex's mercy. He can do whatever he wants.

Did he force himself on me whilst I was unconscious? I feel beneath the duvet, expecting to be naked. But I am still wearing my pyjamas.

I have to get up out of this bed before he comes back and tortures me until I give up my secrets. I reach out to pull open the drawer of the bedside cabinet. To see if there is anything I can use in my defence. But my hand touches tissues and a half-open packet of herbal tablets for indigestion.

What can I do? I can get up and go to the door, banging on it, demanding to be let free. If he does not respond, I can walk to the back window and see if I can somehow climb out and down onto the garage roof. I do not fancy my chances either way.

I could shout for help. But I am not sure anyone will hear me before he comes bursting in. Even if they did, they might call the police, and I can't have them here. Or I can somehow find something to use, maybe break a leg off the armchair, then stand behind the door awaiting his return. As the door swings open, I'll step out and raise the weapon, taking him by surprise. Yes, that is my best chance.

I sit up, wondering how I am going to manage to break off a chair leg.

There is sudden movement from a shape in the chair in the far corner of the bedroom.

"Hello, Laura."

HE IS across the room in seconds.

I turn my head, bracing for a savage blow.

But he does not strike me.

He is close to me, this shadowy figure, with his hands up, palms raised, in front of his face, as he moves to the side of the bed. Then stops and speaks almost frantically.

"I'm sorry, really sorry. I didn't mean to startle you."

A man's voice.

Not Alex's. But Robert's. Or something close to it.

His brother.

He sits on the side of the bed. I am shaking, and it is all I can do not to pull away. I stay still, more from shock than anything else.

"I'm Andrew ... Robert's brother. I saw that man ... he ran off into the night ... like a scared rabbit ... I'd have gone after him, but ... I've been keeping guard in case he came back. He's long gone now. I thought you'd sleep through until morning. I'm so sorry."

I peer through the darkness and can see it is him. The brother. This man in black. I don't know what to say in reply. I am stunned into silence, full of fear.

He sits there, at a respectful distance, his hands crossed on his lap. He seems solicitous, as Robert was at the beginning.

Even so, I want to tell him to go, to leave the house. That this – his just being here – is frightening me.

But the thought of shouting, "Get out. Go!" at him makes me feel sick.

I know how Robert behaved. And Alex. I now know what some men are like.

I must be calm and sensible and talk to him rationally as best I can.

"How did you find me?" I ask, trying to sound curious, as if untroubled by his presence. As if this is perfectly normal.

He smiles. I can see him more clearly now, my eyes adjusting to the dark. And somehow, unexpectedly, despite the strangeness of the moment, it eases my fear a little.

"I followed you," he replies simply and then adds, "I wanted to be sure you were okay. I guessed Robert had left you. I thought you might ... harm yourself. Our mother took her own life. Robert is ..." He searches for words, but then concludes, "... not a good man."

I nod, once, twice, three times, to be sure that he can see me, that I am agreeing with him, indicating that what he says makes sense. In a way, I suppose it does.

"I waited, all evening, over the way, to see if Robert turned up. I was about to leave when I saw a man slip round the back. I thought it might be ... a friend of yours. But I came up the path to ... I don't know ... see if you were all right, I suppose. I stood there a while. And then I heard fighting and banged on the door."

I nod again, thinking I should thank him. For checking on me. For breaking in. For chasing Alex off and staying to watch over me. "Thank you," I say quietly.

Then, my mind in turmoil, still half expecting him to lunge at me, he stands up and steps back and apologises again profusely.

He says politely that he'll sleep downstairs now he knows I am "safe and sound". If that's okay? And that, if it's all right, we can talk over breakfast.

"Put the world to rights," he says. "Well, as much as we can." And, somehow, those last few words make me feel more reassured than I'd ever expected to be.

I LISTEN to him coughing and moving about and then settling down in the living room. But I cannot return to sleep.

I need to wee.

But something else is troubling me too. I'm not sure what it is. Something about Andrew. I can't quite place it. There's a vital detail that I've overlooked.

In these dark hours as daylight approaches, my mind seeks out troubling thoughts, taking them down the darkest passageways, leaving me sick with worry. I think about Alex and when he might – when he will – come back. Harry and his report that he's sent here, there and everywhere. About when there will be a sharp "Open up!" at the door. About Mrs Knox and Sarah, and so many unknown others locally, lining up to berate me whenever I go out. Most of all, I am now thinking of Andrew, Robert's brother, downstairs whilst I am upstairs.

It is the risk of exposure that is troubling me. It's closer than ever. Robert's watch and wallet and mobile phone and laptop are under the bed in the front bedroom, waiting to be found. Downstairs, his body is just two doors away, one into the utility room, two into the garage.

I wonder why Andrew is really here. Whether he truly thought Robert's disappearance had left me pregnant and suicidal. And so he has come to make sure I am safe and well, that I've not been left destitute. Or if, in truth, he has come to find out what has really happened to Robert. Perhaps Robert owes him money. Even worse, perhaps Andrew and Robert are – were – in the scam together. And Andrew suspects something bad has happened to Robert and that is why he is here. Or he thinks that Robert has run off and that he, Andrew, has to hunt him down. There are so many possibilities.

I listen carefully, straining to hear something, some movement, in the still of the night.

To hear Andrew creeping upstairs and into the front bedroom, searching around and coming across Robert's belongings. Puzzling over them. Reaching a conclusion. The only conclusion.

Then searching the house, thinking I am asleep, going from room to room faster and faster until, finally, he goes into the garage, where he uncovers the truth.

The urge to wee cannot be put off any longer, so I sit up, turn and put my right foot on the floor. It hurts a little, but I can stand on it. I slip out of bed and shuffle towards the door. I wonder, after Andrew put me in this bed and then searched for fresh bedding, what he found as he looked around. Whether he is downstairs already trying to get into Robert's phone and laptop, knowing Robert would not have left these behind and gradually realising what I must have done.

I am moving along the landing, slowly but steadily, towards the bathroom, waiting for him to hear me, come upstairs, hold out Robert's phone, saying "What's this? Why did he leave his phone here? What the hell have you done?" But I make it into the bathroom. As I wee, I can hear noises downstairs. Is it Andrew moving about, ready to uncover Robert's body?

I come out of the bathroom, stand on the landing, listening to what is happening down below. He has been moving around, but I can no longer hear any noise. I wait, expecting to hear the door into the utility room creaking open. Then footsteps. The door into the garage opening,

Andrew stepping through. A moment's silence. And then a gasp of horror as he discovers his brother's body.

I am trapped, unable to move.

Listening for the gasp.

I am frozen as he takes his phone and presses 999.

18

W e sit opposite each other at the table in the sunny conservatory, having breakfast. Cereals, toast and a pot of tea that he brings through, back and forth, from the kitchen. It is not how I would have it with old mugs and chipped bowls I never use and a bag of sugar rather than my tube of sweeteners. But he has done his best. And he is cheerful enough.

He tap-tapped on the bedroom door at eight o'clock. I was awake but exhausted, having listened out on the stairs and in my bed for hours before nodding off briefly as the sun came up. He asked if he could help me downstairs, but I said I could manage, and he replied that he'd go and make breakfast.

When he was gone, I made my way to the wardrobe for a change of clothes and then along the landing to the bathroom. And so, finally, to the staircase, where I asked for his assistance, as my right ankle felt sore, and I did not want to risk tumbling down. He took my arm, and we went down the stairs and across to the kitchen and beyond, him half carrying, me half leaning on him as though we were in a three-legged race at school.

He seems a happy person whereas Robert, behind the civilised veneer, was brooding and troubled. Andrew seems less mannered than his brother, more salt-of-the-earth, although he tries to say and do the right things. That down-to-earthness is no bad thing, I think. And so, as we eat and drink, neither of us in a hurry, we go to and fro, talking things over.

He begins, after we have introduced ourselves properly and shaken hands, by apologising again for startling me in the night. Smiles shyly and says, "I'm so sorry." He seems embarrassed.

Then he adds that he thought "the man" – by which he means Alex – was scared off and wouldn't come back, but he stayed just in case. He adds, in a hesitating voice, that he thought I "might take my own life". I shake my head, embarrassed too, and then reply by asking about Alex and what happened.

"I'd come up the path ... I don't know why ... some sort of instinct ... and I heard the noise of the fight and saw you, through the glass, and him. I banged on the door and was about to break it down. But he pulled it open, knocked me to the side and ran off. I could have given chase and arrested him, but ... it was a straight choice ... I came in to help you. I thought you were ..." His voice fades away.

"Did you see where he went, the man? Alex. I wouldn't want you to ... please don't ... arrest him or anything ... he's ... not well in the head, that's all." I don't want Andrew to escalate matters even further out of my control.

"No," he answers and then adds, "I assumed it was what we used to call a domestic." He looks at me, as if to ask, "a fight between lovers?"

I shake my head. "He's the son of the man over the road,

Harry. He invested money, his life savings, in some scheme of Robert's. So did some of the other neighbours. They've not been paid their interest lately, and they are angry. Alex isn't ... he has issues ... he took it too far, coming into my home like that. Please let it go."

"You were unconscious ... but breathing regularly ... peacefully ... and you didn't seem to have banged your head or anything ... your throat and ankle were both ... marked ... bruised. I laid you on the bed, covered you with what I could find and kept watch." He thinks for a moment, sipping tea from his mug. "I wasn't sure where to put you. So I put you in the big bed ... found bedding in the chest of drawers and the shelves in the wardrobe. I'm not sure ... I think you might have been sleeping in another room?"

I swallow. Of course, he'd noted the bed in the main bedroom was stripped bare. And that I was sleeping in the front bedroom. I wonder if he searched around and saw anything else suspicious. I look at him, but he sits there gazing back at me with a guileless expression.

I sip my mug of tea too, giving me a moment to think. "I couldn't bear to sleep in there after ... Robert left me ... but thank you ... I can move back into the other bedroom tonight if my ..." I gesture towards my right ankle.

He smiles reassuringly. "Ah, I thought ... I wasn't sure ... I didn't want to ..."

I laugh suddenly. "I'm not a porcelain doll!"

He laughs too. "I can look at it later if you like, after breakfast. I've seen plenty of bumps and bruises in my time."

"Yes, you're a policeman," I say, feeling a sudden surge of alarm. "What sort?"

He pauses for a moment, putting some butter and then some marmalade onto a piece of toast. "Sorry," he says, pointing at the jar of marmalade. He puts his knife back in, trying to remove a smear of butter he's left behind.

He drops a blob of marmalade on his black jumper.

I smile and point at it.

He laughs and wipes it off with a sheet of kitchen roll by his plate.

"I'm a desk sergeant at a station in Lincolnshire. I deal with drunks and shoplifters and drug addicts, booking them in, the cells if necessary, and members of the public who come in to report a missing cat or a noisy neighbour ... all sorts of stuff ... the stuff of life. Not what I planned. And you?"

"I'm a teacher, early years, reception class, at the local primary school. I've done it since I came out of university. I'm thirty-seven." I don't know why I blurted that out, nerves, I suppose. I change the conversation back to him. "What had you planned? Not to be a desk sergeant?"

"I don't know." He sighs, stirs his tea, thinks a while as he looks out into the garden. Then, at last, he speaks. "I ... I suppose, like most in the police, I wanted to be a detective. I was on traffic for a while. A long time, really. I'm forty-two. But then Jessica, my wife, died in a car accident ... anyway, I took some time off and then moved to various desk jobs and, um, ended up on the front desk ... that's me."

I'm not sure what to say to him, this ordinary sort of man with his head bowed in front of me.

"Do you have children?" I say, regretting the words before I finish saying them.

"No," he answers simply, looking up and around but not at me. "I'd have loved to ... we tried ... but ..." He goes to say something more but stops as if he is about to choke on the words. He shrugs.

There is a silence for a moment or two as we continue with our breakfasts. It seems to stretch to a minute, maybe longer.

"You're expecting Robert's baby," he states with a nod

towards my tummy. "When is ... he or she ... due?" He is trying to sound more cheerful.

"A girl," I reply, smiling at him as he looks at me at last. "She's due on the twenty-fifth of November."

He nods. "I'll find Robert for you, make him pay for the baby at least. He's ..." I can see him thinking how to put it. "He was always the apple of our parents' eyes when we were young. I was the plodder. He was the clever one. The tortoise and the hare, I suppose. He got into a lot of trouble with girls and money ... credit cards ... when he was a teenager. Mum and Dad bailed him out time and again ... it meant they did not have enough money for me to go to ... well, it doesn't matter now, I suppose."

He sips at his mug of tea before continuing, "He went to prison for a while ... for fraud ... but was out halfway through his sentence. His ridiculously short sentence. And ..." He laughs, but it's a sour sound. "He hooked up with this middle-aged woman in the village, a real charmer he was, investing her money ... gambling it away more like ... it broke my mother's heart ... ruined my parents ... they were old-fashioned, see, and it was a small place, and they couldn't bear the shame." He sits a while, moving his plate and his bowl here and there. It seems to soothe him.

"Then my mum took her own life. They said it was an accidental overdose, that she got muddled with new medication for her aches and pains ... but, for me, she took so many tablets that it had to be intentional. It was the night after they moved from our family home to this horrible little bungalow. My dad went soon after, a heart attack, gone before his time. Robert came back then for his half of the money. He got it. Cleared off. Came back again when it had run out. Wanted more. Money. My wife. He got both, one way or the other." He stops again, gazing into space, struggling with his composure and leaving what happened to my imagination.

Then at last he looks at me properly, this sad man with the friendly face. "I promise you I will find him. If there is any money left, if he has squirrelled it away somewhere, I will get it back for you. And you can pay off your friends and neighbours." He stops and looks at me as if it just occurs to him that maybe I have lost money as well. "And the rest you can put in the bank for you and your baby."

I ASSUMED THAT, as breakfast came to an end, he would make his excuses, repeat his promise and leave. And I would never see or hear from him again. But he did not. He suggested a walk. "To get some fresh air ... it's going to be a lovely day." He then added, sensing my uncertainty, that we should talk about Robert and "compare notes ... so we can find him ... get the money back". "We", I noted. Not "I". Not just him. The two of us.

I am not sure how I feel about that. The sooner he leaves, the safer I will be. As long as he is here, the risk of exposure is ever present. Yet I feel easier in his company than I would have expected. There is something about him I like. Not that it matters. I have to live my life alone with my baby, Emily. And Robert, of course. Always there, even in death, standing guard over us. But I could pass the time of day with Andrew; feeling normal for an hour or two would be nice. Still, I will feel safer when he is out of the house. And now he has scared Alex off – he won't reappear whilst we are away.

So I agreed to his request, trying to sound cheerful, and suggested we drive, his car or mine – we settled on mine, as his is "old and leaky" – to nearby Trimley Marshes, where we could walk by the farm and down to the docks and back by the horses in the field. It is a pleasant amble of about forty-five minutes. I think I can manage that slowly even with my sore ankle.

We park by the farm in one of half a dozen dusty parking spaces. I used to walk here with Father and Mother when I was young, up until I left for university. There is a duck pond by the farm where, whenever we saw the ducks, Father would start speaking in Donald Duck's voice.

It made me laugh out loud when I was little. As I got older, he still did the voice every time, and anyone nearby could hear. I'd flush red, cringing with embarrassment. My tall, rather out of time, father. Now, all these years on, I would give almost anything to have him here now, making his rasping noises. Just being here really, silly and steadfast and loving.

Then Andrew stops to look at the ducks on the pond. For a moment, a dreadful or glorious moment, I'm not sure which, I think he is going to do a Donald Duck voice. I seem to stop breathing in that instant. But then he turns and points to the gate that leads us to the wide-open path that stretches out into the distance towards the docks, and the moment passes.

He asks matter-of-factly, "Is it that way?" as he points towards the cranes beyond the path and the fields and the trees ahead of us.

I nod and go to say yes, but thoughts of my lovely old father are in my head again, and I stop, as I would choke on the word.

He gives me a look, slightly puzzled, but does not say anything as he moves to the gate, opens it, and leads us on.

The first part of the walk is along that dusty path with the farm to the left and fields to the right disappearing, after ten minutes or so, into woodlands that skirt around in an upside-down U beside the edge of the docks. The beginning of this walk was always my favourite, with the views so far and wide. And it is nice when it is sunny, as it is today, if a little chilly.

We talk about something and nothing, mostly about the small businesses in the buildings behind the farm and the brightness of the day and what lies beyond the fields to the right. "The river," I say. "It flows that way from Ipswich and that way to the sea at Felixstowe." I point right and then left. I am not sure if the exact position and direction of the river are as I suggest. But I said so with certainty, as I do when talking to small children. If you say something with confidence, even if you are uncertain, it tends to be believed.

I don't know that much about this part of Trimley St Mary even though I have lived close by all my life. But I am familiar with the walk, and I know the trees, the names of the birds and what is growing in the fields. Father would point out everything to me as we went round and then test me next time. Andrew stops and listens to the sound of birdsong, and I do too.

He says, "Tell me, what bird is that, Laura?"

I do not speak. It is, word for word, what Father would ask me. I am almost overcome by emotion again and raise my hands in a "who knows?" gesture. He laughs.

We go by a small pathway, on the left, and he says, "Excuse me a minute," and dashes off. I assume he needs to go behind a bush. Father was a diabetic and was often nipping behind trees "to spend a penny". I carry on walking along the main path, heading towards a bench.

I sit on the bench to rest my ankle and look across the fields towards the cranes at the docks. It is a beautiful day, and I try to live in the moment, forgetting all the horror that has happened and the dangers that are now swirling around me and always will. I am, unexpectedly, at peace in this instant.

Then Andrew is back, and he has a bunch of delicate,

white and pink wildflowers in his hand. Cuckoo flowers. Father would make the sound of a cuckoo calling whenever we saw them on our walks. We never saw a cuckoo nor heard one although it is said that cuckoos are here in the marshes. "Pretty flowers," he says, offering them to me. I almost expect him to add, "For a pretty lady," and am pleased he does not. I smile my thanks. He sits next to me and sighs. "Well, this is nice." I am not sure what he is referring to, the view, the walk or being here with me.

"It is," I say, and I turn and smile at him, and we look at each other. And it really is lovely. I put my nose into the cuckoo flowers. I stop, hesitating, before holding the flowers towards him so that he can do the same. He does, and we smile at each other again.

AFTER OUR SIT-DOWN on the bench, where we rested quietly, taking in the view, we walk on, side by side, approaching the woods that take us on the long curve alongside the docks. He asks me tentatively about my life, and I talk with surprising ease about my childhood and my parents, going to university and working at the local primary school. I don't mention my ex-fiancé or linger on my parents' deaths or mention my feelings of isolation and loneliness – those desperate moments when I thought of death too often – nor do I speak of Robert or the baby. I want to enjoy this brief interlude in my life.

We stop and look across the wire-mesh fence at the lorries and cranes at the docks, such industrial activities at odds with the peace and quiet and beauty of the woods.

He speaks of his own childhood, not mentioning Robert, but his parents, an accountant and a housewife, and their home in Lincolnshire and his schooldays there. He reels it all off up to A levels and beyond, joining the police and all the way through to becoming a desk sergeant. But I detect no joy in what he says. There is a sadness, a sense of failure and longing, I think, for something better in everything he says. Robert, of course, is there in the background, an unspoken, malignant presence.

As we continue our walk, through the woods to the train track and turning towards the horses in the field, the moment arrives as I knew it would – Andrew asks me about Robert and his disappearance. I have now gone over this enough times with the police to know what – and what not – to say. I have to remember that Andrew is a policeman too. And that Robert, for all the horror, was Andrew's brother. Andrew will, without doubt, be bound by feelings of duty and loyalty.

Andrew begins by asking carefully how Robert and I met "... got together?" ... and I mention Harry's barbeque and how Robert walked me to my front door, and we kept in touch, and then he came to stay ... "and ..." my voice fades away as I go to say "... never left ..." and I have an immediate, awful image of Robert's body in the garage in my mind.

Andrew does not seem to notice and goes on to ask if we were happy up until Robert left. I am nonplussed. The question throws me, and I don't know how to answer. It seems such a strange thing to ask.

"We were looking forward to being parents," I say finally, gesturing towards my tummy. He glances at me. I do not look at him. I think he knows I am avoiding the question. But I cannot tell the truth about the mental torture and the physical violence. I am ashamed of it, that I allowed it to happen and then escalate the way it did. I have to lead Andrew away from that and in another direction so he never has any cause to doubt or suspect me.

"How did he leave?" An open invitation for me to move the conversation in the direction I want it to take.

"We went to bed ... I knew he was troubled ... neighbours

had been badgering him about missed payments ... and I woke up in the morning, and he had gone."

After that, the questions come thick and fast.

"Were you surprised ... shocked?"

I say, "Yes." Then add, "Stunned, really."

"Did you wake up in the night? When he was getting ready, moving about, getting dressed?"

I can hear the word "surely?" in his voice. I reply, "No." I now realise how unlikely this sounds, so I add that I'd had a cup of herbal tea before I went to bed, which helps me to sleep. As I say that, I think it sounds ridiculous. I hope he does not ask me any more about it. I would not know what to say. He nods as if to suggest that makes sense. Then asks if, with hindsight, I could now see clues, evidence, that Robert was planning to leave. I say that neighbours were banging on the door, threatening him. He indicates I should go on, but I say, "That's it, really."

We stop by the railway track as a train loaded with containers from the docks rattles by. In years gone by, Father, Mother and I would stand here and guess how many containers there would be – ten, twenty, thirty or more – and there would always be more than any of us ever expected. Forty or so sometimes. To change the subject, to let me gather my thoughts, I go to ask him to guess how many containers there will be. But he does not slow and just keeps walking, ready to ask the next question.

As we walk on, he asks if Robert has been in touch since he left.

"No."

He then asks if Robert left anything behind, and before I can reply, he adds, "That would suggest he is coming back."

I know I cannot mention Robert's wallet or watch or mobile phone or laptop; there is no way Robert would leave any of these belongings behind. To mention them, let alone show them, would sow incriminating suspicions. More than that, really – it would be irrefutable proof of wrongdoing and, in turn, of my guilt.

I wish now I had thrown at least the wallet and the watch away; the mobile phone and the laptop could perhaps pass as my own. I must make sure he never sees them.

"No, nothing," I answer and then remember I told Harry that Robert had left some clothes behind. And that we had gone to bed at eleven even though all the lights were on when Harry knocked at the door gone midnight. I can only hope Andrew and Harry never have a conversation.

"Did he ever talk about places he had been or would like to go ... people he was friendly with ... anything that might suggest where he might go, who he could be with?"

I say that, when we met, he talked of having offices in London and Edinburgh and elsewhere. Bristol, I think. And that he visited clients all over the country to encourage them to invest in his various schemes but that it was all very general, vague even. I do not mention the apartment in Norwich, nor what I discovered there.

Then he asks about the car, Robert's car. "What car did he drive when he first came to stay ... can you remember the plate?"

I hesitate, thinking of saying how, when Robert turned up on my doorstep, he was battered and bruised. For some reason, I do not. I think I want to say as little as possible so as not to risk giving myself away with a careless comment.

I say he drove a Ford Fiesta, and Andrew asks the colour, and I answer green, lime green, and he asks me to try to recall the number plate; he has a colleague, a friend, who can look that up, track Robert down. I say I cannot remember. I don't want him digging about.

I think of saying that Robert drove the car to Trimley St Mary railway station, but I do not. That was another mistake

I made. Andrew will wonder why Robert supposedly drove to a run-down station in the middle of the night when there were no trains running until the morning. I do not think this man is a fool.

And, of course, there are people who saw the car there, and Alex watched me coming home. It would not take Robert much time or effort – knocking on the doors of the houses by the station, perhaps having a conversation with Alex if their paths should happen to cross – to discover this. He will wonder why, and, eventually, he will turn to me and ask me. And that will lead to suspicions and searches and the end of everything.

ANDREW and I stand by the wire fence of the field with two horses in it, close to the end of our walk. We are silent for a few minutes.

The horses come trotting across, tails swishing, expecting us to feed them. I imagine someone from the nearby farm comes along at this time of day, every day.

We stroke the horses, feeling their hot breath upon our arms and hands. When they realise we have nothing for them, they both leave, almost sauntering away. Still we stand there, waiting, I think, for the other to speak.

"I hate him, you know," Andrew says, his voice bitter. He does not look at me, just gazes out across the field as though he is thinking aloud. "He came back, did I say? Robert ... when his share of our parents' money had gone. God knows what he did with it, how he went through it so fast. We let him stay with us ... my wife let him, really ... I was away on a course ... he spun her some sob story, sweet-talked her ... she was too kind ... no, too gullible ... for her own good. Our good. She had ... a thing with him ... let him invest most of our savings, and then ... anyway, off they went."

He pauses, and I am sure he is blinking back tears, but I don't want to look too closely, to embarrass him.

"That didn't last long. He dumped her when the money ran out. She was pregnant too, although ... she could not carry to full term. She came back and ... it was too late for us ... I was so full of anger ... stupid pride ... we sold up and went our separate ways ... and then she died." He spits out the last few words. "It's all so bloody tragic."

I stand quietly next to him for a while, not sure what to say or do. He turns his head and wipes his eyes with his jacket sleeve. Then stands still, gazing at the horses, his head turned slightly away from me. He is regaining his composure before he speaks again.

I take two of the cuckoo flowers I am holding and step forward, thinking to slip the stems into the buttonhole on his jacket. But I fumble, and they fall to the ground.

He laughs, his nose and mouth all spluttery, and bends and picks them up, giving them back to me. I smile and put the little bouquet back together. And we stand, looking out across the field to the horses.

"She told me ... later on ... when she wanted us to try again," he says. "My wife, I mean. What Robert was like when they were together. How kind and attentive he was at the start. How ... he was everything I wasn't." He sounds so sour. "Then, how controlling he was." He stops and thinks what he is going to say next. "He would ask her about me ... and ... us ... our lives together ... he was so jealous." He shakes his head, a mix of bemusement and horror on his face.

"She became pregnant quite quickly. By him. Robert said it must have been mine. That she was lying about how far pregnant she was. And because he'd decided she was lying, he would beat her, she said, with his shoe on her stomach ...

as though he wanted to destroy ..." Andrew chokes on his words and stops. He struggles for a moment or two and then asks, "Was he like that with you?"

I am unable to speak. I incline my head as if to say yes. He turns, tears in his eyes, to look at me. I nod again, more forcefully this time.

I am still unable to say anything, and I imagine he is going to move towards me and hug me, maybe more. I stand there. Waiting.

And then I speak at last.

"Robert ..." I want to say, "I killed Robert. He deserved to die."

I need to take this huge and impossible weight off my shoulders. To share it. But I know I dare not, so I say instead, "Robert ... was a Jekyll and Hyde character."

Andrew turns to go, moving along the path, heading back towards the car. I think perhaps, as he steps in front of me, that he will turn and reach out his hand for mine.

Instead, he turns and says, "If you let me have his phone number and email address when we get back, they'd be really useful. And if you can remember the number plate, I'll use my contacts to track him down."

I look at Andrew's face, now shining with some sort of excitement, and I have the terrible thought that he is not here for me. That this is more about revenge than anything else. To bring Robert down and to ruin him once and for all. The sooner Andrew is gone, the better.

ANDREW SITS IN AN ARMCHAIR, looking out of the living-room window, drinking from a mug of tea I've made. Mine is on the coffee table as I go upstairs to fetch my mobile phone and laptop to check for Robert's phone number and email address. I do not know these off the top of my head other than that the number ends in 007. When Robert first gave the number to me, he said it was my "licence to call". He then laughed at my blank expression and added, "James Bond, 007 ... licence to kill?"

The thought of Andrew digging about alarms me. The sooner he has Robert's details, the sooner he will leave. There is danger while he is here, spotting droplets of blood I may have missed on a skirting board, maybe wandering into the garage looking for a toolbox to do an odd job for me, a loose coat hook, a sticking door, whatever. His presence on our walk was strangely soothing, but I am so uneasy all the time he is here in the house.

I wonder if, as a policeman, he would want me to give him my phone and laptop so he can look at any texts and emails to and from Robert – that these might give him clues, leads really, when seen through a police officer's eyes. I might, with a friend, say "help yourself". But I have a terrible fear of him looking, out of curiosity, at my search history and seeing what I have been reading about – the rate and nature of decomposition of a human body.

There's no need to hand anything over. I will simply give him the mobile phone number and the email address written on paper from the notepad on the bedside cabinet. I wonder how he plans to use them to try to track down Robert. I remember reading somewhere that the police can somehow track a mobile phone if it is turned on. I suspect that is what Andrew is thinking of. I have, since Robert's death, been through his emails to me, and I wonder, if Andrew goes through the police to the internet service provider, what he can uncover that way.

As I come downstairs, the sheet of paper in my hand, he is standing up, waiting for me. "The police are here; they've just pulled up outside in a car."

We look at each other. His face is bland and non-committal. I wonder if it is the two community police officers or whether this will be the senior officer now. She will want to take me down to the station for questioning.

But, of course, Andrew does not know about the previous police visits, I've not mentioned them, so I need to look surprised. I pull a face.

We're still looking at each other. "Do you want me to get rid of them for now?" he asks as I hand him the sheet of paper with Robert's contact details written on it.

He looks at the paper and back at me. Without speaking, we are complicit in that neither of us wants the police involved. I do not want to let them in again.

"If you're not feeling well ... being pregnant ... you want to have a lie-down ... I can try to send them on their way?"

I nod my agreement.

He says, "Wait here," and goes to the front door, stepping out onto the step and shutting the door behind him.

I stand there listening. I hear him walking down the path. He calls out a cheery greeting, "Good day."

I step to the living-room window, moving a slat of the blind for a clearer view. I glance and then step back. It is the community police officers again. I wonder what they want now. Perhaps it will be for Robert's phone number and email address. I don't think they asked for them before. A glaring mistake, for sure. Then again, I suppose they probably already have them from Harry.

They talk for a while, a few minutes, Andrew leading the conversation. He seems to be asking questions, and they answer. Then they seem to be asking questions, which Andrew answers. On it goes, never-ending. It is hard to know which way things are going. I'm not breathing properly.

Andrew reaches into his back pocket, shows them something from his wallet, his police ID card, I think, to prove he is a fellow officer. They may then talk to him on an officer-to-officer basis. That frightens me, the sharing of information I don't know about.

He moves closer to them, and they stand in a huddle. I cannot really hear what they are saying and dare not open a window as I might otherwise do. It as though they are comparing notes, sharing what they know. But that might just be my overactive imagination.

Then the two police officers are stepping back, going to their car, getting in and doing a three-point turn before driving away. Andrew watches them go, then tucks the police ID, or whatever it is, into his wallet and slips that into his back pocket. He comes towards to the house. I have no idea what to think or expect. I seem to be holding my breath.

"They said they've been here before to see you?" he says, asks really, as I open the front door and let him in. I turn and lead the way back to the living room. I shrug, my mouth dry, as I turn back round and face him. As if to say, "I'd forgotten, it's nothing." He looks at me, a strange look. I don't know how detailed the conversation was between him and the police officers, whether he just said I was ill and could they come back another day, or if they'd talked as police, one to another, eager to solve a possible crime between them. The fact is, I don't know whose side he is on.

"What did they say ... have they found Robert?" It is the only thing I can ask. It would seem odd not to. He shakes his head. "They didn't say ... they can't say that much ... in case it compromises ... and I'm Robert's brother. We're different police forces too ... and I don't think they know much anyway; they're just beat bobbies in a car." He pauses. "I said I was here to help you ... you weren't well at the moment ... could they come back ... which they will. They did not say when.

"The special, she said they'd found Robert's car ... more

than she should say probably, but she's keen to make her mark, that one. I think she wanted to pick my brains ... file a report. They've not given me the number, though. He stepped in before she could answer my questions. But they did tell me that there are some women's clothes in the boot, which they think might be yours. I assume they want you to identify them."

That puzzles me, the women's clothes; I'd never thought to look in the boot. But I say nothing and just present an open, slightly curious face.

"One thing they did say, well, she said, was that his car was abandoned at the local railway station in the middle of the night ... and there were no trains until the morning. 'He may have had an accomplice,' she said, looking at me, clearly thinking it was me. I showed them my warrant card and gave them my details, so I expect I'll hear more from someone once it's worked its way up the line."

He sighs, suggesting that it's a pain but nothing more, and then says in a neutral voice, "Robert would have worked alone – so why would he do that? Leave his car there? In the early hours?"

I simply shrug and go into the kitchen to start preparing a lunch of baked potatoes and salad. Noah will be here soon. I tell Andrew about what a beautiful boy he is and how lovely his parents, the tattooed couple, are. By changing the subject, I hope he won't dwell on the car at the railway station.

19

T he little boy comes marching into the house in a blue and white striped tee shirt and navy blue shorts, a rucksack on his back, cute white trainers on his feet.

"Noah," he says when I ask him his name (even though I know it). "I'm four." He replies to my next question almost before I've finished asking it. Then goes straight by me to explore. This precocious boy, so full of confidence.

His parents, Nick and Amy, stand on the doorstep. They have kind and friendly faces. He is tall and thin and has bleach-blond hair and a brown bushy beard. She is startlingly pretty with big blue-grey eyes and full lips. Her sticky-out ears are adorned with little chains and jewels. I like both Nick and Amy a lot. "We won't be long," they chime in unison. "Two hours ... everything is in his backpack ... some notes in a pad ... and our mobile numbers ... we'll be back in a couple of hours, three at most."

I'm not completely sure why they are leaving their gorgeous little boy with me; I assume, from our previous conversation and their excited faces today, that they are off for a baby scan and have nobody else to babysit Noah. I know, from other conversations over the months, that her parents live far away in Littlehampton in Sussex, and he has two younger, single brothers out on the other side of Cambridge. They say as they leave, "Noah will be in your class from September ... it's lovely that you have a chance to get to know each other." Despite the circumstances, I am delighted to have him. I have always wanted to babysit Noah.

By the time I am in the living room, he is sitting on the sofa next to Andrew. The rucksack is between them.

Noah is looking at the blank screen of the television whilst Andrew presses this remote control and that, trying to turn it on. He seems to be struggling to work them out.

I take them from him, and I work my way through to something on YouTube. A young and enthusiastic woman with an American accent is doing some sort of preschool show – it has cats and kittens and songs. It seems to be holding Noah's attention. I think it will keep him occupied for a while as we all become comfortable with each other.

I sit on the sofa next to Noah, opening his rucksack to see what is in it: a notebook with lists of various dos and don'ts, a change of clothes, a brown bread and cheese sandwich cut in four, two cartons of juice and plastic tubs with various cut-up fruits and vegetables in them. Even the blueberries are each cut in two. Such attentive parents. There is also a book about dogs and a pad and felt-tipped pens. I flick through the pad and see Noah's clumsy drawings of cats and dogs and drag-ons, and even with their huge misshapen heads and missing legs and tails, and one dog with six legs, they are awfully sweet.

I am lost in the moment, the joy of normality, the three of us on the sofa together. The little boy looks at the television and then at Andrew and at me and smiles at us in turn before returning his gaze to the screen. He looks round again a minute or two later, to check, I think, that we are both still watching and paying attention and not on our mobile phones. I've often noticed that when parents drop off and pick up from school, some are more interested in their phones than their children. We smile at each other. I ruffle his hair. It is a magical moment. I hope I will be able to hug him later.

I watch Andrew out of the corner of my eye. He sits there with his hands folded in his lap alongside Noah. He looks calm and relaxed and smiles warmly enough whenever Noah or I turn to look at him. But he seems, with his carefully posed position, to be putting on an act. I think police officers often have to do that. I wonder if Noah has made him think about the children he might have had. I wonder if, like me, he just wants to put his arms around the little boy and cuddle him. I note, by Andrew's left eyebrow, a drop of sweat. He may, of course, be puzzling over Robert's car and other mysteries of his brother's disappearance.

I get up, asking Andrew if he'd like coffee and biscuits whilst we sit here and watch TV. I add that, later, maybe he can play in the garden with Noah as I get lunch ready. He turns to me and nods as if to say, "Yes, please".

Noah turns towards me too, and I suggest to Andrew that he get a drink and a fruit snack out of the rucksack for the child.

And then I am in the kitchen, pottering around. This, a little family, the simplicity of it, is all I have ever wanted in my life.

As the kettle boils, I watch Andrew and Noah through the half-open door. Andrew unzips the rucksack and angles the open top towards Noah so he can see inside. Noah leans forward and puts his right hand in, rummages around, and pulls out a plastic tub. Andrew takes it from Noah, holds it up to see what is in it and says, "Ugh, squashed spiders." Noah laughs and says something in reply that I don't quite catch. "Blueberries," Andrew says. He pulls a face as if to say he'd prefer squashed spiders.

It is a happy scene, and I watch for a while longer, listening to them chatting away. Andrew takes out the pad and pens for Noah and does a drawing. They are getting along well. I step back and stand in the kitchen, and for a minute or two, maybe even longer, all sorts of happy thoughts go through my head. Of this moment. Of how things might somehow be. I am daydreaming, of course, as I always do, but I am happy.

At last, reluctantly, I shake myself from my reverie. I rummage in and out of cupboards and drawers for mugs and plates and spoons and biscuits. I only have a half-eaten packet of Rich Tea, and I wonder if Noah would like these. I think they might be rather boring. I suddenly remember that when Father had Alzheimer's and was dying, he would munch on a Rich Tea biscuit and push the mush out between his teeth as if to amuse me. I was in my early thirties at the time, but I still loved him for it.

If Noah comes round again, I could buy a packet of Garibaldi, which my father used to call "squashed fly biscuits". I wonder if they might make Noah laugh, or it might be better to just get a packet of pink wafers. I shake my head free of my silly, happy daydreams.

As I come back into the living room, carrying a tray of coffee and biscuits, I see Andrew leaning forward on the sofa with his head in his hands. He's counting, "Sixteen, seventeen …"

There is no sign of Noah. I stop, confused, as Andrew counts to twenty and shouts, "Ready or not, here I come!"

I drop the tray, mugs cracking, coffee splattering, biscuits flying across the floor. I feel my stomach rising towards my throat.

"WHAT ARE YOU DOING?" I shout, louder than I mean to, already knowing the answer and what it means.

Andrew gets slowly to his feet, chuckling away, and then bends down to reach for the tray as if we have all the time in the world, putting the broken mugs and plate and biscuits onto it, saying, "It's no matter ... you'd better get some kitchen roll ... I'll mop this up."

Such nonsense when my life is about to come to a shuddering halt. "You're playing hide-and-seek? Where's he gone?" He points to the door that opens to the hallway that leads to the utility room and the door that opens into the garage. I am moving now, as quickly as I can, out into the hallway.

I am calling, "Noah! Noah!" to stop him from going into that garage, climbing under that big shelf to hide and seeing what is there next to him.

I realise, as I get to the door opening into the utility room, how my reaction must seem to Andrew: a woman on the brink of insanity. But then I am.

I am in the utility room, moving through, the washing machine and tumble dryer both on, the noise masking the scream that will come any second from Noah as he encounters the dead body so close to his face.

I must grab him, cover his mouth, stop the scream before it starts. Andrew will come running if he hears the boy's terrified cry. What will I do then?

I stop as I get to the garage door, my fingers on the handle, stunned at the realisation of the decision I have to make in the next few seconds.

I lean my head against the door, drawing breaths, my mind blurring. I will open this door and see Noah there, his hand on the plastic sheeting lined with blood.

He will turn towards me, his mouth hanging open, and then he will throw back his head and scream and scream and scream.

Andrew will be there in seconds, by my shoulder, looking at me and the little boy and the wrapped-up body of his brother. And then it will all be over.

I open the door.

I know that this is the end of it.

I step into the garage.

HE IS NOT THERE. He's not under the shelf. He is not in the garage at all.

I sink to my knees, overwhelmed by thoughts of the choice I'd have faced if Noah – and then Andrew – had seen the body.

No choice at all, really. I could not have touched a hair on that little boy's head.

I hear Andrew coming out of the living room, into the hallway, calling politely to me.

I get to my feet. I cannot let him see me in this state. I cannot let him in the garage. Anything more than a cursory glance and he will see what is in front of him.

He will step forward, tug at the plastic, alarmed by the blood.

He will see what it is there, hidden away, out of sight.

And that will be that. My lifelong hell of losing my baby will begin. My life will end.

As he comes into the utility room, I am back on my feet, out of the garage, shutting the door behind me.

He looks at me and asks, worried, "Are you alright? What's the matter?"

I have to sound as though I am not on the brink of tears,

feeling as though I am about to collapse. "I was worried about Noah, that he might hurt himself in here ... it's just the teacher in me ... where is he?"

"Upstairs," he replies. "I heard him on the steps. I was going to say, but you had already gone. Are you sure you're okay? You look like you've seen a ghost."

I wrap my arms around my tummy and mumble something about the baby and not feeling well. I am sweating now, but he does not seem to notice.

He takes my arm, a kind, old-fashioned gesture, and guides me back through into the hallway and then to the living room. I lean on him as we go, and the mix of firmness and gentleness reminds me again of my dear father.

I sit down on the sofa as he bends to tidy up the broken mugs and plates and then goes to make me a cup of tea, calling cheerfully to Noah that he's got one more minute ... so hurry up and hide! I try to relax. To recapture those happy thoughts. To be at peace. But I feel sick with worry, overwhelmed by the feeling that everything is close to crashing down around me.

"I'll just give him a chance to find a good place to hide." Andrew chuckles, handing me a cup of tea. "Then I'll go and search for him. Lots of noise. I'll make a proper game of it."

I smile as best I can, taking the tea from him. My hands are barely shaking now, but still I take the cup and saucer with two hands so they don't clatter together.

He sits next to me on the sofa, holding a glass of orange squash. "I helped myself. I hope you don't mind." I smile again, although I don't seem to be able to speak, so I just nod my agreement.

I listen for Noah moving about. I can hear the pitter-patter of footsteps and a door creaking open as he finds himself somewhere to hide in this unfamiliar house.

I worry that he might hurt himself, trapping a finger in a door or falling down the stairs. He is four and full of mischief. I am a schoolteacher who has spent years filling out risk-assessment forms and never letting small children out of my sight.

But it is more than that. Upstairs, hidden away beneath that single bed in the front room, are Robert's watch and wallet, mobile phone and laptop. And I have a sudden image of Noah coming back down holding the watch in one hand and the wallet in the other and giving them to Andrew and Andrew turning and looking at me, his face showing utter shock.

I put my cup of tea and the saucer down on the coffee table and am on my feet, about to go upstairs to find Noah and take anything belonging to Robert from him before Andrew sees it.

But Andrew puts his glass of squash down too and puts his arm out, blocking my way. "Wait!" he says. "Listen! He's coming back down the stairs"

I hear a thump, thump, thump noise. I think Noah has sat on the top stair and is now coming down on his bottom one step at a time.

Thump.

Thump.

Thump.

I go to push by Andrew, but he puts his hand on my arm. "Don't spoil his big moment," he says. I hesitate. If I knock his hand aside and keep moving, he will wonder why. If I wait, I have no idea what Noah will have in his hand.

Thump.

Thump.

Thump.

I can bear it no longer. I step forward, and Andrew drops his hand.

Thump.

Thump.

Thump.

Little footsteps in the hallway. Then the door swings open.

Noah stands there with a clenched fist held towards us.

He lowers his hand and opens it.

20

The three of us sit at the kitchen table, eating our lunch. Baked potatoes and salad and bottles of water for Andrew and me. An assortment of little sandwiches and fruit and vegetables with a carton of juice for Noah. He is propped up on two cushions. Even then he only just sees over the edge of the table with his big, saucer eyes. We have to steady him now and then on his cushions, and we all laugh.

He hums a song I do not recognise and looks at – no watches – the pile of three £1 coins by his plate. He came downstairs with one coin, all shiny-faced and proud, clutched in his little fist. I took him upstairs, and he showed me where he found it in the carpet close to where I had hidden Robert's belongings. Just so close. I helped Noah to find two more coins by the skirting board, and I gave them to him, and he seems so proud of them. He touches them now and again.

Noah is such a sweet child, well mannered and nicely behaved. He rocks back and forward and wobbles on the cushions on purpose. I steady him. He laughs, eats more food and then does it again. Andrew reaches out as he wobbles

and shakes him as if he really will fall off the chair. He laughs.
We repeat this on and off throughout the meal.

This contented time seems to last for ages. But it is now
coming to an end, as his parents are due back at any moment.

We have been in the garden, chasing each other and then
kicking a ball about before playing hide-and-seek with him
in the bushes, just his little legs and trainers showing. We
came back in and watched the television for a while as the
potatoes baked. "Ting!" Noah called out when the microwave
made its noise.

"Ting."

"Ting."

"Ting."

We all went, echoing the noise one by one. Those parents
who have children may take them for granted. I don't. This
silly stuff fills me with joy and excitement for when I have my
own child. It is enough, for now, to shine bright sunlight on
the dark, ever-presence of Robert.

As we get down at last from the table, none of us seeming
to want to break the magic spell, I open my arms to Noah,
and he steps towards me, and I hug him, and he hugs me
back. It is a perfect moment.

And then Andrew and Noah, clutching his coins and
dropping them and picking them up and dropping them
again, go into the living room to watch television until Nick
and Amy return. I glance at my watch; it won't be long now. I
take the plates from the kitchen table to the dishwasher. I put
the kettle on to make mugs of tea for Andrew and me.

As I go back and forth, from the table to the dishwasher
and the kettle and the cupboards, I stop now and then to
glance into the living room. Andrew and Noah are on the
sofa, Andrew at the far end, Noah slumped on him, looking
at another of the jolly American woman's sing-song videos. I
think he is nodding off. All the exertions of the day! Running

around the garden. Too much hide-and-seek. I will put him on my lap for a cuddle when I sit down.

Andrew turns and smiles at me. He looks down at Noah and then tips his head back and pretends to snore. We both laugh. Andrew adjusts himself to reach into his back pocket to get his phone, checking the news or the weather for this afternoon or perhaps looking at the latest about football or golf or whatever sport he follows. A rugby man, I think. I smile to myself as I put tea bags and pour hot water into the mugs. This – this everyday existence – is all I could have ever hoped for. I feel my eyes filling with tears. Sentimental fool that I am.

I am about to put the mugs onto a tray but cannot resist one last look at Andrew and Noah. As I move towards the door, I hear a mobile phone ringing – from further away. I wonder if someone, a police officer from work, is calling Andrew, and he has slipped out from underneath Noah and gone upstairs to take the call in private.

I panic for a second, thinking Noah may roll off the sofa and bang his head on the floor. I dash in, the noise of the mobile phone still ringing out, expecting to see Noah slipping off the edge of the sofa. He is as I last saw him, slumped and asleep on Andrew, who has his mobile phone to his ear.

"I'm ringing Robert's number," he says and then looks upwards to where the mobile phone is calling out from the bedroom.

In that split second, I think the pretence – my pretence – of Robert disappearing in the dead of night is over. Andrew will get up and turn and run upstairs and find the mobile phone and the watch and the wallet and the laptop pushed as far as I could under that bed.

Then he will come down and hold them out to me – the phone, the watch and the wallet laid out on top of the laptop – and ask in a shaking, incredulous voice, "These are all

Robert's ... what are they doing here, hidden under the bed?" And he will think about the car abandoned at the railway station in the middle of the night when there were no trains for hours, and he will have his answer. Then his face will change, hardening in front of my eyes.

But I am saved by the ding-a-ling ling of the doorbell and excited noises from Nick and Amy on the step and Noah waking and running to the door.

"Go with him," I say to Andrew, who looks at me, confused for a moment, as I brush by him and run up the stairs towards the ringing of the mobile phone.

By the time I get to it, Andrew has stopped the call, and the phone is no longer ringing. I stand there for a moment, feeling sick, listening to the joyful noises downstairs.

I come down, Robert's mobile phone held out in my hand, my face full of surprise, ready to bluff as best I can. There is bedlam in the living room. Nick and Amy are on their knees, hugging Noah, chatting with him and showing him a photograph. Andrew stands over them, smiling. He glances at me, but it is not the look of a man who is now suspicious of me. Not unless he is a supremely good actor. I hand the phone to him, and he takes it without comment, distracted by what's happening around him.

"Um. Er," he says good-naturedly, stumbling over his words. He gestures towards Nick and Amy, clearly not remembering their names even though I talked about them several times over lunch. "Noah's parents," he says, "are having a baby ... another baby." He seems ever-so-slightly embarrassed and not sure what to do. He waves his hands as if he is about to clap them. Then he wrings them together a little awkwardly.

I say, "Ditto," towards Amy and point to my tummy, glad to have my earlier instincts confirmed. "A girl, Emily, due the twenty-fifth of November."

Amy stands up and hugs me. Nick reaches out and shakes Andrew's hand as though they are both fathers-to-be. Noah stands in the middle, bouncing back and forth off Amy's and Nick's legs. "A baby ..." she says to me, "a baby brother or sister for Noah ... due 2 December ... "

She stands back and hands me a photograph of a baby scan from her handbag. It is a 3D one, like the one I wanted of Emily, taken at a private clinic in Colchester rather than the flat, 2D one I got from the NHS Hospital in Ipswich. Even now, in this moment of joy, Robert is ever present and casting a long shadow. I smile though, moved by the scan.

Amy adds, "It took ages ... sorry to have been so long ... but it was worth it in the end ... we got such a lovely scan of Bump ... we call the baby Bump. Our little Bump."

We stand there smiling at each other, Amy and I, two mothers-to-be bonding over this little splodgy-looking photograph. It tugs at my heart, a mixture of sadness and joy. And then Nick is picking up Noah and, glancing at Andrew and me, says, "Well, we'll let you get on." As they move to the door, Noah waves and smiles back at us. Amy laughs. "Wait a minute!" and then, to me, "Men!" as the two of us walk around gathering up Noah's bits and pieces and putting them back into his rucksack.

She hugs me again and kisses me, quite unexpectedly, on the cheek. "Congratulations," she says. I have always thought of myself, like Father, as someone who people are not drawn to in an emotional or demonstrative way. I am touched by Amy's gesture and respond the same way. We walk to the front door, and she says, "Goodbye," to Andrew, and he smiles and says, "Congratulations," back at her.

She swings the rucksack over her shoulder and hugs me one last time. "Our babies will be playmates ... best friends forever." I look at her, and she's just so full of excitement and emotion that I give her one last long hug.

I shut the front door and turn and walk towards Andrew now standing in the living room with his back to me, his head bowed over Robert's mobile phone. I stop behind him, not knowing what to expect. Robert would have gone very quiet – as Andrew now is – and then suddenly swung round and hit the side of my head with his right fist. He would have done it again and again until I fell and was cowering at his feet. I stand there now, waiting, determined that I will put my arms up to defend myself. I have been through so much. It has toughened me, made me stronger.

Andrew turns, and I flinch instinctively, looking at him, trying to judge his expression. He still has his head down, a puzzled look on his face, as he taps at Robert's mobile phone. "Everything is in here, but I can't get into it ... not yet ... I've tried all the combinations I think he might have used." I don't respond, expecting him instead to have been asking me why Robert had gone off and left his phone behind ... and why he drove and left his car at that back-of-beyond railway station. But all he says is, "I know someone who can get into it ... back in Lincoln ... unlock all his wrong-doings."

He looks up at me at last, a neutral expression on his face, so bland that it unnerves me. He should be asking me angry questions, pushing me, pulling my story to pieces. But he does not. I don't understand why.

And then he says, "Let's go for another walk ... it's a sunny afternoon ... over towards where you used to live." He pauses for a moment, almost theatrically, and then adds, "I've been working things out ... about Robert ... this phone ... his car ... and you know what, Laura? I know exactly what happened."

I SHUT the front door behind us, pushing and pulling to make sure it's secure, and then look around the close to see if anyone is watching. Habit now – I think it always will be. I wonder whether I should have insisted that Andrew told me what he thinks happened there and then. I could have wandered casually into the kitchen as he spoke, and he would have followed me, and I could have then turned and faced him. But he was keen to leave, and I went after him. If I did not, he might have gone straight to the police station in nearby Felixstowe to tell his story. And I'd be sitting, once more, waiting for the police to come for me.

Instead, I now follow Andrew as he strides out, leading the way, to the top of the close and then right. I indicate as I catch up with him, to go along the high road, by the village store and the roundabout and the sausage shop, up towards Grimston Lane, where I used to live. I have talked about it and its woods and fields and hiding places, but still I wonder why he wants to go there – and whether he will confront me in hidden-away woodland about the conclusions he has reached.

He slows his pace, as if remembering me, and we walk side by side for a few minutes along the high road. I wait to hear what he has to say. I do not know what I will do if he has worked out the truth. I might have had a fighting chance if it were the two of us face to face in the kitchen. Him big and strong. Me protecting myself and my baby. Out here, with people on the pavements and cars passing by, I cannot do anything. But then neither can he. Andrew cannot confront me here in full view of everyone.

As we approach the village store, he turns to me and smiles, such a strange sort of smile, and then starts talking. "I know just what happened," he says emphatically, glancing towards me. "I've worked it out."

I glance back at him but do not answer. I'm not going to incriminate myself.

He waits, expecting me to ask, "Oh yes?" or something like it, the fear showing in my face.

I note the village store is now just five, six, seven strides away, and as he reveals the truth, I can dash inside. I don't know where I will go from there, though. I can shout to staff that he, this man, has frightened me; please help me to get away. Then perhaps whoever works there will hurry me out the back whilst others stand between me and Andrew.

What then? I have nowhere else to go. Any happiness in my life ending, crouched on the ground by the bins of the village store, waiting to hear the sirens that mark the arrival of the police as they come to arrest me.

"Robert was a charmer," Andrew says. "Good-looking. Very smooth and believable. Yes?"

I hesitate by the entrance to the store, ready to go in, but instead I keep walking. "Yes," I reply.

"He went from one woman to another. Left as soon as he'd sucked the last one dry. Yes?"

"Yes," I reply again.

Andrew reaches out and takes my hand. "He's taken all your money ... bled you dry ... and now he has gone on to his next victim."

I glance at him. I hold on to his hand.

"He had another woman lined up ... he always did ... and she texted him in the middle of the night ... whilst you were asleep ... when he left suddenly ... maybe he was responding to some sort of cry for help from her."

I nod as if that makes sense. I think it does to him.

"He left in a hurry, dropped his phone by your bed and didn't dare come back in case he woke you. Drove to meet her at that railway station ... their rendezvous ... perhaps where they met regularly for ... anyway ... he had some of her clothes in the boot of his car."

I nod again and try to look upset. As a woman scorned would be.

"They then went off to wherever she lives ... a widow, I'd

guess ... with her big house and her life savings ... and he's out there somewhere now ... starting the whole thing again."

He turns to me at last and smiles, a big, reassuring smile. "It's not your fault, Laura ... He's been doing this for years ... He's such a smooth-talker ... so convincing. He's got away with it for so long, but this is the last time, I swear it." Then he leans – almost lurches – forward and hugs me. I hesitate for a moment, surprised and not sure what to do. I put my arms around his back and pat him. I am conscious of my baby between us, the three of us squashed together.

Eventually, I step back, and he does too, and we continue walking up the high street to the roundabout, crossing it and going by the sausage shop. He looks at it and laughs. "Just sausages? A shop that just sells sausages?"

I smile and laugh too. I think he is going to hug me again or maybe take my hand, but he does not. Even so, we walk on in companionable silence.

"I can use his phone," he says, "to find out everything ... where the money is ... perhaps where he is now ... and I can get the money back for you and your baby ... for others too."

I stop and ask him if that means bringing in the police. "I'd feel humiliated," I add. "Please don't."

"No," he answers firmly, encouragingly. "It would all be taken out of my hands ... be passed upwards ... and sideways ... and round ... and round again ... by which time he's gone again. I'll catch him now. Mark my words."

———————

WE STAND at the top of Grimston Lane in Trimley St Martin, where I used to live as a child, and we look out across the fields. I have not been here nor done this in years. If I shut my eyes, I could almost imagine Father and Mother standing behind me.

"Come on, Dolly Daydream, let's go for a walk," Father would cry, startling me. The memory makes me feel sad, melancholy.

To our far left, we can see the cranes at the docks. Years ago when I was a child growing up in Grimston Lane, we had a clear view across countryside for miles. But the docks have long since encroached further and further on everything in Felixstowe and its surroundings, ruining the beauty of the landscape.

Ahead and to the right, we can see towards the A14 taking lorries to and from the port and out across the country. I can hear the traffic today; the wind is blowing this way. In summer, when I was young, I would sleep with my bedroom window open and fall asleep to the soothing hum.

"How has Robert got away with what he's done?" I ask suddenly, curious to have the gaps in my knowledge filled in. "Not just ... women like me, but other investors too."

Andrew glances around and sighs. "He'd not be satisfied with one woman's savings at a time ... not when there are other people out there ... I'm no expert, but I imagine he'd set up some sort of bells and whistles website full of promises of high rewards and no risks ... case studies of those people who've made a small fortune ... all made up of course. He'd then start posting, under many names, positive comments about the website and the money to be made on different forums and all over the internet ... driving people to the site.

"He'd then maybe hold meetings for would-be investors in smart hotels, turn up in a nice suit and flashy car, one or two other people with him pretending to work for him, making notes, passing him files, fetching his coffee ... hired hands for the day. Lots of charts and numbers and big profits. All smoke and mirrors. He could be very charming and persuasive ... and it's easy enough to fake almost anything, bank statements, trading statements. And, of course, people like the idea of doubling their money with little or no effort ... they're greedy and stupid, many of them.

"And he will have created a company, registered its office at an upmarket address in London, paid someone to set up a company bank account, answer the phone and send on post. The investors' money is paid into the company account and then transferred to Robert's personal account somewhere, maybe overseas. Europe. America. He pays some interest to the original investors with newer investors' money used to keep everything going as more investors come in. After a while, when the regulatory forms aren't filed, Companies House will strike off the company.

"And that completes the scam. Robert removes the website, takes the money and starts over sometime down the line. Investors don't know which way to turn, as the money has gone to a company that no longer exists. The taxman's not involved, as the company was shut down before filing accounts. Convenient, that. The police aren't really interested. They don't have the expertise, not at a local level. They'll tell investors to go to one of the financial regulatory bodies; and they're far too busy focusing on the big stuff, the high-profile criminals."

I turn slightly and start walking further down Grimston Lane towards the house where I used to live. Andrew follows, and I ask him, "So, has all the money gone, so many thousands of pounds?"

"I don't know, Laura, really I don't. I won't know until we get into his phone. I'm sure we can do that ... at least I have a colleague who can ... and we can hopefully have a look through his contacts and messages and maybe his emails too. We might have access to his bank accounts through the phone as well ... that would be interesting.

"Still, it would have been better if he had taken his phone. If he was using it, it could be tracked and we'd know where he was. We then drive there and simply wait for him to appear. Even so, if he's left the phone behind by accident, we have a good chance of getting information from it ..." He stops, rummages in his pocket, takes out the phone. "When we get back, I'll see if we can open it.

"Robert was a gambler, went through money like water. If he's sensible, he'd have only taken small, five-figure sums from investors so that, after a while, they'd write it off as a bad experience. Six-figure sums ... from this Harry and ... others ..." He looks at me, and I nod and say, "Life savings," and he takes my meaning and adds, "People don't write off those sorts of sums. They can't afford to. They've been ruined.

"I have a suspicion that he has been funnelling most of this money overseas, maybe America, Florida ... Orlando. He always loved the idea of living there. Maybe, once he's accumulated enough, he'll quit while he's ahead and move there, living off other people's savings for the rest of his life." He pauses and looks me in the eye, then takes my hands in his. "So," he says, his voice so animated now, "what we need to do is to get into this phone and take the money back before he can ... we need to whip it away from under his nose."

"So this is where you were brought up ... it's very *Anne of Green Gables*," he says conversationally as we wander along the lane, looking at the houses to our left; some are smart; others look rather tatty.

I laugh, recognising many comparisons to that simpler, old-fashioned time and place. "My perfect childhood," I reply. He does not say anything, so I go on, my inner thoughts spilling out. I have the strangest feeling, a happy one – as if I have known him for years.

"I thought it would last forever. That I'd live here with my father and mother and my husband and my children as one big happy family and ..." I am suddenly overcome with emotion.

I point to the fields to our right, and after a few moments, I go on. "We used to walk out here so many times in the evenings and at weekends and summer holidays. Listening to the birds, foraging, watching the wildlife with our binoculars ... I'd pick wildflowers, press them in books, turn them into bookmarks, give them as presents." I smile at the memories before continuing.

"It was an old-fashioned childhood, yes ... making home-made lemonade and baking cakes and reading *The Secret Garden* and *Black Beauty* and *Little Women* ... imagining I was Meg or Jo or Beth or Amy ... creating scrapbooks and climbing trees and chasing rabbits and watching them disappear into their burrows. I loved every minute of it.

"Father and Mother were ... from another time and place. We had a television but only really watched it on occasions; Father preferred the radio ... I remember we watched it when Princess Diana died ... and we enjoyed old BBC comedy videos at Christmas. We didn't have computers or much in the way of technology ... any technology until quite late, really ... I had to get a computer for schoolwork, I remember. And Father had a fax until he was quite elderly, and he would ask people for their fax number even though no one else still had one, and they would laugh at him. Younger people didn't even know what a fax machine was." The thought makes me smile again.

We walk on and get to our old house. I barely recognise it. There have been so many changes since I last saw it. I had not realised. I wish we had not come here. I hate the look of it. My memories were a comfort, but the reality is wiping out my past, everything I held so dear.

The house looks to have been rebuilt by a subsequent owner with more money than sense – it's futuristic, all wood and metal and smoked-glass windows. It looks like something you'd see in Los Angeles not rural Suffolk. The garage has gone and been replaced with a wide, artificial driveway that will never see weeds poking through. Had I not been on this spot where I stood so many times as a child, kicking stones and waiting for my parents to come out for our evening walk, I would never have known the house.

"That was my bedroom," I say, pointing top left. "Before it ... ah, it's so different ... it's not my home anymore." I stop then, and Andrew sees how upset I am and takes my arm gently, guiding me away and back up the lane.

He asks me if this is what I want for my baby; I assume he means this sort of rural setting of trees and woods and fields. I carry on talking, surprising myself at how open I am. "I'd like to sell up, move away, far from anywhere, to a cottage with roses round the door and a long back garden full of wildflowers – cuckoos singing in the trees. That would be bliss." I stop and pause, then add, "I don't like this modern world very much. It's not my world, really."

Then he asks, as we walk back towards the high road, how I will manage with the baby on my own and, hesitating a little, if I had always wanted a child. I think, for a moment, that I will tell him of the endless days and nights after my parents had died and I had parted from my fiancé, and I was sad and lonely and depressed and imagined my own death so many times. Lying there at three a.m., looking at packets of Anadins I'd been storing up for that moment.

"It's all I've ever wished for," I answer. "My own little family. I've always wanted to have what I had when I was a child, just the three of us." I hesitate and then add, "Yes, I'll manage on my own. I'll have to. I'll probably spend my life where I am, managing on little or no money. But I'll have my baby ... I'll have Emily."

We walk along in silence again – our companionable silence – back to the high road and along by the sausage shop. He takes my arm, that lovely old-fashioned gesture my father used to make, as we get to the roundabout. And I am pleased to take it as we step out into the road.

By the time we walk by the village store, we are holding hands. Madness, I know. But it somehow feels right, and it comforts me. I will grab these brief moments of contentment as and when I can. God knows, Andrew will be gone soon enough, and I will never see him again. And plenty of horrors lie ahead of me. A whole lifetime of them.

Neither of us says anything much, just idle chit-chat about the two churches – Trimley St Mary and Trimley St Martin standing opposite each other – and the lane where the actor Roger Moore was said to have once lived many years ago. Not that anyone ever seems to have seen him here. Then we are at the top of the close, and at just the same instant, we let go of each other's hand.

HARRY IS BACK. I see him straightaway. He is on my doorstep, bending down, crouching over to peer through my letterbox. He's shouting my name too. Once. Twice. Three times.

It would be comical if it weren't so alarming. He's so bloody incessant. So endless. Will he ever stop chasing me for what Robert did to him? No, he never will. And I cannot move away. This will go on forever.

He stands up and turns round as he hears us approaching. Looks at Andrew, glances at me, does a double take, looking at Andrew again, thinking it is Robert.

Andrew takes charge immediately, tugging his driving

licence, maybe even his police ID, from the wallet in his back pocket, showing it briefly to Harry, who looks towards it but does not study it closely. I can tell he is thrown, bewildered by Andrew's presence and perhaps by his physical similarity to Robert.

"I'm looking into the matter," Andrew tells Harry. "Seeing what we can do. I'll be filing a report," he says. What he says – which is nothing much really – is expressed with such absolute authority that I think it will stop Harry in his tracks, send him on his way.

Harry looks at Andrew again, really looks at him, and I am not sure if he believes Andrew and Robert are related or not. There is a certain similarity, but they do not look like twins. They are not peas in a pod. Andrew is older and taller and less smooth, more rugged. Harry might think it is just coincidence. And he is old, and his eyesight is fading.

Harry turns to me and speaks. He is more polite and less aggressive in Andrew's presence than he has been before. But the sheen of sweat, the twitch of his face and the shaking of his hands show that these manners come at some cost. He looks like he might have a stroke at any minute.

"We're having a meeting tonight, Alex and I ... at my house ... seven thirty. Sarah and her daughter ... Mrs Knox and her young men ... they are very angry. ... We will discuss what's happened and agree a way forward. We want you there." It is more of a demand than a request. An "or else".

"If not, if we can't agree a way to get our money back from you, we are going to club together to pay a barrister to take you to court ... make you sell your house to pay us back." His eyes swivel from me to Andrew and back again. A flash of anger. "Do the right thing," he instructs more aggressively.

I turn to go. I can't face this again, the endless threats, the going round and around.

Andrew says something to him. I catch the end of it.

"You'd have contracted with Robert Wilkinson ... his company. This matter has nothing to do with Laura Curtis ... nothing at all."

There are more words between them, angry from Harry, emphatic from Andrew, as I walk away, sick of everything.

"You say you're looking into it," Harry shouts after Andrew as he follows me. "Ask her why she says she went to bed at eleven o'clock that night when I saw her up and about at gone midnight. Ask her about that ... And when you're checking, check what she was doing walking back home on her own at four in the morning. Eh? Ask her about that." Harry is standing on his own now, his face scarlet with indignation. "She's a bloody con artist. She's up to her neck in this. She's behind it all. She's got our money, and we want it back."

I am at the front door, struggling with my feelings as I step inside. I heard all of Harry's accusations, he must have spoken to Alex by now, and Andrew will have heard them too. He will want some answers from me. The thought fills me with dread. Andrew steps into the hallway, shutting the door behind him. I almost flinch as I imagine how he is going to turn to me, demanding to know, "What's all that about? What were you doing up at midnight and walking at four in the morning ?"

But he does not. Instead he puts his arms around me and holds me tight. I feel crushed against him, me and my baby, and I wonder what he is going to say when he releases me. Which way he is going to go.

But in my heart I know.

He's on my side now.

I am sure of it.

21

SATURDAY, 5 JUNE, THE EVENING

We sit here, Andrew and I, at the kitchen table, eating microwave meals – cauliflower cheese for him, macaroni cheese for me – with salad and a bottle of fizzy water. Trying to be humdrum, boring and just plain normal for a while.

But it is not easy. We talk of this and that: plants in the garden, the colour of the fence panels, stuff and nonsense. It's all forced, and we both know it. We are, in a way, both holding our breath; we are listening and waiting.

Over the way, Harry and Alex, Sarah and Lucy, Mrs Knox and her horrible boys are all holding their meeting at this moment. They'll be talking about me, all their financial losses, working themselves up to righteous anger. I fear what Alex and the two Knox boys might be egged on to do; if not now, then at night as I sleep.

Andrew suggested, soon after we got back, that we could simply pack up, leave in his car straightaway, and go back to his place. "Get you out of the line of fire," he said. "Lie low for a while."

I said no, that I would not be chased away. Besides, I still have my job at the primary school, which I could not leave until the end of the summer term. I cannot just disappear. The reality, of course, is that I have no choice but to stay. I cannot go anywhere with Robert's body in the garage, especially not with the possibility that Alex might break in again.

Andrew shook his head and said, quite firmly, that I did not have to put up with "this nonsense, this bullying". He reminded me that I have all sorts of options, I could go to the police, and there are various legal remedies. He even implied that he could arrest them! Of course, I do not want any of that – none of it – as it would draw so much unwanted attention to me.

If I am honest, we came close to an argument. I did not want to do anything. He wanted to do something. I stuck to my guns, and finally, reluctantly, he shrugged and said he'd stay the night "to be on the safe side". The look on his face made it clear that he'd rather be more gung-ho about it. But that was the last thing I wanted.

As we finish our makeshift meal, I scrape the remains into the kitchen pedal bin, and, as it is now full, I put it out by the back gate. Andrew goes into the living room, sitting in the armchair that allows him to see out through the slats of the blind into the close.

I load the dishwasher and then go round checking that all the doors are locked so that no one can break in without making a noise. I then make mugs of tea. As if this is any old evening in front of the television.

I sit down on the sofa, mugs on coasters on the coffee table, this continued sham of normality. It is getting dark outside, and it is growing chilly in here. I put my hands on my tummy. I am waiting for what is to happen soon.

Andrew did not ask me about Harry's accusations. That I was up gone midnight when I had told him I was in bed at eleven. I believe Andrew has assumed they were the ramblings of a confused old man who's angry enough to stir things up.

Nor did Andrew ask me about Harry's claim that I was out and about at four in the morning. Maybe Andrew thinks it is a lie. Or perhaps he suspects that I have not been truthful but is choosing not to confront me.

I can't help but hold on to my feeling that Andrew is on my side, come what may. Sometimes I think he is too good to be true. But his equilibrium and his sense of calm make me trust him. Yet I still have moments of doubt. There are things that jar; I just cannot bring them to the front of my mind yet.

We sit there sipping our tea in our ever-extending pretence of normality. Everything else – the darkness, the silence, the imminent threat – reveals that this is anything but normal.

"Here they come," he says finally, lifting himself up out of his armchair to get a better view. "All wound up." I can hear "told you so" in his tone.

I get up and move towards him, next to him, as though he is protecting me. Or, perhaps, I him. I see Harry on his doorstep. Sarah and her daughter walking back to their house. Mrs Knox to hers. They all look this way, watching as Alex and the two Knox boys cross and stand on the pavement outside my house.

———

THREE HOURS on and I am in bed in the front bedroom, the one that will be Emily's room. Andrew is downstairs in the living room. I think he will stay awake all night if he can.

I cannot sleep, ever restless, listening out for the side gate being unbolted slowly, footsteps on the patio, a shoulder on the conservatory doors, determined pressure cra-a-acking them open. Then Alex and the Knox boys will be in the house, coming for me.

I hear Andrew moving about downstairs, clearing his throat, pouring water from the kitchen tap into a glass, coughing on his way back into the living room. His presence should reassure me, but it does not. He has no reason to go into the garage, but I cannot shake the fear that he might for some reason.

Alex and the Knox boys did not do anything when they stood outside my house after Harry's meeting. At least, they did not come up shouting and banging on the front door as I had feared. Perhaps that would have been best. What they did was, in its way, more frightening.

Alex stood there, pointing at the living-room window as if he knew we were there, watching.

"Don't react," Andrew warned me, so we stood there unmoving. "I don't think they can see us. He's just acting big for the others."

Maybe so. But it was enough to spook me.

I could sense that Andrew wanted to do something, to charge out there and get stuck in and sort it all out. I put my hand on his arm as if to say, "Please don't." And, then, more firmly, "No."

Then Alex and the two Knox boys struck some poses and strutted back and forth. And we stood and waited, Andrew impatient, me sick with fear, until they strolled away.

I look at the bedside clock, the illuminated numbers showing 2.23 a.m. I am worried sick and exhausted. I can't imagine how I might do this night after night, how I can endlessly live with the fear of what might happen next.

Andrew is down there, sitting on the edge of the armchair so he can see the front of the house. He gets up regularly, prowls round, checking that everything is still locked and that nobody is out the back.

I hear every noise outside the house, each of them amplified by my fear. I jump, startled by the howl of a cat somewhere in the fields beyond the back fence. Then a similar screech from another cat, responding. I wait to hear them hissing and yowling and fighting. Wondering whether, whilst all this is happening, Alex and the Knox boys are carefully unbolting the gate and creeping into the back garden.

It occurs to me that these yowling noises are actually being made by Alex and the Knox boys, that they are out there somewhere, beyond the fence, knowing I am awake, and tormenting me. That they are enjoying terrifying me in some sort of twisted, sadistic way.

Then there is unexpected silence. It is always quiet here in this close. That now makes me uneasy. My ears strain to hear any noise. I hear the gate creak open and footsteps coming around and onto the patio. I think it is my mind playing tricks, imagining my worst fears coming to life. But I am sure I am hearing the sound of oh-so-careful movements.

Andrew will talk to them, I think, if or when they arrive. As a police officer, he will have spent years dealing with angry and threatening people. But I think there is a huge difference between a member of the public shouting at you across the front desk of a police station and three violent and aggressive young men breaking into your house at three in the morning. And so I have a knife under my pillow in case I – we – need it.

"Thing is," he said thoughtfully before I went up to bed, "if we can somehow access some of the money through Robert's phone, we only need to pay off your neighbours ... no one else will come after you ... nobody knew he was here. If we can pay them off, your troubles are over." He did not mention the rest of the money.

"If they come, I'll say we'll get their money back in the next week. We'll make them go away, wait ... and we then have a week to see what happens." I told him that Sarah and Mrs Knox are owed relatively small sums, but that Robert took Harry's life savings. "He must be in his eighties," Robert replied. "We can pay him a little each month, as Robert was going to do ..." He did not finish the sentence. He did not need to. I understood his meaning. "Until Harry dies."

Bang!

My thoughts are broken by the thump of a fist on the conservatory doors. I am up and out of the bed and onto my feet. I was not mistaken; I did hear Alex and the Knox boys coming in the back gate, carefully sliding back the bolt at the top, and creeping slowly step by step to the conservatory.

There is another bang a few seconds later.

I move to the bedroom window and look down. It is the older Knox boy, the nasty one, thumping on the glass with a gloved fist. The younger Knox boy and Alex are standing behind him, twitching and jigging about and giggling as though this is fun to them, something enjoyable.

Bang!

One more, another few seconds later. Still I look down, watching. The younger Knox boy now seems to be doing a bizarre dance, laughing to himself as if it is the funniest thing ever. Alex is moving in time with him and is singing some sort of song. The older Knox boy turns his head up suddenly, and we look at each other. I see the glint of a knife.

I hear Andrew call out almost cheerfully from downstairs, "Don't worry, Laura ... I'm going ..."

I STAND THERE at the window, looking down, not knowing what to do.

I go to call out to Andrew, "Don't, he has a knife," but the words choke in my throat.

I know what will happen. Angry words exchanged. Pushing and shoving. The knife. Andrew on the ground, dying. Alex and the Knox boys running away.

I cannot let that happen. No matter what.

I have to try to stop it.

I hurry downstairs as fast as I can, full of dread.

The conservatory doors are open. Andrew stands there with his back to me. I cannot see the older Knox boy with the knife. Andrew's body is between him and me. I see Alex and the younger Knox boy, behind and to the sides. They are silent now, watchful; they have stopped jigging and giggling and dancing.

I hear Andrew talking to them, but I cannot make out the words, only the tone of his voice, steady and reasonable, as he tries to talk sense to them.

I imagine the words he is saying as I take one and then two steps forward. He is telling them what he told me. That he is going to get the money back, and their parents will have it within the week. They just have to be patient.

I hear him as he says the words, "Just be patient."

The older Knox boy responds, shouts threatening words, showing off for the other two.

Alex and the younger Knox boy start jigging about again, a grotesque rap, encouraging the older Knox boy to "do it, do it".

He is about to step forward and plunge the knife into Andrew's heart.

I am up to Andrew's shoulder, now next to him, as Alex and the Knox boys catch sight of me. They pause for a moment, waiting to see what I do. I look at the older Knox boy, who has his arms down by his side, his hands in an unnatural position as he shields the knife. He looks back at me, holding my gaze. I don't know which way he will go.

And so I step forward and move in front of Andrew,

between him and the older Knox boy. I place my hands on my tummy, and I take a breath as I think what I am going to say. I need to say it firmly and clearly. But I am frightened, and my hands, if they were not clasped together, would be shaking.

"I promise ... I promise you that we will get the money back in seven days. Andrew" – I turn my head slightly towards him – "is going to the police first thing in the morning with Robert's mobile phone and all his details. He will access his accounts and get your money back."

Alex and the younger Knox boy stand there, waiting to see what the older Knox boy says and does.

There is a long, agonising wait. As the seconds pass, I watch the expression change on the older Knox boy's face. He wants the chance to back off but without losing face in front of the others.

"Please ..." I say. "I promise," I add.

One more long and endless wait, and then, suddenly, the horrid older Knox boy nods and turns. "Seven days," he says. "We'll be back." And then he goes, leading the way, the other two following him.

"He had a knife," I say, turning towards Andrew as Alex and the Knox boys get to the gate and leave.

"I know," Andrew answers. "I'll let it go ... just for now ... until we've sorted the money out ... but I can't let him get away with that."

A pause as we take in the enormity of what just happened. Not just the knife but between us. We hug. I'm not sure which one of us went to hug the other first. Both at the same time, I think.

I am shaking now, realising that I could have so easily been stabbed. That it could have been me – me and my baby – lying on the patio, my life, our lives, ebbing away. And then Andrew would have been attacked, too, before Alex and the

Knox boys ran off. I saved Andrew, and I know why, and it wasn't because I didn't want ambulances and police cars coming here in the dead of night, Robert's body being discovered.

"Let's go back to bed," Andrew says, releasing me from our hug. "I'll sleep on the sofa. Then, in the morning, I'll head on back to Lincoln, get this phone opened up and see what we can do ... whatever happens, I'll be back by the evening, eight or nine at the latest ... if I've got into it, we can get all of this sorted out. If not, we'll have to think of a plan B ... getting you away from here until everyone's cooled down. Don't worry, everything will be okay."

I wait to see if he will say, "I promise." But he does not.

6.45 a.m. and Andrew is about to leave for the three-hour drive back to Lincoln.

I woke at 6.35 a.m., hearing him coming up the stairs, going along the landing, into the bathroom and out five minutes later.

By then I was up from my bed and downstairs, boiling the kettle for two mugs of tea.

"Would you like a cooked breakfast?" I ask as he comes into the kitchen to say goodbye. "Before you go?"

He smiles, comes across, hugs me briefly and says, "I'm hot and sweaty, sorry ... and it's a bit early for a full English, maybe tomorrow."

"Toast, then? Couple of slices. Marmalade or jam?"

He shakes his head. "I need to get going ... meeting at nine thirty ... I'll stop on the way somewhere if I get a chance." He pulls off his black jumper, throws it over his shoulder. He has a grubby white tee shirt underneath that looks like he's worn it for ages. "I'm so hot," he says. "I don't know why."

I offer him a mug of tea, which he takes and then turns to go. He's in a hurry to leave.

I stand in the living room, angling the blind so I can watch him at the car. He throws his jumper on the passenger seat, puts his mug of tea on the roof and then leans back into the car and pops open the bonnet.

I guess, being a former traffic officer, it's force of habit to look over your car before setting off, especially on a long journey. I can't remember when I last checked mine. I can't even recall when it had a service. I just drive it until a warning light comes on.

He has the bonnet propped up and is looking at the engine. Making sure everything is just so. I watch him as I sip my tea. Then he drops the bonnet down. All is well. He is good to go.

He stands by the car, drinking his tea, looking around the close. It's as though he is cooling himself in the breeze.

Then he turns and looks back at my house, at me, I think, watching him through the blind. He raises his mug in a celebratory manner.

I raise mine back at him although I am not sure he can see me. In fact, I don't think he can. I'm not sure why he did it, really.

Then he is walking back up the path to the house. I open the front door and let him back in. "I'd forget my head if it wasn't screwed on." He puts the empty mug on the windowsill. Then moves to the sofa, picking up Robert's mobile phone from the armrest. I had not even noticed it was there.

"Well," he adds, a moment of awkwardness about saying goodbye twice, "I'll be off then."

I go to ask him for his mobile number so we can stay in touch through the day until he returns tonight. But he is already turning and going out the front door once more.

I stand by the front door and watch him back at the car, getting in and shutting the door. I wonder if I should wave him goodbye. But he is already getting out of the car again, moving to the front, lifting up the bonnet. I should have offered to make him some sandwiches for his journey. I have some thick slices of ham in the fridge. And I have a flask underneath the sink, at the back somewhere. I could make him some coffee for when he stops off.

He is doing something under the bonnet, pushing something in, pulling it out, looking at it, pushing it back in again. I expect him to drop the bonnet back down, get in the car, turn it around and drive away. But he does not. He stands there and turns towards the garage. I know why.

I stare, unable to move. I know what it is.

He needs oil to top up his engine. He will go to the garage, pull up the door, and go in to see if I have any there.

There is a tub of oil at the back by the work unit, right next to the body. I should rush out to try to stop him, to say I haven't any oil, that there is a petrol station five minutes down the road in Felixstowe. But I cannot move.

Instead, I watch as he goes to the boot of his car, takes out a tub of oil, goes back to the engine, tops it up, checks it, returns the tub back to the boot and then wipes his hands on a cloth. I breathe a sigh of relief. At last, he is good to go.

But he looks up again, over towards the garage, then takes a black bin bag out of the boot and walks to the garage with it. I move suddenly, quickly, to see what he is doing.

There is rubbish scattered by the garage door. Alex and the Knox boys, leaving in the early hours, must have kicked the bag I'd left out down the alleyway and on to the driveway.

I watch as Andrew picks up the empty cartons, packaging and what's left inside the pedal bin bag. He puts all of it into the black bin bag. There is a moment of agony as everything – my whole life – hangs in the balance.

He can leave the black bin bag on the driveway for me to sort out later.

He can go and put it in the big grey bin for me.

He can lift up the garage door and tuck it inside, out of sight.

He lifts up the garage door, walks inside. Ten, twenty, thirty seconds pass.

And he is still inside the garage.

I AM on the far side of the kitchen, facing the door, my back against the work surface, as Andrew stumbles in and stands in the doorway.

He looks stunned and horrified. Trying to take in what he has just discovered.

I stand there waiting, one hand on my tummy, the other behind my back, not sure what he is going to do; nor what I will do.

An endless moment, stretching out.

I watch him shake his head, making sense of it all. I wait an age. To see which way he goes. What else can I do?

He swallows, about to speak.

"He forced himself on me," I say quietly.

"Tortured me.

"He made my life a living hell."

I keep talking as calmly as I can. Andrew stands still, his head down.

"He tried to drown me in the bath.

"He pushed my head under. Held it there.

"He punched my stomach. My baby. So I would miscarry."

One more thing to say.

"He came at me that night ... to strangle me ... to kill me."

My voice is rising, jagged now and full of anger and fear. "I stabbed him to save myself ... my baby ... I did not know what to do after ... I cannot be parted from my baby ... I hid him away." I choke on my words.

Andrew looks up at me now, and I look back at him, trying to hold his gaze.

I cannot tell from his face, still so full of shock, what he is thinking. Which way this will go.

He steps towards me, then stops as I shift my position against the work surface.

"You knew him, what he was like," I say, desperate now, my voice and my heart breaking.

"How he behaved. How he treated people.

"What he did with women."

I hesitate. This is it. Andrew is about to make his choice.

"Your mother took her own life because of him.

"And your father died of a heart attack – a broken heart.

"Your wife left you because of him ... your own brother ruined your life."

One last thing to say.

"You know he was a bad man. You hated him for everything he's done to you. And you should hate him for everything he did to me ... and my baby, Em ..." I stop speaking, choking up again now.

He takes one, two, three steps forward.

His head is down. Lunging at me.

I bring the knife up and round from behind my back.

"You poor thing," he says, grabbing and wrapping his arms around me. My right arm is behind his back, my right hand holding a kitchen knife.

Not "I love you". Nor "Darling Laura". Just "You poor

thing." But it is enough.

He has made his choice. He has chosen me.

I pull my right hand away, twisting to the side as though embarrassed, and putting the knife back on the work surface behind me. He is full of emotion, and I don't think he notices.

We stand and look at each other.

There is nothing but compassion on his face. Relief, I suspect, on mine.

Neither of us speaks for so long.

Eventually, he steps back, lets go of me, but then puts his hands back on my arms and starts talking. Gabbling, really. A stream of consciousness pouring out of him.

"Laura ... I know you had no choice ... with Robert ... it was you or him ... you and your baby. He would have ..." Andrew stops, thinks, then carries on. "... not wanted to share you." He gulps, as though realising what he is saying. "I understand why you had to do it ... self-defence. We can ... I'd love to ... the three of us ..."

He glances at me, my uncertain expression, stumbles over the words he is trying to say.

"I ... am here for you ... if you want me ... need me ... to look after you ... and your baby." His voice, over this last sentence, drops almost to a whisper. As if he is unsure how I will react. Maybe he thinks I will reject him. I smile at him. He carries on.

"I know where I can put him, Robert, somewhere safe where he will never be found. Then maybe, if, you know, one day ..." He looks at my face for reassurance. "You could sell this place ... me mine ... and we could start over somewhere far away."

I'm not sure if this is a question or a statement, but I smile and nod gently, and I think for one moment he is going to move forward and kiss me. But he pulls me gently towards him and hugs me long and hard.

The thought of Robert hidden away forever almost overwhelms me.

I hug Andrew back.

I will be safe. My baby too. With Andrew. Perhaps there may be some money as well.

Finally, he lets me go, saying he will get the phone looked at by this work colleague who will open it and reveal all of its secrets. He'll be back later this evening. Before bedtime. He looks at me as he says "bedtime", and I smile and nod again.

Then, as he turns to go, he asks if there is anything else of Robert's here. "A laptop?" he queries.

I pause and look at him and then say, "Yes, there is." I fetch the laptop, wallet and the watch and give them to him.

He takes the wallet and watch and, without looking at them, slips them into his jacket pockets, one either side. Then holds the laptop. "Between his mobile phone and this ..." he says, "the Aladdin's cave will be opened."

Then, at last, I hold my breath, expecting him to take a step forward and kiss me.

But he does not.

Instead, the laptop in his hands, he turns and is gone. He is in a hurry.

I SPEND the morning cleaning and washing, getting everything nice and just so for Andrew's return. I have such a sense of joy and relief but am so tired by my exertions that I sit down on the sofa before lunch and fall asleep.

I awake an hour or so later and lie here in this oasis of calm for ages and ages. No one rings the doorbell, bangs on the door, shouts for me. I don't think anyone will ever bother me again. The world feels at peace.

I dream of happier times ahead. My baby. Andrew. A

family. A new home and life somewhere, maybe the York-shire Dales or Devon; I had such happy holidays there with Father and Mother when I was small. Money. Robert gone and eventually forgotten.

He still intrudes into my thoughts when I am not keeping busy. I am ashamed of what I have done, what I have become. A murderer. The guilt eats at me. I can rationalise killing Robert. I had no choice. It was him or me. Him or me and my baby; me dead on the kitchen floor, my baby dying in my womb. It was a life-or-death decision.

But I know that I would have killed Alex too. For what? This man coming into my home, threatening me, trying to get Harry's money back, his inheritance. Those actions did not warrant his death. He is mentally unwell, and he knew nothing about Robert. Yet I was prepared to kill him. If neces-sary, I would have killed him and dealt with his body. What have I become?

And Andrew. This man – this good and decent man – whom I am now planning to spend my life with. Who has offered to be the father of my child. This man who will hide Robert's body away forever. Who will come back to me with the money that Robert stole. He will give me and my baby the opportunity to live a long and happy life. I was ready to kill him too. What sort of monster am I?

I get up to make myself a salad for lunch. I have to stay as normal and as busy as I can. I cannot sit and wallow in these terrible thoughts. I did what I did with Robert, Alex and Andrew. It was the right thing, the only thing, each time. I know that, really. I did what I had to for my baby.

After lunch, I bake cakes, lots and lots of cakes; some-thing I loved to do with Father when I was little. Fairy cakes, topped with creamy icing and sprinkles. I am absorbed in what I am doing, imagining how one day soon I will do this with Emily.

Later, hot and tired, I sit back down on the sofa and gaze out of the window. I have the feeling that the neighbours and the local police are leaving me alone. All I have to do now is to relax a while, have a bath and something to eat at teatime as I await Andrew's return later this evening.

I go back to my daydreaming. I imagine how, sooner rather than later, I will sell this house and Andrew will sell his. With the proceeds of one, we will buy a little cottage somewhere in the wilds of Yorkshire or the moors of Devon. We will live, for a while, as Emily grows and goes to school, off the proceeds of the other. This will be our happy life.

I wonder whether, from the mobile phone or laptop, we might be able to access the money Robert has hidden away. Some to be repaid to the likes of Harry, Mrs Knox and Sarah. The rest, perhaps even a substantial nest egg, allowing us to live out our lives reading and painting and walking and being contented.

There will come a time, near the end of our lives, with Emily and our other children and their children, our grand-children, living close by, when we will look back over every-thing. We will see a glorious life lived together, and we will barely remember this terrible time, let alone be tormented by it.

In the evening, as I sit back on the sofa with a glass of sparkling water after my meal, I am determined to put all of my sad and troubled thoughts behind me. I await Andrew's return, with news of restored riches, and we will snuggle up in bed together.

The fact is, we will have everything. Robert will be gone. There will be money in the bank. A new life will stretch out in front of us. I could almost weep with joy. After all of this utter horror, happy-ever-after lies ahead.

It is 11.10 p.m. I am in the living room looking out through the window blind and across the close.

I had expected Andrew to return by 9 p.m. Then 10 p.m. And finally 11 p.m.

Now I hope he will be home by midnight. I am so tired that I think I will be asleep by then.

I look at the beautiful woman in the painting above the fireplace. This is the moment I need to be like her; strong and calm and steadfast.

I work out how long it will have taken him to drive back to Lincoln. To see his colleague and wait while he hacks into the mobile phone and laptop.

I guess that Andrew would then have had to extract the information he needed: accounts, usernames, passwords, balances. Lunch and a pint and some cash as a thank you to the friend; these things would have taken up maybe another hour or two.

Then he would have gone back to his house, where he would have picked up any post, checked all was well, packed a suitcase, and headed back down the A1 and along the A14 to me. Even if he did all those things, he should have been here by nine at the latest. Earlier, really.

I wonder if the car has broken down and he is waiting for a breakdown service to rescue him. I have no way of knowing.

There is nothing I can do but wait.

I do not have his mobile phone number. I did not ask for it.

I wonder if he might have been in an accident on the road. That he might now be in hospital somewhere.

As I stare out into the night, worrying, my mood gets ever darker. He may, of course, have got into the phone and laptop, accessed everything, the "Aladdin's cave" as he called it, and now be sitting on a huge six-figure pot of money that he wants to keep for himself. More money than he could ever dream of. There may be enough there for him to start a new life in Europe or America, withdrawing or transferring money as he needs it over the coming years. He is a policeman. He'd know about these things.

As I sit here now, Andrew may be getting on a plane to somewhere far away. A sunny hotspot in Greece or Italy, or Turkey perhaps.

I wonder what it means for me if he has simply fled with the money. I know in my heart that it can only mean one thing.

I am back where I started. No money, of course. And the body still in the garage. And the neighbours coming back at some point. The police too. There is no happy-ever-after future for me and my baby. Life could not be worse.

I could weep. I feel sick.

And I wonder if I have been conned all along by Andrew.

My mind reels back over everything, and my thoughts turn into suspicions and then into something more certain. I remember how he called me "Laura" when I woke after Alex's attack and he was sitting in the chair in the bedroom. How did he know my name at that time?

He said he followed my car back from Lincoln, but – it hits me with some force – he was wearing different clothes. A white shirt replaced by a white tee shirt and a black jumper. So he must have stopped at his home to change. I do not know how he could have followed me as I left. He must have seen my car's numberplate and accessed information – my name and address – from the police database.

When he discovered Robert's body, he asked straight after if there was a laptop, and that strikes me now as odd, that this would be one of his first thoughts. And when he left, he did not hug or kiss me or say when he would be back or give me his mobile number. He just went as quickly as he could.

It strikes me suddenly that it could be worse. Much, much worse. Really it could.

Andrew could simply take the money and run. It occurs to me that the house he lives in may be rented, a police house possibly, and that he has no real money and no family or friends to keep him here. His house, his clothes, his leaky old car all suggest he is not a wealthy man. The money – sudden riches – might well overwhelm him.

He may simply leave me be. Or he could, if he wishes, tell the police – somehow, anonymously, he would know how to do it – that I have killed Robert and the body is in the garage.

As I mull over these terrible either-or scenarios, I glance up, and my spirit soars as I see the lights of a car coming into the close. Andrew, it is Andrew, and I am now sobbing with joy and relief.

Behind that car is another. And then one more. Three in all.

They make their way to my house and park along the way. Police from one car will go round the back of my house to block off my escape. Police from the two other cars will go to the left and right of my house, preventing any chance of me getting away.

I look again at the beautiful woman in the painting above the fireplace. After all my imaginings, over all these years, I must now draw all the strength I can from her.

Two senior police officers will then walk up the path and knock on the door and shout out.

And I will open the door and stand there tall and strong, cradling my baby, my Emily, in my tummy.

"Laura Elizabeth Curtis," they will say, "we arrest you for the murder of Robert James Wilkinson."

EPILOGUE

I am on my back. The sun is in my face.

I am relaxed.

We live, Andrew, Emily, Baby Grace and I, in a stone cottage miles from anywhere on the edge of Dartmoor in Devon. It is a wild and desolate place, but, in summer, as it is now, its bleakness has a certain beauty to it.

There is magic here. This morning, a deer stood and looked across at us having breakfast in the back garden before turning and walking slowly, majestically, away, disappearing into the still misty moor.

We are in the garden now, on this glorious summer day. I am stretched out on a blanket, sunbathing. Andrew sits next to me, feeding Baby Grace. Emily is playing with a toy watering can and bucket in a paddling pool close by my feet.

I can hear noises, shouts, somewhere in the distance.

But I ignore them.

Nothing can disturb the joy of this moment.

It is usually so quiet here, just the sounds of birdsong in the trees. I can hear Baby Grace sucking greedily at her bottle. Emily is splashing away in the water.

I will, when Baby Grace has finished, ask Andrew to make a pot of tea and a beaker of orange squash for Emily.

We can then sit together on the blanket and eat some of the cupcakes that Emily and I made this morning.

There is banging now, much closer.

I take no notice of it at all.

This is my lovely, happy time.

I take Baby Grace from Andrew and sit her on my knee, gently rubbing her back. Andrew lifts Emily out of the paddling pool and wraps a towel around her.

After drying Emily, Andrew sits her on the blanket, kisses me, and goes into the cottage to make our tea. Emily reaches across for a cuddle.

Andrew returns with a tray loaded with a pot of tea, mugs and plates, a jug of orange squash and colourful cupcakes for our impromptu picnic. We all sit on the blanket close to each other.

There is louder banging, and shouting too.

I hear the sounds of keys jangling.

I keep my eyes shut, enjoying every last second of this moment.

I squeeze my babies tight, breathing in the smell of their hair and the suntan lotion on their skin. My beautiful, gorgeous babies. They are all I could have ever wished for.

Andrew wraps his arms around Emily, Baby Grace and me, and says, "I love you."

My beautiful family. This wonderful father. The perfect husband. My happy-ever-after life. For ever. And ever. Always and forever.

I look up as the door swings open. The warder stands there, her face hard and uncaring.

She gestures to me to get up off my bed, to move away from the sun shining through the bars of the cell window. I have another assessment today in the mental health unit of this prison.

I'm crying. Sobbing really. She gazes back, unblinking and indifferent.

I'm only ever happy now in my daydreams.

I was charged with Robert's murder. Andrew told the police.

He handed them the mobile phone and laptop and walked away scot-free.

My baby was taken from me. If I can get out of here, I will go and find her.

Until then, my daydreams are all I have to keep me sane.

THE END

ABOUT THE AUTHOR

Did you enjoy *The Perfect Husband*? If you could spend a moment to write an honest review on Amazon, no matter how short, we would be extremely grateful. They really do help readers discover new authors.

Iain Maitland is the author of four previous psych thrillers, *The Girl Downstairs* (2021), *The Scribbler* (2020), *Mr Todd's Reckoning* (2019) and *Sweet William* (2017).

He is also the author of two memoirs, *Dear Michael, Love Dad* (Hodder, 2016), a book of letters written to his eldest son who experienced depression and anorexia, and (co-authored with Michael) *Out Of The Madhouse* (Jessica Kingsley, 2018).

Iain is an Ambassador for Stem4, the teenage mental health charity. He talks regularly about mental health issues in schools and colleges and workplaces.

He is currently writing two further psych thrillers for Inkubator Books for publication in 2023.

Find out more about Iain and engage with him at:

www.iainmaitland.net

AUTHOR NOTES

The Perfect Husband is my second psych thriller with Inkubator Books, following 2021's *The Girl Downstairs*, and I thought I'd write a little about the book, providing answers to some of the questions I'm often asked at author signings, book events etc. I'll not write too much though, no real spoilers, just in case you are looking at this before you read the book!

My stories often come from a single idea that catches my eye and my imagination then rolls it out. The idea here – a man making his partner write down her sexual experiences in a notebook and then testing her about them – came from a report I read in a newspaper on holiday years ago. I suspect, sadly, there are many such stories. It stuck in my mind and then rolled outwards into what is now, give or take, an 80,000-word book.

Laura, my main character, is at heart a kind and loving person but, like most of the leads in my books, given my background, she has mental health issues; relating to loneliness, feelings of isolation and being out of touch with the modern world. She also has what she calls her 'rainy-day' money inherited from her parents (and that may be a blessing or a curse).

Robert Wilkinson then arrives – handsome and wealthy and full of love so it seems; Laura's life is transformed overnight and everything she has ever wanted – love, a child, a happy family – looks as though it will all be coming true. Riches too as he is an investment adviser who can double or triple her money; maybe even more.

We join the story – the prologue – about six months after Robert has moved in with Laura. We see what has happened over that time in flashback – I did not want to start at the very beginning of their story and kind of go all the way through it. I did not want to dwell on all that took place getting to the prologue.

I've tried not to be too graphic in the book although I felt there were moments when I needed to set out some events. Much of what we see – all of it really – is through the eyes of Laura. She is, for the most part, a reliable narrator, although she is prone to daydreams and flights of fancy. She does have mental health issues and so she does not always act or react in the ways that someone without these issues might do.

So, mental health. All my leads – and some of the others too - have issues of some kind. My eldest son, Michael experienced anxiety, depression and more and spent five months in The Priory. I wrote a family memoir, *Dear Michael, Love Dad* (Hodder) and, with Michael, *Out Of The Madhouse* (JKP Publishing) based on those days. We went on to become ambassadors for the teenage mental health charity, Stem4. So mental health issues - across the board - are always there in everything I write.

I set my books where I live or have lived. I just like to have the roads, the trees, the woods etc, all in my mind as I write. Laura lives in Trimley St Mary, a village in Suffolk, next to its twin village of Trimley St Martin. I lived in Trimley St Mary with my family for 10 years before moving a few miles down the road to where we live now.

My wife Tracey and I have walked by the farm and Trimley marshes many times, especially when our three children were small. I still walk our dog Dolly there now and then. We used to have friends in Grimston Lane in Trimley St Martin, where Laura lived, and we visited there often. We still go to Rendlesham Forest, as a family, walking Dolly and my daughter Sophie's dog, Zack and, before that, our lovely Jack Russell, Bernard.

I rarely begin a book with an ending in mind. With my last psych thriller, *The Girl Downstairs*, the pivotal moment was going to be where the young female lead stole a baby from a pushchair in a shop. As I started writing – and the characters took me this way and that – a whole new, rather more dramatic, twist took place.

Laura and Robert and the other characters in the book all feel real in my head – I've known two or three Lauras and plenty of Roberts over the years – and I let them take me where they wanted to go. The story does not always make comfortable reading but it's where I think it would go and how it would end.

The ending! I submitted the MS to my publisher, Brian, who

knows more than a thing or two about publishing psych thrillers, and he suggested a slightly different ending. A tweak and a twist you might say. So that's the ending we have – and I hope you like it. (If you're curious about the original ending, feel free to drop me a line and I'll send it to you).

So what next? If you've enjoyed *The Perfect Husband,* please do let me know. And maybe leave a review somewhere? Thank you. *The Girl Downstairs* was my last psych thriller if you're looking for another read. I'm currently writing *Call Me Mother* (A working title that will change) for Inkubator Books and, all being well, that should be out in early 2023. I do hope you'll read that too.

Thank you – I hope to see you again soon.

Iain

23 September 2022

PS. Ginger – I'm sorry! But it is consistent with the characters and the story and I did try to avoid making it too graphic – and, of course, there is nothing to say that it wasn't old age and peaceful. Even so, I won't do it again ...

ACKNOWLEDGMENTS

Thank you ...

Brian and Garret and all at Inkubator Books for publishing *The Perfect Husband*.. You've done a grand job as always.

Dee Dee Design – for your cover. I love it.

Barbara Nadel – for the cover quote and your ongoing support. Looking forward to our next lunch!

Emma Hargrave – for your line edit. It was thorough and challenging – exactly what I would have wanted.

Pauline Nolet – for reading the proofs so well.

Alice Latchford – for seeing the MS so smoothly through production.

Tracey, Sophie, Glyn and Georgia – for answering my questions about school stuff and pregnancies and babies and the different shades of orange etc.

Ruth Goudy – for answering my questions about flowers.

Matthew Smith at Exprimez Literary Agency – for being my fab agent. We must have lunch again soon!

My family, Tracey, Michael, Georgia, Sophie, Glyn, Adam, Sophie, Jonah and Halley, Dolly and Zack – for being there.

ALSO BY IAIN MAITLAND

59319947R10173